*             [LARGE PRINT]
Mi  Michaels, Barbara
    The walker in shadows.

# The Walker in Shadows

Also Available in Large Print
by Barbara Michaels:

*The Sea King's Daughter*
*Wait for What Will Come*

# Barbara Michaels

# *The Walker in Shadows*

## G.K.HALL &CO.

**Boston, Massachusetts**

1980

**Library of Congress Cataloging in Publication Data**

Michaels, Barbara, 1927–
  The walker in shadows.

  "Large print."
  1.  Large type books.    I.  Title.
[PZ4.M577Wal    1980]    [PS3563.E747]  813'.54  79–27833
ISBN 0–8161–3060–4

Copyright © 1979 by Barbara Michaels

Published in Large Print by arrangement with Dodd, Mead & Company

Set in Wang graphic systems 18 pt Times Roman

To Peter Mertz

Any resemblance between whom and
any character in this book is slightly
more than coincidental

# One

The house next door had been empty as long as Pat could remember. Old Hiram, the caretaker, did not really occupy it; he camped in it, buying his food at one or another of the quick-food outlets and sleeping — so rumor reported — on a folding cot in one of the vast, echoing bedrooms. No chest of drawers would have been necessary, since he appeared to own only two shirts — one checked, the other plain blue — and two pairs of pants. Presumably these were replaced periodically, since they never progressed beyond a certain stage of decrepitude. Hiram had been heard mumbling to himself as he walked the streets, on those occasions when he emerged to dine on Big Macs and French fries. The soles

1

of his shoes, inadequately secured by rubber bands, slapped the sidewalk as he proceeded. Sometimes he burst into a loud shrill laugh, as if he had told himself a particularly witty joke.

The neighborhood children called him a witch, ignoring his sex, which was, admittedly, hard to determine at a casual glance, for his long gray hair straggled to his shoulders. It was Pat's son Mark, trained to verbal accuracy by his father, who pointed out that male witches were more properly known as warlocks. The other kids liked the sound of the word and adopted it; thereafter, when old Hiram appeared on the street he was followed by a crowd of imp-sized tormentors, chanting the noun and a variety of selected adjectives. These became richer and riper and more decidedly Anglo-Saxon as the children grew, and their mothers shook their heads and wondered where the little monsters picked up such language.

Hiram's persecutors called him names, but they stayed at a safe distance, and after one or two unpleasant episodes they did not venture onto the weedy, overgrown lawn of the house next door. They claimed Hiram had chased them with a nail-studded club, spitting blue fire.

The adults dismissed the blue fire and were inclined to place the club in the same doubtful category. No child ever showed convincing wounds, so the other parents followed the example of Jerry Robbins, husband of Pat and father of Mark. His reaction to Mark's complaint was a stern lecture on the meaning of private property. The lecture was reinforced by the method immortalized by Dickens' Mr. Squeers — wall, noun; build, verb active. Mark built the wall between the two houses, assisted by his father. It took him three weeks of playtime, and got the point across.

A high iron fence, complete with spikes, surrounded the rest of the forbidden property. Rankly overgrown trees and shrubs formed a further barrier; on summer nights the shrouding honeysuckle scented the entire neighborhood, and poison ivy added its charms to brambly roses and other foliage. Normally these barriers would only have been a challenge to the children. It was not the wall, or the fence, or the poison ivy that kept them out; it was old Hiram, and the effect Jerry's lecture had had, not only on his own son, but on the other children.

Jerry had been dead now for over a year.

Pat's mind touched this thought and twisted away. She had survived that year only by refusing to let the knowledge surface any oftener than she could help; by concentrating compulsively on the tasks of each day; and by seeking chores that kept her mind fully occupied and her body exhausted enough to sleep.

It was spring again, and that made it worse. Spring is always cruel, with its false promise of resurrection, and Jerry had enjoyed the season so much — the return of the migratory birds, the emerging green spears of bulbs he had planted the previous fall, the first freezing afternoon on a soggy golf course. Yet as Pat sat by her window

4

looking down on the hard-knotted potential flowers of the lilac bushes by the front door, she was thinking of something other than the treachery of spring. The house next door had been sold. A month earlier old Hiram had vanished into that mysterious limbo from which he had come, and a series of workmen had descended on the old house, supervised by a bustling lady from the local realtor's office. This morning the moving vans had lumbered up the street and stopped before the house, and Pat had decided that her cold was so bad she couldn't possibly go to work.

She blew her nose and dropped the tissue into a wastebasket conveniently at hand by her perch on the deep, padded window seat. Nurses were supposed to be immune to any disease short of bubonic plague; but she was entitled to some sick leave, the office was well staffed that week — and she was curious. She was cultivating that curiosity the way an injured person might encourage the first signs of movement in a paralyzed limb.

It was a dreary day, with low gray clouds and occasional drizzles of rain. A stiff breeze rattled the branches of the trees. If these had been fully leafed her view would have been cut off; even now, the only way she could see what was going on was from the second floor of the house. Her room was on the corner; she could see not only the street but, over the fence, into the neighboring yard. The first van had opened its rear doors and men were lifting out furniture swathed in protective cloths.

Pat wriggled into a more comfortable position, her feet up on the seat, her back supported by cushions. Mark had gone off to his morning classes at the junior college after fussing over her till she was ready to shriek. He prided himself on his culinary skills; the breakfast he had brought her included enough food for one of the husky moving men next door — bacon and eggs, English muffins, fried potatoes, grapefruit, and a big glass of orange juice. He made sure she ate all of it, standing over her with his hands on his

6

lean hips and his dark brows drawn together in a forbidding scowl, until she swallowed the last bite. The fact that he looked so much like his father didn't make it any easier for her to swallow.

Now, thank God, he had gone, and Pat was able to relax with coffee and cigarettes. She had not dared to admit to him that she was curious about what was happening next door, for he took a dim view of gossip and snooping, as he called it. Albert the cat prowled the room hoping Pat had overlooked a scrap of bacon. Mark's dog, Jud, a big black Labrador fondly known as the laziest dog in Maryland, was sprawled on the braided rug before the fireplace.

It was a charming, if slightly bizarre, room. Pat's eyes, accustomed to its eccentricities, passed over without heeding them, but a stranger would have been amused or appalled by some of the details. The large, high-ceilinged chamber was half-paneled, in the Georgian style, but the carving on the wooden chimneypiece was pure Gothic, with fantastic pointed arches supporting the mantel. Equally fantastic was the oriel window on whose wide cushioned seat Pat had settled, with its leaded panes and trefoil arches. The architecture demanded massive furniture, like the heavy four-poster bed; but the hangings and spread were of flowered print whose colors matched the lavender and blue and rose shades of the braided rug where Jud snored in canine comfort. Pat doubted that the dog had any notion of guarding her; Mark had lighted the fire before he left and Jud had simply sought out the warmest place in the house. Jerry always said Jud was an ideal watchdog. He was so clumsy and so affectionate that a burglar would be bound to trip over him and break a leg, giving them plenty of time to telephone the police.

Resolutely Pat turned her eyes from the room she and Jerry had shared to the view out of the window. The moving men had removed the shrouding cloths from some of the objects before they carried them into the house. What she could see was prosaic enough: a bronze standing lamp, sections of a steel bookcase, rolled rugs, their patterns indecipherable. A few of the pieces of furniture were transported still swathed in their wrappings. Pat tried to make out their shapes and failed, catching only a glimpse of curved chair legs that ended in the characteristic Queen Anne ball. Perhaps the newcomers shared Jerry's love of old things, antique furniture, aged houses.

The fact that they had bought the house next door suggested that they did. Like her house, it was an anomaly on glossy, modern Magnolia Drive, with its rows of split levels and Williamsburg reproductions. Jerry had hated the new houses. A house wasn't even *mature* till it was a century old, he claimed, stressing the adjective as he always did when he had found a word that pleased him.

When they first came to Washington, ten years earlier, they had lived in an apartment for a while, but it soon became apparent that Mark's nine-year-old energies could not be confined within four walls, particularly walls built of plasterboard. He thundered up and down the stairs, smuggled in all the stray animals he encountered, bounced balls off passing neighbors (accidentally, of course), and generally raised Cain. They decided to hunt for a house. The prices in the District of Columbia were appalling, so they investigated the neighboring counties of Maryland and Virginia.

It wasn't until then that Pat realized her husband had a passion for old houses. He was a history buff, particularly interested in military history, and Pat had already tramped all the old battlegrounds within driving distance of Washington. She got a bad case of poison ivy at Bull Run, twisted her ankle at Gettysburg, and was stung by wasps at Yorktown, after Jerry, trying to locate the site of Rochambeau's unit, had disturbed a nest. But she had not known that Jerry's interest in the past extended to architecture until they found the house near Poolesville.

In those days the Williamsburg reproductions and the split levels were still in the future, and the future Magnolia Drive was only a graveled country road. As the real-estate agent's car bounced along the rutted surface, Pat felt a stir of misgiving.

"It's awfully isolated," she said, glancing uneasily at the empty fields on both sides of the road. "Aren't there any other houses?"

"Not since the old Johnson place burned down, couple of years back," Mr. Platt, the realtor, replied. He winced as the bottom of his sleek yellow Thunderbird scraped a boulder. "But it's not that far from the highway, Miz Robbins; only about a mile. You folks said you wanted privacy. . . ."

A mile or so from the highway the road divided. The right branch passed between tumbled piles of rock that had once been gateposts and plunged into a jungle of shrubbery. The left branch seemed to disappear entirely after a few yards. Pat paid this little heed, for above the trees to the right she had caught a glimpse of something that left her openmouthed with surprise. It appeared to be the top of a medieval stone tower.

The house would have looked more at home on a Scottish mountaintop or a wild Cornish moor. Someone had recently mowed the weedy lawn and trimmed the bushes back so that it was possible to reach the porch steps — barely possible. The brick walk had been laid in an elegant herringbone pattern; now many of the bricks were missing and the others had been dislodged by tree roots and weathering. As they stumbled along it the boxwood pressed in on either side, yellowed with neglect and smelling abominable. At least it smelled bad to Pat. Jerry sniffed the cat-litter-box aroma as if it were incense.

The closer they got to the house, the more incredible it appeared. There *was* a stone tower, with battlements. There was also an oriel window on the second floor. An equally Gothic bay window on the first floor still retained some panes of stained glass. Across the front of this hybrid monstrosity stretched a typically American front porch, though the wooden posts that supported its roof were carved into medieval curlicues.

Mr. Platt led them quickly across the creaking porch and into the house, hoping, no doubt, that the interior would be less remarkable than the outside of the place. In that he was mistaken. While Jerry exclaimed over the pointed Gothic doorframes and carved wainscoting and marble fireplaces, Pat saw the hideously stained tub in the old-fashioned bathroom and the antique appliances in the kitchen. Surprisingly there were plenty of closets, as well as a room-sized pantry next to the kitchen. "Lots of storage space," Mr. Platt said cheerily, opening one of the cabinets in the pantry — and slamming it hastily shut upon a pile of mouse droppings.

So far as Pat could see, the only other advantage the house boasted was that it was not so unmanageably large as she had expected from its pretentious exterior. A parlor, dining room, library and kitchen on the first floor; four major bedrooms, plus several odd little chambers tucked in here and there on the second. There were more bedrooms, small but well lighted, on the third floor. "We wouldn't have to use this level," Jerry muttered, "Close it off . . . save on heating. . . ."

"We should save quite a bundle on heating when the furnace breaks down, as it is on the verge of doing," Pat said. "Radiators! I haven't seen those things since —"

"Wonderful to sit on when you come in out of the snow," Jerry said, a faraway look in his eyes. "And to hang your wet coats and things on."

Mr. Platt beamed approvingly at him.

"Few repairs here and there, not much . . . considering you should get the place cheap. Old Miz Bates' heirs are anxious to sell. Make 'em an offer."

Jerry did — an offer so low that Mr. Platt's expression lost its poorly concealed contempt and became one of pure pain.

"Well, now, Mr. Robbins, I dunno. . . ."

" Won't do any harm to ask," Jerry said.

Not until then did Pat realize he was

serious about buying the house. Her protests rose to high heaven. It was too far from his job, he'd have to drive for hours every day. There were no neighbors; whom would Mark play with? The house was in terrible condition. The porch steps were crumbling, the ceilings were water-stained, wallpaper hung in peeling strips, floors sagged. . . .A howl of glee from Mark, somewhere in the overgrown garden, prompted her to add, "And there's probably a well somewhere he can fall into, and old rusty nails he'll get tetanus from, and . . ."

She saw Jerry's face, and her protests died. There was no use trying to talk sense to him when he looked like that. Sighing, she turned for another look at the Gothic battlements. Her shoulder brushed Jerry's arm, and it was as if his emotions brushed off into her mind. For a moment she saw the old house as he saw it — its grotesque charm, its underlying solidity, the inevitable suggestion of courage in its resistance to time and neglect.

"It has the original hardware and some

of the original glass," Jerry muttered. "The American Gothic revival — mid-nineteenth century — there aren't many of them left, Pat. I'll bet under all the layers of paint the banisters are solid walnut."

"The yard," Pat began.

Jerry surveyed it with bemused pleasure. "Sensational, isn't it? This boxwood must be a hundred years old. And the magnolias —"

"And the poison ivy, and the weeds," Pat groaned. The house was surrounded by high green walls of undergrowth. Over the trees at the left side she saw something that made her wonder if consternation had unhinged her mind.

"That can't be!" she exclaimed.

Mr. Platt followed her glance.

"You aren't seein' double, Miz Robbins," he assured her, with a chuckle. "That's a tower, all right. There's another house over there. The twin to this one."

"Don't tell me there are two houses like this." Pat said. "One would be bad enough."

The two men, now allied in a common aim, exchanged amused glances; but Jerry was as intrigued as Pat.

"Twin houses, Mr. Platt? I've heard of such things, but only in fiction."

"Well, this is fact. Old Mr. Peters built these houses for his girls, when they got married. Back before the War Between the States, that was. He was quite a character, Mr. Peters. Read a lot. He got some fellow out from Scotland to build the houses, they say. I'd sell you Halcyon House," Mr. Platt went on, grinning, "only it's in worse shape than . . . . That's to say, it's tied up in some court fighting, the heirs can't agree." His eyes went from Jerry's rapt face to the barely visible top of the tower of the neighboring house, and he said thoughtfully, "Better see about getting a caretaker in there. One of these days I just might . . ."

"Find another sucker?" Pat inquired pointedly.

Mr. Platt made deprecating noises, but Pat knew that was precisely what he was thinking. It had never occurred to him, until Jerry walked into his life, that anyone would be fool enough to buy either of the old houses. Where there was one, there might be another.

And of course there were others, many of them. Pat and Jerry were among the first of the frustrated city dwellers to move out, seeking lower prices and country air. They bought up the old houses that dotted the countryside and remodeled them; builders caught on to the trend and constructed streets of little modern boxes amid the cornfields and pastures. Among these sharp businessmen was Mr. Platt. He had not mentioned to them — why should he, after all? — that he owned all the property along Bates Road. The year after they bought their house the bulldozers moved in, and by November there was a new street, named Magnolia Drive, lined with houses. The homes in Magnolia Estates (Mr. Platt was not a man of imagination) had only two basic floor plans, but by painting them different colors and changing details such as shutters and rooflines, Mr. Platt managed to give them a simulacrum of individuality. Jerry swore at the houses and their builder at least once a day. But Pat rather liked the "new people," though she saw little of them. She had gone back to work part-time by then. Mark was in school all day, and Jerry's beloved house was draining them financially, even though he did most of the work himself.

For a solid year he worked every night and every weekend and every day of his vacation. Under his direction Pat wore the skin off her fingers scraping and sanding and painting. When Jerry put on the new roof she stood clutching the ladder, an ineffectual gesture, as he laughingly pointed out, though of course he appreciated the thought.

The end of the year did not mark the end of Jerry's labors, for by that time he was so infatuated with the house that improving it had become a pleasurable hobby instead of a duty. But the worst of the work was done by then; the house was habitable, and Pat had moments when she admitted that she was getting rather fond of the place herself. The newly plastered walls had been painted in pastel shades, Delft blue and sunny yellow; the floors gleamed with wax. The newel posts and banisters *were* walnut. Azaleas and rhododendron emerged from the weeds and bloomed brilliantly, as if grateful for their new freedom. As Jerry's salary rose he bought gifts for the house — new bathroom fixtures, a modern kitchen — and, cautiously and with care, a few treasured antiques.

All those years the house next door stood empty, tied up in legal complications — or perhaps, for Mr. Platt was no fool, being held for the inevitable rise in price. The shrubbery grew taller and ranker every year. Occasionally old Hiram hacked some of the weeds down, but he did not discourage the growths that ensured his privacy.

As Pat sat sipping her coffee and watching the moving men struggle through the windy weather with their burdens, she could deduce where many of the pieces of furniture would go. The houses were not only duplicates, they were mirror images of one another. The oriel window in her bedroom faced the oriel in the master bedroom next door. Unfortunately the Gothic tracery and small panes made it impossible for her to see inside the room, but she assumed that the heavy carved headboard of the Victorian double bed would be placed in the master bedroom, along with the matching dresser and marble-topped washstand. The smaller dresser, painted white — French provincial probably, though she couldn't make out the details — must belong to a girl child, unless husband and wife had separate bedrooms. The second-best bedroom, corresponding to the one Mark occupied, was at the back of the house, on the same side as the master bedroom. Perhaps the white furniture would go in that room. She had seen only two dressers carried in, which didn't necessarily prove that only two bedrooms would be in use. . . .

At that point in her speculations her front-door bell rang.

Pat peered through the spyhole in the door before she opened it. When they first bought the house, she didn't even bother locking the doors most of the time. But the city was moving out to join them, and with it came fear.

What she saw through the spyhole, grotesquely distorted by the glass, was a face set in a hideous leer. Fingers wriggled at each ear and a long pink tongue protruded.

Pat opened the door.

"Nancy. How nice to see your lovely face."

Nancy's hair was bright red — the result of art, not nature. She was twenty pounds overweight, and was always on a diet. That morning she was wearing a padded jacket belonging to one of her large sons. It did nothing for her figure.

"Have you seen the new neighbors yet?" she asked, shedding the jacket. "What kind of furniture do they have? I didn't realize you were home; why didn't you call me? If I hadn't seen your car when I happened to take a walk —"

"On a day like this?" Pat grinned at

her neighbor, whose dislike of healthy exercise was as notorious as her constant dieting.

Nancy grinned back. She had very large white teeth; in any other woman the dental display might have been alarming, suggestive of werewolves. Combined with Nancy's snub nose and plump cheeks, the teeth were rather endearing.

"Damn you, you're always catching me in my little lies. All right, I came because I was dying of curiosity. I planned to break a shoelace or something outside their gate. But this is better. Don't tell me you weren't looking."

"Of course I was. Let me warm up the coffee and then we'll go back to my room. I've got a beautiful view from the corner window."

Perched on a kitchen stool, Nancy continued to chatter while Pat heated the coffee and toasted English muffins. She was Pat's closest friend on "the street," as its inhabitants called it. She was also the neighborhood gossip, and proud of the title. When you wondered why the police cars had been parked outside Number 146 last night, you called Nancy. She always knew, just as she was the first to know that the Andersons had finally split up and that the funny-looking white dog that knocked over your garbage can belonged to the Dunlaps on Azalea Court. But she had a heart as big as her curiosity; hurt children and weeping wives carried their problems to her, and every stray dog and cat in the area arrived at her back door, as if the Humane Society had drawn them a map.

Pat poured coffee and offered cream and sugar. Nancy took both, and helped herself lavishly to raspberry jam, heaping it on the toasted muffins. A raspberry patch had been one of the amenities to emerge from the weeds when Jerry started his yard work; Pat made jam every summer, and pies too. Jerry loved red raspberry pie.

Carrying their snack, they went upstairs and sat down in the window seat. Jud sat on Nancy's feet, drooling in a disgusting fashion. Like all dogs, he knew a sucker when he met one. Nancy fed him scraps of muffin, but her eyes were glued to the window.

"A piano! A baby grand, no less. . . . Somebody is musical."

"Brilliant deduction," Pat said affectionately. "Maybe the daughter plays. You did say there was a daughter?"

"Mm-hmmm. High-school age. Most of them take piano lessons, don't they?"

"Some of them do." Like Pat, Nancy lacked female children. She had four boys, ranging in age from ten to eighteen. Nancy pretended to know nothing of the habits of young girls, although her home often overflowed with them. Her boys were handsome and popular, and, as Nancy often complained, young girls these days had no modesty at all, the way they chased the boys.

"Maybe Friedrichs plays himself," she went on indistinctly, through a mouthful of muffin and jam. "No reason why a lawyer shouldn't play the piano, I guess. A baby grand seems a little lavish for a teenager, unless she's a juvenile Myra Hess.''

''Maybe it belongs to Mrs. Friedrichs,'' Pat suggested, knowing that this game of endless, fruitless speculation was one of Nancy's favorite activities. Pat rather enjoyed it herself. Had not Jane Austen written great novels about the minutiae of neighborhood life?

''My dear, didn't I tell you?'' Having finished her muffin, Nancy gave Pat her full attention. Her black eyes widened. ''There is no Mrs. Friedrichs. Or if there is, she's sick, or in Europe, or something. I've seen him — Friedrichs — several times. When the painters were here, last month. I tell you, sweetie, if I weren't happily married to my darling fat little bald husband, I'd set my cap for Mr. F. He's rather gorgeous — tall and muscular and longlegged. And he's got hair. It's beginning to turn gray, but it's so nice and thick.'' Nancy paused for a deep breath, and continued before Pat could comment on this ingenuous description. ''Norma — you know how nosy she is — Norma introduced herself to him one time, imagine her nerve. He told her his daughter was in school —"

"Ah, so that's how you found out about the daughter," Pat said, highly entertained. "Didn't Norma ask him about his wife?"

"Yes, she did. Not that bluntly, of course; even Norma wouldn't have so much gall. She said something about looking forward to meeting Mrs. Friedrichs. . . .Well, my dear! Talk about black looks! He just glared at her and walked away, at least that's what Norma said."

"So maybe he's divorced. It's common enough."

"Or maybe he's a widower." Nancy gave Pat a candidly speculative look. That was one of the things Pat liked about her. Paradoxical as it might seem, widowhood was easier to endure if people took it for granted, without apologies or excessive delicacy. But this time Pat shook her head, smiling.

"Don't matchmake, Nancy. It's a repulsive habit."

"You don't need anyone to make

matches for you. Once you make up your own mind. . . ." Nancy left it at that. She turned her attention back to the window. "That chest of drawers looks like Sheraton. Handsome piece of furniture."

"Could be a good reproduction." Pat pressed her forehead against the glass, squinting, but details were hard to make out. They were all more or less interested in antiques. The whole neighborhood was history-conscious, especially since the Bicentennial.

The movers began carrying in carton after carton, anonymous in their brown cardboard concealment. But Nancy could speculate even about cardboard boxes.

"China and glassware? No, the boxes are too small. Books, maybe. He's got a lot of them, hasn't he? Anyhow, Norma figured something nasty had gone wrong with the marriage, and fairly recently, or he wouldn't have looked so angry. After Norma told me he was a lawyer I asked Sol Jacobs if he'd ever heard of him, and he had. He's from Chicago. Friedrichs, I mean, not Sol. Had his own practice there, Sol said, quite a good one. Now he's come to work for the Justice Department."

"A political appointment?"

"I guess so." Nancy dismissed this with a shrug of her plump shoulders. Her husband was a contractor, and she shared the nonpoliticals' mild contempt for those who ate from the government trough, as she put it. "He must have money, don't you think? I mean, a grand piano, and the house wasn't cheap. . . . And look at that!"

It was a massive sideboard, black with age and covered with ornate carving, so heavy that the whole crew had to lend a hand to transport it.

"Jacobean," Pat guessed, her nose flat against the glass. "If that's genuine, it is a magnificent piece of furniture."

Carved chairs and a trestle table followed the sideboard. The two women were so engrossed they failed to hear Jud's whine of welcome, or the footsteps ascending the stairs. Mark had been tiptoeing — purposely.

"Aha," he shouted, in the bass tones

of a villain in a melodrama. "Caught you!"

Both women jumped. Nancy banged her head on the paneling and swore.

"Damn you, Mark, what's the idea of sneaking up on us like that? You scared me out of a year's growth."

"You ought to be ashamed of yourselves," Mark said. "The Snoop Sisters! Haven't you anything better to do with your time?"

He flung himself onto the chaise longue and swung his leg over the end.

"Take your feet off the couch," Pat said automatically.

Mark frowned at her, but obeyed. When his black brows drew together he looked unnervingly like his father, which was odd, because all his features were his mother's, from his curly brown hair and pointed nose to his full-lipped mouth. Only recently had Pat realized that she had let him get away with too much this past year because it was easier for her to cope with Mark's smile than with Jerry's frown, on Mark's face.

"It's almost noon," he went on.

"Here's the starving student, back from class, no lunch ready, not even a piece of bread defrosting. And here's his doting mum with her nose glued to the window, spying on the next-door neighbors. Helluva note."

"You cook your own lunch most days anyway," Nancy said unsympathetically, "And when your poor mother is home sick in bed —"

Mark let out a wordless hoot of derision.

"She's a malingerer," he said, dwelling pleasurably on the syllables. "She conned me into getting her a magnificent gourmet breakfast, and now look at her. Blooming with health. It was a trick, wasn't it? Just so you could stay home and snoop on the new neighbors. I mean, women are really —"

"Spare me the analysis," Nancy interrupted. "I get enough of that kind of juvenile impertinence at home. Isn't there something you should be doing, Mark? Homework, or baseball practice, or —"

Mark rose to his full height, which was

considerably over six feet.

"I see through your machinations, Mrs. Groft," he said crushingly. "You know full well that basketball is my game, not baseball. You ought to know, since your own son is on the team. But I can take a hint. I do not need to have a brick wall fall on me. As a matter of fact, I have many worthwhile things to do. I am meeting a friend for a spot of lunch. Are you sure, dearest mother, that I cannot do anything for your hypochondria before I leave?"

"No," Pat said, "I mean, yes, I'm sure. Don't be late for dinner."

"When am I ever late?" Mark ambled out before she had time to deliver the crushing reply his question deserved. Jud trailed hopefully after him. Sometimes Mark took him for rides. He liked going in the car with Mark. They went nice and fast, with loud music playing and the windows down, so that the wind blew delightfully through his ears.

But this time Mark abandoned him. The women upstairs heard the door slam, and a mournful howl from Jud.

Then they saw Mark saunter down the walk.

He had parked his car, a cherished antique Studebaker, on the street, instead of going to the bother of opening the gate. The whole lot, something over two acres, was fenced. It had cost a small fortune, but Jerry had insisted on doing it when they bought the dog. The county leash law was seldom observed in that semirural area, but Jerry had had strong views on letting animals run loose, to annoy neighbors and endanger themselves on the highways.

The boxwood hedge along the front fence had been trimmed in the fall and had not yet gained its spring growth. Pat and Nancy had a clear view of Mark's head and shoulders as he strolled toward his car, rather more slowly than was his wont. Then they caught a glimpse of something else, something as bright gold as sunshine on a summer day, moving along on a level considerably below Mark's gangling height. Nancy nudged Pat.

"That must be the daughter."

She was blond — that much was apparent. Something else became equally apparent as the two women watched, although they saw no more of the girl than the top of her shining hair. Mark saw her at the same time the overhead watchers did. He came to a stop, so suddenly that he rocked back on his heels. The shining fair head stopped too, facing Mark. It was on a level with his shoulders,

Mark turned slightly and leaned against the fence, folding his arms in what he probably hoped was a pose of sophisticated nonchalance. Tilting his head attentively, he seemed to listen as the invisible girl spoke. Then he burst into laughter, his shoulders shaking, his mouth opening wide.

"It's as good as an old Laurel and Hardy silent film," said Nancy, enthralled. "Pretty soon another suitor will come along with the custard pie."

"She must be very pretty," Pat said, trying to raise herself high enough to see over the hedge, but failing. "Mark wouldn't react that way unless she was —"

"I knew it!" Nancy hooted with laughter. "Here comes the third angle of the triangle."

"He's too old to be a suitor," Pat said. "He's wearing a hat. Have you ever known a nineteen-year-old boy to wear a hat? Or a raincoat?"

The newcomer's height almost matched Mark's, but he was heavier and broader of shoulder. Rain had begun to streak the window, so the snoopers were unable to see his face clearly, shadowed as it was by the hat brim. Pat got an impression of strongly marked features, heavy eyebrows, and a general air of disapproval — though she could not have specified the precise reasons for that impression.

"It's Friedrichs," Nancy said, swiping vainly at the wet pane. "I think. . . . Damn this rain."

"Whoever he is, he's the winner," Pat said, as the blond head turned and retreated, side by side with the raincoat and the hat. Mark stood staring after them, oblivious of the rain that was falling more heavily, streaking his face and flattening his hair.

"He hasn't got an umbrella," Pat said, swinging her feet down to the floor.

Nancy caught her arm.

"Does he own an umbrella? Mine wouldn't be caught dead carrying one. He won't take cold, they never do — at least not from getting wet. Doesn't he look ridiculous?" Nancy chuckled. "That's why he came home, the little hypocrite. One of the boys must have told him about the girl. Lecturing us on snooping, and then —"

"You're mean," Pat said, watching her son slouch slowly toward his car. His head was still turned in the direction of the house into which the fair head had disappeared. He stumbled over an obstruction of some kind and kept his feet only by a comic series of contortions.

Nancy's laughter increased in volume.

"Serves him right," she said heartlessly. "I hope he's thoroughly smitten. He's broken enough hearts in his time. He's ripe for a painful love affair."

"Maybe you're right," Pat said, smiling.

Later she was to remember Nancy's comment, and wonder whether she would have agreed with it if she had had any premonition of how peculiarly painful this affair would be, not only for Mark, but for the others who were about to be drawn into its perilous course.

## II

As Pat suffered through the first months of widowhood she realized that the greatest thing Jerry had done for her was to help her cultivate independence. Bad as those months were, they would have been worse if she had not learned to think of herself as a complete person in her own right. In losing Jerry she had lost the most joyful part of her life, but she had not lost part of herself. She was not maimed.

Not that it came that easily, or was that consciously acknowledged. It had never been conscious, on either part.

Jerry had been that rare creature, an adult human being. He gave freely and accepted only willing gifts. They fought, of course. Like his son, Jerry had a quick, indignant temper and a loud voice. He was as impatient of cruelty as he was of deliberate stupidity. But their arguments were always about acts or ideas, never about personalities, and some of the loudest concerned Pat's tendency — as her husband viewed it — to let other people take advantage of her.

Mark was the most consistent offender. Jerry admitted that it was natural for a child, the most egocentric of all creatures, to demand unreasonable concessions from parents; but he maintained that the only way to teach people consideration for others was to force them to be considerate. One of his pet hates was what he called the guilty-parent syndrome.

"You've been reading that damned child-behavior column again," he would roar at Pat, when she agonized over some imagined failure in dealing with their son. "Damn it, you're a good mother! You know a lot more about how to raise a child than some fool psychologist who sits in his office all day writing columns. You're not guilty! Stop feeling guilty or I'll rap you!''

At four o'clock on that rainy day when the new neighbors moved in, Pat went down to the kitchen and began cooking a large, elaborate dinner. Maybe Mark had not meant his criticism to make her feel guilty. On the other hand, he probably had.

Pat shook her head, smiling ruefully, as she gathered the ingredients for Mark's favorite, made-from-scratch muffins. At least she knew why she was going to so much trouble, on a day when she really didn't feel too great.

Her guilt feelings had not been severe enough to remove her from her post at the upstairs window until after the moving vans left. Nancy had departed several hours earlier, cursing the dental appointment that took her from the scene of the action. They had seen no more of the Friedrichs, who were undoubtedly inside trying to sort out their belongings — a horrible, tiring job, that one. And no woman in the house. . . .

The ensuing developments were really Pat's own fault — or, as Jerry might have said, "You asked for it, kid." She would have done the same thing, though, even if there had been a Mrs. Friedrichs. It was only neighborly. She had been through the moving routine herself, and knew only too well what it was like. She was preparing her own dinner; it was not much more trouble to make a double batch of muffins, and two casseroles.

At five she had the casseroles ready for the oven, and the muffins were done. Mark had not appeared. Snuffling, for her cold had reached the drippy stage, Pat got into boots and raincoat and scarf, piled the extra food into a canvas carry-all, and went out.

There was no gate between the two properties, so she had to go along her front walk and out the gate onto the street. With an umbrella in one hand and the carry-all in the other, opening and closing gates became a major chore, especially since the Friedrichs' gate stuck, rusted from disuse, no doubt. Rejoicing in her noble motives, Pat was not too saintly to observe, with considerable interest, that the armies of workmen who had come and gone in the past weeks had done wonders for the appearance of the old house. The carved porch pillars had been repaired and painted, the front door had new hinges and a fancy brass knocker, the broken windowpanes, boarded over by old Hiram, had been replaced. There was even a doormat. It did not say "Welcome."

Pat put down her dripping umbrella and used the brass knocker. Virtuously she refrained from looking through the glass panels on either side of the door. The panels on her door were of stained glass, old fragments acquired by Jerry at an antique auction. They gave more privacy than clear glass, and suited the period — or so Jerry claimed.

Lost in the mental fog that still tended to cloud her mind when she thought of

Jerry, she did not hear the approaching footsteps. When the door swung open she jumped.

The expression on the face of the man who stood looking down at her did nothing to make her feel at ease. Pat was suddenly conscious of the brilliant red of her nose, and the lock of hair that had escaped from under her scarf to drip on her cheek. She had meant to buy a new raincoat, only the prices were so awful. . . .

"Hello," she said. "I'm Pat Robbins, from next door?"

Now why had she made that statement sound like a question? She knew who she was.

Friedrichs continued to stare at her in silence. He had a long, prominent nose and a thin mouth. Though not conventionally handsome, his face had distinction and character, and his thick dark hair, streaked with silver at the temples, was as attractive as Nancy had claimed. Pat wondered what he would look like if he smiled. He was not smiling now; his expression of cold disinterest made her feel even grubbier and shorter than she really was.

"I just dropped by to welcome you to the neighborhood," she said. "If there is anything I can do . . ."

"Thank you," Friedrichs said, after an interval that was, surely, deliberately prolonged. "There is nothing."

By that time Pat knew she was in trouble, and that there was no way to get out of it gracefully. But she was damned if she was going to carry the casserole back home, like a rejected kitten.

"Here," she said, thrusting the carry-all and its contents at Friedrichs. He had to take it, but his expression was that of a man accepting a parcel from the garbage man: contents unknown, but highly suspect. "I thought you might not feel like going out for dinner on such a wretched evening," Pat went on desperately. "And I know what moving day is like; the pots and pans are always at the bottom of a carton marked 'Books.'"

Friedrichs peered into the carry-all. Pat saw that her apple-cinnamon muffins had escaped the twisted silver paper in which she had wrapped them, and were sprawled dissolutely on top of the casserole like rejected leftovers.

"How kind of you, Mrs. Robbins," he said, drawling his words. "It's delightful to meet a woman who believes in the good old adages."

They stood staring at one another for a moment, Pat in bewilderment, Friedrichs smiling faintly. Pat knew that the smile, like the enigmatic comment, was not intended to be friendly.

"Well," she said. "Please let us know if there is anything we can do. Good night."

If she had been a little less upset, she would have seen that Friedrichs' cynical mouth relaxed, and that his lips parted as if he were about to speak. But she was in a hurry to get away.

Naturally, she forgot her umbrella. She didn't remember it until she was at her own gate, and the rain was running down her face. By then she would rather have drowned than go back. She didn't understand Friedrichs' comment, but there was no mistaking his general attitude. Antagonistic? Hostile? Suspicious? She couldn't decide on the right word — words had been Jerry's hobby, not hers — but any of them might apply.

After she had hung up her raincoat and changed her wet shoes, she went to the kitchen to see how dinner was coming along. Contrary to her usual habit — solitary drinking was a danger she consciously avoided — she poured herself a glass of sherry and sat down at the kitchen table to think about adages. What the hades had the man meant? Adages were sayings, like, "There's many a slip between the cup and the lip," or "A stitch in time saves nine. . . ."

Then the answer struck her, and she felt a wave of color flood her face. "The way to a man's heart is through . . ." Oh, no. He couldn't have meant that one, he couldn't be so rude!

But he had been rude. Everything he had said, every change of expression had been designed to offend. And he knew who she was. He had called her *Mrs.* Robbins. The workmen he had employed, painters and plumbers and electricians, were local men; she had recognized their trucks. They would have gossiped. "Nice lady next door, Mr. Friedrichs; lost her husband last year." Or would they say that? Maybe they didn't think she was a nice lady. Maybe they said something like, "Watch out for that widow next door, Mr. F.; you know women, she'll be looking for a new mealticket. . . ."

When Mark came in the back door he found his mother with her head down on the kitchen table, emitting horrible snorting noises.

Being a young man of practical bent, he checked the stove first. Nothing was burning. Having ascertained that his dinner was not in danger, he put a large, oil-stained hand on his mother's heaving shoulder and said gently, "What's bugging you, chick?"

"Oh!" Pat sat upright. "I didn't hear you come in. Why is it that you sound like a thundering herd most of the time, and then walk like Natty Bumppo when I would appreciate some notice of your approach?''

''Who's Natty Bumppo?''

''Never mind.'' Pat took a napkin from the holder on the table and wiped her eyes.

Mark sat down opposite her. He refilled her sherry glass and then lifted the bottle to his lips.

''Mark!''

''Thought that would get you.'' Mark put the bottle down and indicated her glass. ''Drink up. What's the problem, Mom? Is it . . . Dad?''

''No,'' Pat said, mildly surprised. She managed a feeble laugh. ''Mark, you wouldn't believe it. I have been insulted. How about challenging somebody to a duel?''

''Sure,'' Mark said, looking relieved. ''Custard pies at fifty paces? Two falls out of three? Who insulted you, dear gray-haired mother of mine? When is dinner?''

Pat started to laugh, and hiccuped. ''You horrible person,'' she said.

"Hey, Mom. . . ."

Pat pushed him away.

"Being embraced by you is like being hugged by a grizzly," she complained. "I'm sorry, bud. This rotten cold is making me weepy. I had a fit of neighborliness, and took a casserole next door. I was not well received."

"If he refused one of your casseroles he's out of his skull," Mark said tactfully. "It smells great."

"Oh, I'm being silly." Pat gave her nose one last swipe and rose to her feet. "What do you want, corn or green beans?"

"Both. Please." Mark was on a vegetable kick. He added, finishing Pat's sherry, "Seriously, Mom, what did the guy say? I mean, if he really was rude to you —"

Pat stood stock-still, the packages of frozen vegetables in her hand, and stared thoughtfully at Mark.

"He was rude," she said, after a moment. "But in a strange way. He wasn't rude to me personally. How could he be? He doesn't even know me. He's hurt and angry at the whole world."

"His wife left him last year," Mark said.

"How do you know?"

"Kathy told me."

"Oh, her name is Kathy, is it? How did you elicit such personal information from the girl in such a short time?"

"Aha!" Mark leaped from his chair like Dracula preparing to swoop on a victim. "You and Mrs. Groft were snooping, weren't you? I knew you were watching me. Honest to God, a person has got no more privacy around here —"

"That's one of the little problems of community living," Pat said. She was feeling better, and was inclined to laugh at her own sensitivity. "What is the girl like, Mark? We couldn't see anything but the top of her head."

Mark drifted to the cupboard and began foraging in the cookie drawer. His mother made no comment; to call his appetite voracious was to understate the case, and she knew he could consume an entire box of cookies and still eat an excellent dinner.

"Very foxy," he said, his face averted. "Blond?"

"If you saw the top of her head —"

"Small."

"Five-two, a hundred and one pounds."

"Mark —"

"Just a rough estimate," Mark said, grinning.

"I don't care about her measurements. What is she like?"

There was a pause.

"Nice," Mark said. His mother stared at him. "Well, dammit," Mark said, "isn't that what you're always saying? 'She's such a nice girl,' and like that? She's . . . nice."

"Hmmm."

"If you're going to act like that. I'm leaving," Mark growled. He caught Pat's eye, and after a tense moment he suddenly burst out laughing. "Hey, cut it out, Mom."

"I love you," Pat said.

"Me, too," Mark said, and laughed again. He sat down at the table with a box of chocolate-chip cookies. "We didn't have much time to talk. I just introduced myself and I said welcome to the neighborhood and like that, and I told her about my — my family, and she told me about hers. . . . She's going to Princeton next fall.''

"Princeton!" Pat was properly impressed.

"Yeah, well, I guess she's pretty bright," Mark said thickly, swallowing a cookie whole. "Changing schools in your last semester of high school is tough. She's finished her course work already. Only her dad thinks it's better for her to be in school, so she's going to Willowburn."

Willowburn was a private school, one of the most highly regarded in the area, and very expensive. Pat nodded thoughtfully.

"They are on the trimester system, aren't they? March . . . The last trimester must be starting about now. But I wonder why —"

"I'm not Mrs. Groft," Mark said. "Spare me the groundless theories."

"I suppose he didn't want her sitting

51

around all day with nothing to do," Pat went on, ignoring the comment. "That makes sense."

The casserole was ready. She put it on the table. " 'Sensible' is one word for Herr Friedrichs," Mark said. Without rising he took two plates from the shelf of the cupboard above his head and slid one across the table toward Pat. Then he began folding the napkins into the shapes of tulips, an archaic and useless skill he had picked up from a former girl friend. Like his father, Mark had a weakness for esoteric knowledge.

"That's right, you met him," Pat said. "What did he say?"

"It was what he didn't say. Oh, he was polite. Kathy introduced us and I said 'Howdy-do,' and practically genuflected. He said, 'Hello, young man; come in, Kathy, I need you.' And, man, that was it. Not exactly your warm neighborly greeting. I am beginning to get the impression," Mark concluded, "that he doesn't approve of people in general."

Pat served the vegetables. Now she understood Mark's reaction to the news that Friedrichs had been rude to her. He too had seen his friendly advances wither under Friedrichs' frigid stare. It was easier for Mark to accept rejection if he thought it was not directed at him personally. In fact, Pat was inclined to wonder whether her reception had not been affected by Friedrichs' obvious antagonism toward Mark. He had pounced on the two young people like a dragon, refusing to give them time to talk (although Mark had certainly managed to learn a great deal during that brief encounter)!

Pat smiled wryly to herself. She was reacting just as Mark had — trying to blame Friedrichs' hostility on something other than herself. To hell with him, she thought. Who does he think he is, Paul Newman?

"I guess maybe we had better give up on the Friedrichs," she said.

"I would certainly advise you not to waste your well-known charm on that cold fish."

"But you are going to waste yours on Kathy?"

"It wouldn't be wasted." Mark grinned broadly and heaped his plate.

"I don't know, Mark. If Mr. Friedrichs doesn't want —"

"Oh, come on, Mom. It's up to me to make the overtures, isn't it? I mean, Women's Lib and all that, but she's new around here, and. . . . Maybe you and I are over-reacting. Moving is hell, and he was probably tired." Mark took a large bite and was rendered temporarily speechless. He chewed with such energy that his mother deduced he had more to say, so she waited, and finally Mark went on, his eyes twinkling. "If he gives you any more grief, let me know, and I'll sic the ghost onto him."

"Ghost! What ghost?"

"Oh, they have a ghost," Mark said calmly. "Old Hiram used to see it. He told Dad about it. We were going to check it out. . . ."

He stopped speaking and buttered a muffin with exaggerated concentration. Pat did not pursue the subject. She and Mark were still tiptoeing around one another's feelings, and, as people are wont to do in those circumstances, they kept tripping over their own grief. But this was the first time she had heard Mark display the same bitterness she felt about Jerry's unfinished plans and frustrated hopes.

They ate in silence. Mark's eyes were lowered, his face shuttered, and she knew better than to prod at his reserve. But beneath her remembered pain another green shoot of healthy curiosity thrust itself forth. Jerry had been a confirmed skeptic. He had also been one of the few people in the neighborhood old Hiram condescended to notice. What had the old man said to him? And why hadn't Jerry mentioned the conversation to her, so they could laugh together over poor crazy Hiram's imaginary ghost?

# Two

Spring came early that year. An unseasonably warm spell brought crocuses and daffodils leaping out of the ground in sunny splendor and encouraged the cherry blossoms to bloom on schedule for the first time in ten years. When the women met in the supermarket they gloated over the lovely weather, and hoped frost wouldn't blight the blooms of peach and cherry and apple. Fruit prices were as high as Everest already.

Mark's fancy did not lightly turn with the season. It had focused on its goal even before the daffodils appeared. Actually, according to Nancy Groft, spring didn't make young men turn to thoughts of love. They thought about it all the time, winter, fall, and summer. If "love" was the right word . . .

Pat smiled dutifully at Nancy's jokes, but she wasn't really amused. Although she would never have admitted it to Nancy, who had been rendered callous by the love affairs of four sons ("you have to get tough, honey, or you bleed to death,") she was worried about Mark. He wasn't eating. Even Nancy would have agreed that was a bad sign.

To say he wasn't eating was an exaggeration, of course. He ate what a normal human being would eat — about half of his usual capacity. Pat knew what was bothering him, and in her opinion, it was only about fifty percent love. If "love" was the right word . . .

The other fifty percent was outraged ego. Mark was a fast worker — as Pat's generation might have said — but in this case he didn't even get a chance to start working. Kathy's father drove her to school every day. It was a long drive, almost thirty miles, and they left before seven. After a week or so Mark became desperate enough to rise at six thirty — a hitherto unheard-of concession for a girl — but it did him no good. Kathy and Friedrichs emerged from the house together, got in the car, and drove off. Their garage was on the side of the house away from Pat's, so Kathy didn't even see Mark draped over the fence like a pensive gargoyle. Pat saw him, though, and she didn't know whether to laugh or cry.

Friedrichs also drove his daughter home. Usually they didn't arrive until six or seven P.M. Some nights it was even later. Presumably they ate out a good deal of the time. The Friedrichs' telephone number was unlisted, and Mark didn't have quite enough nerve to march up to the door and ask to speak to Kathy.

The weekend, for which Mark held high hopes, was equally unproductive. It rained both days and Kathy scarcely left the house. Mark shut himself up in his room, which just happened to overlook the house next door; he had virtuously announced his intention of catching up on schoolwork, but Pat knew he spent

58

most of the time staring morosely out his window. One of Friedrichs' first acts upon moving in had been to hang curtains, so Mark was denied even a glimpse of his new flame.

It was typical of the perversity that pursues lovers that his mother should see more of Kathy than Mark did. Once, between showers on Saturday, she caught sight of the girl wandering in the wet garden. Mark was out, rendering emergency assistance to a friend whose car had run out of gas on the highway. Another day Pat actually met Kathy as she left for work. Mark had given up his early-morning vigils by then, and was still asleep. The girl had just time enough for a smile and a shy "good morning" before her father's peremptory voice called her to hurry.

She was a darling, Pat had to admit that. Petite and dainty as a Meissen shepherdess, even in the navy-blue skirt and tailored jacket Willowburn required of its students, she had charm as well as beauty. The shy smile and nod had been quite delightful. Obviously, Pat thought, she had not inherited her father's rotten disposition. Nor had she inherited his looks; her features were delicate, unlike Friedrichs' craggy bones and jutting nose, and her eyes were as blue as cornflowers. No wonder Mark was smitten (and how he would have jeered at that word and all it implied)! Pat rather suspected that Kathy was not indifferent. When she walked in the garden she kept glancing at the wall between the two houses, as if hoping to see someone there.

In the middle of the third week Mark's vigilance was finally rewarded. When Pat came home that Wednesday night she was tired. The flu season was upon them and the office had been full of coughing, sneezing victims. But one look at Mark's glowing face made her forget her fatigue. He had started dinner, and insisted that she sit down, put her feet up, and sip her sherry like a lady while he finished concocting his specialty — spaghetti. Pat did not argue. It was lovely to relax, with the cat's heavy warmth sprawled across her knees, listening to the cheerful noises from the kitchen — pans clattering, water boiling furiously, and Mark singing at the top of his lungs, stopping only to swear when he dropped or spilled something. He had a perfectly terrible voice. Jerry had been tone deaf, and his son had inherited this trait.

Pat tickled Albert under his lowest chin. He was a tabby — the best color for a cat, Jerry always said — with a white bib and three white paws. He had come to their door one rainy night and kicked it — at least, that is what Mark claimed. His parents found it hard to believe that a shivering, wretched three-month-old kitten could kick a door that hard, but they agreed solemnly that it was probably coincidental that Mark happened to be at the door at that precise moment. As Albert grew in bulk and dignity, it was not difficult to believe he could kick a door if he felt like doing so. The necessity did not arise. He had his own door and often brought friends to lunch, for he was a gregarious soul, in a perfectly Platonic way. He had been altered at the appropriate age, Jerry commenting that his estimation of his own virility did not rise or fall on the nocturnal habits of a tomcat, for God's sake, and there were already too many stray kittens in the world.

Albert purred. Pat sipped her sherry. She felt wonderful.

Mark came in to announce that dinner would be ready in ten minutes. Pat gestured toward a chair.

"Join me, kind sir. And tell me why you're in such a good mood."

"I'll have a beer," Mark said. "As for my mood, why shouldn't I be in a good one?"

"Because it's muggy and warm and your paper for that psych course is overdue."

"I do hate omniscient mothers."

"You can do it this weekend, if you work every minute," Pat murmured.

Mark pulled the ring on the beer can and stopped the overflow with his forearm.

"Shirt's dirty anyhow," he said

cheerfully, anticipating his mother's protest. "You're a sly one, aren't you? How did you know?"

"Know what?"

"That I have a heavy date Friday night. With Kathy."

"You're kidding!" Pat registered appropriate surprise and admiration.

"Nope. The old Robbins magic did the job. I met her at the gate this afternoon. . . ." Mark hesitated. Pat kept her face straight with an effort. She knew Mark was wondering whether to admit that he had lurked in the yard all afternoon, as he had for days. He decided not to admit it. "I just happened to be there when they got home," he went on casually. "They were early today. Teachers' meeting, or something. Anyhow, he went on in the house, and she sort of hung around, and I asked her, and she said yes."

"That's wonderful. Every boy — I mean, young man — on the street has tried to date that girl."

For a moment Mark looked as smug as Albert.

"I know. I won five bucks from Rick."

"Mark! You didn't!"

"Bet? Sure. Why not? Let's eat. I think the spaghetti's done."

They had barely sat down when the telephone rang.

"I'll get it, it's probably for me," Mark said.

It usually was for him. Pat went on eating. She heard him say, "Hello," and then, "Well! Hi, there." The tone of the second greeting made her look up. By then Mark had disappeared with the phone. It was on a long cord, and Mark carried it with him into the hall or, when even greater privacy was required, into a closet. This call was of the latter variety. Pat heard the door close and grinned. The caller must be female. Kathy, no doubt. No other girl could arouse quite that degree of enthusiasm just now. Then her smile faded. That the girl should telephone so soon after accepting an invitation from Mark might not be a good sign.

When Mark reappeared in the doorway

she knew her hunch had been correct. He stood for a moment holding the telephone as if he didn't quite know what to do with it. His face was a mask of bewilderment.

"She can't go out with me."

"That's too bad. A previous engagement?"

"No." Anger replaced Mark's initial surprise. He slammed the telephone back onto its wall holder. "I asked how about Saturday night, or Sunday. She finally admitted her dad says she can't go out with me. Ever."

"Oh, Mark. Did she say why?"

"She was crying," Mark said. He turned. "I'm going over there."

"Mark, wait!" But he was gone. The front door slammed.

Pat stared miserably at the remains of her spaghetti. It was all very well for Nancy to talk about becoming hardened to the troubles of one's children. Pat only wished she could. Her anger against Friedrichs flared, and she fought to control it before Mark returned. She would have to help him overcome his anger, not add to it. She hoped he didn't lose his temper and say, or do, something unforgivable.

He was back in five minutes. The door slammed again and Mark's footsteps pounded down the hall, making bric-a-brac rattle. He took his seat without speaking; his face was white with rage, his mouth pinched together.

"Break something," Pat suggested sympathetically. "Those glasses are expendable; dime-store stuff."

Mark's tight lips relaxed slightly.

"The guy is sick," he muttered. "I mean, really sick."

"What did he say?"

"He answered the door. I bet he never lets *her* do it. She might meet somebody who could contaminate her." For the first time Mark appeared to see his mother's worried look. His eyes lost their flinty glare. "Hey," he said. "Relax, will you? The Robbins honor is untarnished. I did not punch the old devil in the nose. I didn't even say anything rude. All I said was I thought a condemned man had a right to defend himself.''

''Cute,'' Pat admitted. ''The legal touch. What did he say?''

''He stood right there in the doorway and told me what he had against me. Honest to God, Mom, you never heard such garbage. The guy is a hundred years out of date. He should be living in 1880.''

*''What did he say?''*

''Well.'' Mark abandoned any pretense of eating. He pushed his chair back and pondered briefly. ''As near as I can remember, he said he didn't want his daughter going out with a guy who drove too fast, drank too much beer, played rock and roll too loud, didn't mow the lawn or help around the house, stayed out till all hours instead of studying, and was too stupid or too lazy to get admitted to a decent college. There may have been a couple of other things, but I forget them.''

''Of all the unreasonable, unfair. . . .'' Pat's voice rose. She counted to ten and tried again. ''How does he know all that?''

Mark began to laugh. His temper was quick to explode and as quick to cool off. He reached out a long arm and patted his mother on the shoulder.

"Thanks a lot, Mom."

"I didn't mean that. I meant — "

"I know. He must have been watching us all this time.The grass did get pretty long last week. And you had to go and mow the front, where everybody could see you. . . . Okay, okay, I know I should have done it before you had to. And a couple of the guys did leave some beer cans along the driveway one night. And that warm night when the windows were open I guess I did have my hi-fi turned up pretty loud. . . ."

Pat said nothing. She was shocked at the intensity of her rage. Hearing Mark recounting his little sins, with that compulsive, touching fairness of his, she was thinking of the cruelest accusation of all and resenting it even more bitterly than she had resented Friedrichs' sneer at her. Mark had had his choice of several excellent colleges. He had turned them all down when his father died, in order to stay with her. She pushed her chair back from the table.

"I'm going over there and tell that —"

"Mom!" Mark grabbed her and hugged her till her breath came out in a gasp. "Cool it," Mark said. "What a termagant you are! I can defend myself, you know. I'd look like a damned fool if my mommy went running over there to scold the mean man for hurting my little feelings." His voice changed. "Seriously, Mom, I appreciate it. But it wouldn't do any good. He'd just be rude to you. The man is neurotic. He's going to ruin that chick's life, but it's not your problem."

"You're right," Pat said. She put her arms around Mark and hugged him back. "I'm sorry for the girl, but there's nothing we can do about it."

All the same, she spent the rest of the evening thinking about what Friedrichs had said, and inventing horrible fates for him. Not until she was in bed and almost asleep did she isolate the odd feeling of uneasiness that had plagued her since dinner. "It's not *your* problem," Mark had said. Just a casual pronoun — only somehow she suspected its choice had not been casual at all.

## II

A few days later she decided she had let her imagination run away with her. Mark had apparently accepted the situation with perfect equanimity. He was eating, and drinking beer — and, his mother admitted to herself, playing his hi-fi too loud and perhaps driving just a little too fast — just as he had done before Kathy entered his life.

Friedrichs' unjust criticisms continued to haunt Pat, though she knew she should dismiss them with the lofty contempt they deserved. Any man who would judge a boy by the college he attended had to be the worst kind of snob. The slap in the face — or rather, the plural slaps — irked her all the more because she had hoped so much for congenial neighbors. The two old houses at the end of Magnolia Drive were isolated not only in space but in character from the new houses on the block. It would have been so nice to have Halcyon House occupied by a pleasant woman who shared some of her interests, who would drop in for coffee on Saturday morning or perhaps invite her over for a drink occasionally. Early evening was the worst time. If Mark didn't have basketball practice he had other activities to occupy him, and Pat was often alone at that most melancholy hour of the day, when the body is tired and the mind yearns for communication.

Of course, she reminded herself, all single women had to come to terms with that problem. In some ways it was easier for women who had never been married. Such a woman was accepted as complete in herself; she had never been one of a partnership. But she knew she was luckier than most, not only because of the nature of her relationship with Jerry, but because Mark had given up a year of his life to help her make the painful transition from two to one.

As the lilacs opened lavender spears and the azaleas produced clumps of rosy bloom, Pat continued to brood. Like the flowers, she had been dormant for months. Now she was coming to life, jarred by the annoying presence next door. The process was painful, but perhaps it had a certain potential. Pat wondered wryly if the flowers really enjoyed the act of blooming. Maybe the azaleas ached too.

The problem of what to do about Mark bothered her more and more. Was it too late for him to apply to another college next fall? He had said nothing about it; he seemed quite content with his life, with his friends and girl friends at the junior college, and his undemanding routine. Was he hiding his real feelings or — worse — was he getting into a comfortable rut which would be harder to break as time went on? Pat realized only too well that, beloved as he was, Mark was no substitute for Jerry as a companion. The generation gap was not fiction. She liked Haydn, Mark liked Jimmy Hendricks. To her cars were a means of transportation; to Mark, they were practically a religion.

Ballet was not one of the interests they shared, and it was to the ballet Pat went on the following Thursday, picking up a friend in Chevy Chase and going on to Kennedy Center, where Barishnikov was appearing in *Swan Lake*. After the performance she stopped for a cup of coffee with Amy, then drove home through the perfumed spring night in a dazzle of remembered pleasure. The white dogwood trees slipped past the car windows like slim Swan maidens fleeing an enchanter, and the lovely, saccharine music echoed in her ears.

Friday was not a working day for her, but it was for most of the residents of Magnolia Drive. The street was dark and quiet when she turned off the highway, with only a few squares of lighted windows burning against the dark. The drive curved. Not until she neared its end did she see something that made her foot move instinctively from gas pedal to brake.

Normally Halcyon House was as dark as the other houses on the street by this time of night. Now lights began to blaze out, one after the other — first the big oriel in the master bedroom, then the windows of the upper hall, then the fanlight over the front door, as if someone were running through the house pressing the light switches as he went.

Pat glanced at the clock. It was after one A.M. She looked then at her own house. Everything was normal there; Mark had left the porch light on for her, as he always did when she was out late.

Her car had just had its spring tune-up, courtesy of Mark. The engine purred softly. When the first scream ripped through the night, there was no louder sound to combat it.

Pat was out of the car before the sound died. In fact, she was through the gate and halfway up the walk before it stopped, as abruptly as if it had been cut off. It was a terrible sound — wordless, but requiring no words — a peremptory demand for help. And the voice had been that of a woman.

The ground-floor windows of Halcyon House were open to the spring air. No wonder the voice had carried so well. As Pat bounded up the porch steps, taking them two at a time, the scream came again. She threw her weight against the door and was somehow not surprised when the heavy portal yielded.

# III

The mind works far more quickly than conventional measurements of time can reckon. Pat's mind had already painted a picture of what she expected to see; the reality was so like the vision that she was momentarily paralyzed, as a dreamer would be to find his dream a reality.

The hallway of Halcyon House, the duplicate of her own, was as wide as a normal room, with the carved walnut balustrade of the stairs rising at the rear. The hardwood floor, dark with age but freshly waxed, reflected the bulbs of the antique crystal chandelier. On the floor, practically at her feet, was a tableau that might have come out of *Popular Detective,* or some other sensational sex-and-violence tabloid.

Kathy's fair hair spilled like shining water across the dark floor. Her thin blue nylon nightgown was twisted around her hips and her slim bare legs thrashed, kicking the floor. Friedrichs knelt beside her, his hands on her shoulders. As the door burst open he looked up. His face was ashen, bleeding from scratches that marred one cheek, and his expression was so distorted that Pat scarcely recognized him. For a moment the hope flashed through her mind that the man attacking the prostrate girl was not that girl's own father, but a stranger, an intruder. . . . But the shock of black hair was Friedrichs', the heavy shoulders and hard, bruising hands . . .

Her paralysis could not have lasted more than a second or two. She saw the marks of fingers white against the girl's blotched cheeks, and knew why the scream had been cut off so abruptly. Kathy drew a long, choking breath and again cried out. Her father struck her across the mouth.

Pat launched herself like a missile, all one hundred and ten pounds of her body, straight at Friedrichs. He wasn't expecting it; he went over backwards, hitting his head with an ugly thud, and Pat gathered the sobbing girl into her arms. Kathy fought her at first. Pat quieted the flailing hands by pressing them against her body, cradling the golden head on her shoulder and talking as she had talked to Mark years ago when he had had a bad nightmare. "It's all right now, it's all gone — no one can hurt you, I'm here, I'll not let it hurt you. . . ." Kathy's body finally relaxed. Her light bones and quivering muscles felt no heavier to Pat than Mark's eight-year-old body had felt, so long ago.

When the girl's gasps had subsided to low, moaning breaths, Friedrichs sat up. Pat eyed him warily. She was still so shocked and angry it was hard for her to speak, but she knew what tone she must adopt. Very calm, very firm.

"Just what is going on here?" she demanded.

"I wish to hell I knew." Friedrichs fingered the back of his head and winced. "How did you get — no, never mind that. Is she all right?"

"No thanks to you if she is." Pat clutched the girl tighter and tried to move away from Friedrichs, no easy task from a squatting position, with a now limp weight encumbering both arms.

Friedrichs' eyes blazed. He made an instinctive move forward. Seeing Pat's equally instinctive withdrawal, he sat back and took a deep breath. His shirt was crumpled — the sleeves rolled up, the neck open. His thick wavy hair stood out around his face, unkempt and uncombed. One of the deeper scratches on his cheek oozed blood. He needed a shave. He looked like a drunk who had been in a brawl. But when he finally spoke his voice was quiet and controlled.

"Okay, I know what you're thinking, and in all fairness I can't blame you for leaping to conclusions. The important thing — "

"Leaping to conclusions!"

"Just hear me out, please. The important thing is Kathy. She ought to see a doctor immediately. I don't suppose there's a physician in the country who makes house calls, and I'm equally certain that you would scream your head off if I tried to touch her; so perhaps I could impose on you to drive her to the nearest hospital."

Pat stared at him, openmouthed. Her heart was still thudding so hard that her chest ached, but the cool reason of Friedrichs's speech impressed her against her will. Kathy was a dead weight against her shoulder. She was breathing almost normally now.

Friedrichs went on, "I'm going to stand up and move back out of the way. If you like, I'll go into the library and you can lock me in. Only — for God's sake, Mrs. Robbins, do something for her right away. If you can't carry her, maybe . . . maybe your son. . . ."

That last appeal affected Pat more powerfully than anything else the man had said. Surely Friedrichs would not have asked for Mark's help if he hadn't cared more for his daughter than for his reputation. So — as Jerry used to say — so maybe your premises are wrong, kid.

"I think she's all right," Pat said

slowly, tilting Kathy's head back so she could see the girl's face. It was relaxed in the peace of deep sleep. A little too deep, perhaps. . . . Pat looked at Friedrichs, who had risen and was backing away. His eyes were fixed on Kathy's face, and his expression . . . "Are you telling me you didn't attack the child?" Pat demanded.

"I was sitting up in bed reading when I heard her scream," Friedrichs said. "Not really a scream — not then — more like a choked, gurgling moan — a horrible sound. I froze for a second. The next thing I heard was a crash from her room, and then the sound of her footsteps running like a crazy thing. By the time I got out of my room she was halfway down the stairs. I turned on the lights as I followed; that slowed me down. She went in a headlong rush, stumbling and sliding. I thought sure she'd break her neck. I didn't catch up with her till she reached the front door. She had the chain off and the key turned —"

"So that's why the door was open?"

"That's why. When I touched her she

let out the most god-awful yell and turned on me like —'' Friedrichs touched the scratches on his cheek. "I had to grab her hands, hold her, or she would have run straight out of the house in her nightgown. She — she didn't know me. Her eyes were absolutely empty of recognition — empty of everything except mindless terror. I guess I lost my wits too, it was so damned awful. . . . I tried to stop her from screaming, the sound cut right through me, and then I remembered they slap people sometimes, when they get hysterical. . . .''

The damp night air was cool on Pat's arms and cheeks. Friedrichs was sweating. Great clammy drops stood out on his forehead.

Pat came to a sudden decision. If Friedrichs was faking that look of agonized love and concern, he was a better actor than Olivier. And he was right; Kathy's needs came before any other issue.

"Close the door," she said. "Then we'll get her to bed."

Friedrichs obeyed, circling Pat and Kathy with the caution of a leper. Pat's fingers sought the girl's pulse. Strong and steady. Now that her nerves were settling down she found the incident more and more unbelievable. What had gone on in this house tonight?

"Here," she said brusquely. "I can't carry her. You'll have to do it."

Their hands touched briefly as she transferred Kathy's limp weight to her father's arms. His fingers were as cold as ice. Pat followed him up the stairs and along the hall to Kathy's room, the equivalent of the one Mark occupied in her house. It had the same deep bay window and fireplace, and it was decorated in a frilly, flowery style suitable for a girl much younger than Kathy. The dainty wallpaper and matching drapes, the canopied bed and white-painted furniture would have looked pretty if the room had not been such a mess. Papers were strewn about, books had been thrown from the shelves flanking the fireplace, and the bedsheets trailed onto the floor.

Pat touched the light switch and an overhead chandelier flooded the room with brilliance. She picked up the lamp lying on the pillow, a serviceable reading lamp with a bronze base, and restored it to the bedside table. Friedrichs put the girl on the bed. Pat bent over her, checking pulse and respiration again, lifting an eyelid. A blank blue orb stared back at her.

"She seems to be all right," Pat said slowly.

"A doctor —"

"I'm a nurse, you know. I don't think she's in any immediate danger." Pat tucked blankets around the girl's body and straightened. Friedrichs stood on the other side of the bed, his arms hanging limply. Pat was conscious of an unwilling surge of sympathy.

"Look," she said. "If what you told me was the truth — and I'm beginning to think maybe it was — well, there's one obvious explanation for what happened. Are you sure you want the publicity of a doctor and a hospital?"

"Publicity?" Friedrichs stared at her.

The perspiration on his forehead was a slick, shiny film. Large drops ran down his lean cheeks. "What do you mean?"

"Drugs. Her behavior suggests one of the hallucinogens."

"No," Friedrichs said. He wiped his forehead with his sleeve. "No. You mean LSD, something like that? She doesn't take drugs."

"Will you search her room?"

"No. I've never done a thing like that. I wouldn't insult her so."

Pat felt a wave of utter exhaustion, partly physical but primarily emotional. She had been through this before, too often, when she had worked briefly at a local hospital. Six months of night duty in the emergency room had been enough; she had quit and found a job as an office nurse. There were tragedies in that job too, but not like the hospital. It wasn't the blood and mess, or the pain of seeing a life slip through one's hands, a nurse got used to that. But she couldn't get used to the young people, mangled and smashed in needless car crashes, staggering drunk, or spaced out on some drug. Some of them had looked as young and innocent as the girl on the bed. And the parents had usually reacted just as Friedrichs was reacting — "Oh, no, not mine. I know there's a problem, but my child never. . . ."

"You must search," she said. "In justice to her."

Intuitively she had touched the right note. Friedrichs thought it over for a moment and then, without a word, turned to the dresser drawers.

The harsh, unpleasant job took quite a long time. Friedrichs hated what he was doing; his mouth was a thin line of disgust. After a while Pat said, "Shall I . . . ?" and the lawyer nodded silently. So Pat searched the adjoining bathroom — hamper, medicine chest, even the tank of the commode. She didn't enjoy the task either, but it was easier for her than for the distressed father. She found nothing except the usual patent medicines and cosmetics.

Then a sound from the bedroom sent her running back to Kathy. The girl was twisting uneasily and muttering in her sleep. Her eyes were still closed. Pat bent over Kathy. She could not make out distinct words. Then Kathy's eyes opened. They moved around the room, passing over her father as if he had been a piece of furniture. Then she saw Pat; and the light of normal, sane intelligence transformed her face.

"Mrs. Robbins . . . What —"

"Thank God," Pat said, the worst of her fears removed. "How do you feel?"

"Tired. I'm so tired. . . ."

"Kathy. Did you take anything?"

"Is something . . . missing?" Kathy asked.

"No, I didn't mean that. Pills. Did you take anything like that?"

"No." Kathy's hand moved, groping. Pat took it in her own and the girl's slim fingers tightened on hers. "Don't go away. Stay here. Please."

"Of course, if you want me. But you must tell me —"

"Thank you . . ." The words trailed off in a long sigh. Kathy slept again.

Still holding the girl's hand, Pat caught Friedrichs' eye.

"Is she —"

"She's sound asleep," Pat said. "It looks like normal sleep. Mr. Friedrichs, it's up to you. I'm not going to advise you, but —"

"If she were yours?"

"I'd let her sleep it off, and see how she is in the morning."

Friedrichs nodded. He looked like a man who had just finished running twenty miles.

"I have no right to ask this, but — could you stay?"

"I have no intention of leaving. Didn't you hear me promise?"

"I heard you. But I didn't expect. . . ." He sat down quite suddenly, not as if he had intended to do so, but as if his knees had given way and there just happened to be a chair behind him. Pat freed her hand from Kathy's grasp and started toward him, but Friedrichs shook his head.

"I'm all right. Why don't you lie down on that chaise longue, where she — she can see you if she wakes. Would you like some coffee?"

"Yes, thanks. And have some yourself — with plenty of sugar."

"I'm all right," Friedrichs repeated. "I'll get the coffee. Is there anything else you would like?

The meticulous formality of the speech sounded so incongruous that Pat smiled unwillingly.

"Yes, as a matter of fact. I'd like to leave a note for Mark, in case he wakes and wonders what has become of me. Perhaps you could take it next door."

"Certainly. There is paper here —" He indicated Kathy's desk, which was piled with books and other student impedimenta. Pat took a pen and a sheet of notebook paper and scribbled a brief message. She handed it to Friedrichs without folding it.

"You'll see that I didn't mention names, only that someone was ill and I was needed. Please stick it on the refrigerator door with one of the little magnets."

The lawyer's eyes flashed briefly, as if he appreciated the implied permission to read the note. He did not do so, only took the key Pat gave him and left the room, after a final glance at the sleeping girl.

Pat took off her coat and hung it over the back of a chair. Her purse was still in the car. She should have asked Friedrichs to get it, but it didn't seem important. Her house keys were in her coat pocket, and she made it a rule never to carry much cash when she was out late at night.

She went back to the bed. Kathy had turned on her side, her cheek pillowed on her hand. Pat brushed strands of silky hair away from the girl's forehead; Kathy's lips quivered as if she were about to smile. She sighed deeply.

Pat had no intention of lying down on the chaise longue or anywhere else. She had done a foolish thing — a damned fool thing, Jerry would have said — in advising Friedrichs not to call a doctor. Oh, she hadn't actually said it, in so many words, but she had implied as much, and the responsibility weighed heavily on her mind. She would watch the girl's every breath until she woke; at the slightest sign of trouble she would call the rescue squad. In the meantime . . .

Her lips set in an expression, if she had but known it, very much like Friedrichs' when he searched his daughter's possessions, Pat pulled out the top desk drawer and sifted through its contents. Friedrichs had seemed to search thoroughly, but perhaps he had missed something — something he really didn't want to find.

As she went through the room, finding nothing except a little dust and the more or less blameless records of a young girl's school and social life, she was thinking, not about Kathy, but about Kathy's father.

She had been prejudiced against Friedrichs from the start, and therefore ready to think the worst of him. Still, that didn't mean that her assessment had been wrong, or that his performance that night had been genuine. She had seen people lie just as convincingly — girls with eyes as big and blue as Kathy's solemnly swearing they had never heard

90

of heroin, though their arms showed the damning marks of injection; cultured men in expensive clothes denying indignantly that they had ever laid a hand on their wives, while the women nursed black eyes and broken bones and flinched at the very sight of their husbands. Yes, Friedrichs could be lying. So why was she now as prejudiced in his favor as she had formerly been biased against him?

That was easy. She was sympathetic because, if his story was true, she knew how he must be feeling. In a perfect agony of terror and doubt, that was how — just as she would feel if this had happened to Mark. To have the one you loved best in all the world turn on you, striking out with hate, rejecting the help you wanted to give. . . . And the fear — the wild, terrible theories. Drugs? Brain tumor? Paranoia, mental illness? The fear of losing the only one you had left.

Her hands were shaking so badly she decided to abandon the search. She had dropped one delicate little china figurine;

it would have broken if it hadn't fallen on the rug. She had searched every place she could think of and found absolutely nothing incriminating, except a paperback copy of *The Joys of Super Sex* under Kathy's mattress. Pat smiled weakly as she returned it to its place. Nothing abnormal about that.

It began to appear as if Friedrichs were right. The kids weren't that smart or that careful. They usually left some evidence lying around. So if it wasn't drugs, what on earth . . . ?

When Friedrichs returned she had settled into a comfortable overstuffed chair, her hands folded in her lap. He was carrying a tray — and her abandoned purse.

"I hope you don't mind," he said, handing it to her, "but I took the liberty of putting your car in your driveway. You had left the keys in the ignition, and I thought —"

"You were quite right," Pat said, with a smile. "I didn't even park it; I just stopped in the middle of the street. Thank you."

Friedrichs acknowledged her thanks with a grave inclination of his head, and offered her coffee. Pat took it, marveling at the man's strength of will. He had been on the verge of collapse when she burst in; now he had acquired enough self-control to collect her belongings and restore them to their proper places. And the way he had retreated, instantly, when she took over with Kathy — offering to lock himself in the library. . . . Was that consciousness of guilt, or evidence of a mind that was both rigorously logical and intuitively sensitive to other peoples' feelings?

"She's sleeping," Pat said, as Friedrichs turned toward the bed. "I'll watch her, don't worry. The rescue squad can be here in five minutes, if. . . . You don't have to stay."

Friedrichs' lips twisted. He sat down at the desk.

"Do you suppose I could sleep? I don't expect you to believe me, Mrs. Robbins, but I told you precisely what happened. I almost wish what you suspect were true. It would provide an explanation." His eyes went to his daughter, lingered, and then moved around the room as if he were really seeing it for the first time that night. "You didn't have to clean up in here. Merely staying is kindness enough."

"I just put a few things back in their places," Pat said. "books and ornaments — not much. She must have knocked them down when she ran."

"Would it be out of place for me to suggest that fact substantiates my story? Or do you suppose I came in here to attack her?"

With an effort, Pat forced her eyes away from his tormented face. At least he had had enough experience to know that things like that did happen, that horrified outrage was no defense. His hands were gripping the arms of the chair so hard the knuckles showed like naked bone. They were big, hard hands, and the arms bared by his rolled-up shirt sleeves were the arms of an athlete. He must play tennis or handball, she thought to herself. If he had attacked the girl in her bed she would have had a poor chance of getting away from him.

"If I really thought you had tried to hurt her I wouldn't be sitting here now," she said. "Mr. Friedrichs, have you —"

"My name is Josef. With an *f*."

Pat had to smile.

"Yes, I suppose we have progressed to first names. Mine is Pat. You needn't fear that I'll take advantage of it."

A wave of red swept over Friedrichs' face. She hadn't realized how pale he was until the flush gave his cheeks their normal color.

"Drink your coffee," she said. "You're still in a state of shock. It won't do Kathy any good if you pass out, or — or have a heart attack."

"My heart is perfectly sound." He gave her a startled look. "I'm sorry. I didn't mean to touch on —"

"I touched on it," Pat said steadily. "My husband died of a heart attack a year ago. We thought his heart was perfectly sound too."

"I owe you an apology, Mrs. — Pat. Not for what I said just now; for my behavior the other evening, when you most generously offered new neighbors. . . ." He hesitated, and the ghost of a smile curved his thin lips. "Bread and salt, shall we say?"

"Pasta is basically flour, like bread," Pat agreed. "And there was plenty of salt in that casserole."

"Whatever the ingredients, the intent was the same. It was a kind gesture and my response was boorish. I regretted it at once. I tried to call to you, but apparently you didn't hear me. That's no excuse, however, I might have telephoned to express my regrets — or, at the very least, returned your umbrella! My apologies are belated, but, I assure you, heartfelt."

"Forget it," Pat said, amused at his carefully constructed sentences and meticulous grammar. Mark was right; the man should be living in the nineteenth century.

"Thank you." He relapsed into silence, as if to free her of the obligation to talk. Maybe he didn't feel like talking either. The apology had been made with a certain grace, although he had offered no explanation for his boorishness, as he called it. But the omission had its own decorum. Excuses would have necessitated personal references, and perhaps, if Nancy's hunch about his marital misadventures were correct, an appeal to sympathy or an expression of self-pity. Pat glanced at him from under lowered lashes. He must be in his forties; his cheeks and forehead showed the harsh lines of experience, harsher now with strain. No, not the face of a man who indulged in self-pity or allowed others to pity him. Nor, unless all her instincts were false, the face of a man who would mistreat his daughter.

They did not speak again. The night wore on, with the deadly slowness of all vigils. Pat had long since learned the art of sleeping with one eye open; she did so now, drifting in and out of half-slumber, her senses always alert for any untoward sound or movement from Kathy. Once she slipped deep enough into sleep to dream. It seemed to her that the light from the lamp on the bedside table burned low, and that in the shadowy corner behind the bed something moved. A long arm, skeletal in its pallor and bony thinness, reached out toward the sleeping girl.

Pat woke with a start, to hear Kathy moaning. Friedrichs was sound asleep, his head on the desk, resting on his folded arms. Pat got up, stretching stiffened limbs, and tiptoed to the bed. When she touched Kathy, the girl's breathing resumed its quiet pattern.

Pat went back to her chair. The night had turned quite cold. The thin curtains shifted eerily in the breeze, like formless shapes of ectoplasm. She shivered, and wondered, half-seriously, if nightmares lingered on in the room where a dreamer's mind had shaped them. That pale skeletal arm . . . If Kathy had dreamed of something like that reaching out for her, no wonder she had fled in terror.

Of course the explanation was more prosaic. In her drowsing state she had heard Kathy moan, and had conjured up an appropriate horror.

But she did not sleep again. The birds

roused before the sun, raising a racket in the old apple tree outside the window, and finally the sky began to brighten. The sun was not yet up, but the room was fully light when Kathy awoke.

Her father woke the moment she did, sitting up with a stifled grunt as his stiff muscles protested. His sleep-heavy eyes went straight to Kathy. The girl had turned so that her back was toward her father. She was facing Pat, and after a moment recognition replaced the haziness of waking that clouded her eyes.

"Mrs. Robbins — it is you. I thought I dreamed you." She yawned like a sleepy kitten, her even white teeth sparkling.

"Kathy?" Josef's voice cracked. Kathy rolled over in bed.

"Daddy. Did I oversleep? What time . . ." Then she really saw him. "What's the matter? You look so . . ."

She sat up and held out her arms. Josef dropped to one knee beside the bed. Even then he did not embrace her; he took her hands in his and held them tight. Pat, who had moved to the foot of the bed so she could observe what went on in those first, revealing moments, was reassured — about the Friedrichs, if not about their immediate problem. The girl's candid face showed fear, but only for her father, not of him. She turned to Pat.

"Mrs. Robbins, what happened? He's hurt — his face is all scratched and. . . . Is that why you're here? Oh, Dad, you look terrible!"

Pat sat down on the edge of the bed.

"He's fine," she said. "Josef, I could use some coffee, and I'll bet Kathy is hungry."

"Right." Josef rose to his feet, freeing his hands from Kathy's agitated grasp. "I'll just . . . I'll be right back."

He knew, of course, why Pat had dismissed him. Kathy's bewildered blue eyes followed him as he stumbled from the room.

"Mrs. Robbins, what —"

"Now we talk," Pat said. "You're the patient, Kathy, not your father. What happened last night?"

"Last night? I don't understand."

"Are you taking drugs, Kathy? Pills?

Pot? Peyote, or seeds, or —"

Hoping to catch the girl off guard, she made her voice hard and inquisitorial. She would not have been surprised, or convinced, by an indignant denial. Instead, Kathy blushed guiltily.

"I've smoked pot a few times . . . at parties. . . . Please don't tell Dad, he thinks I'm a virgin saint or something. Hey. Wait a minute. You mean last night? Honest to God, Mrs. Robbins —"

"It couldn't have been marijuana," Pat said, half to herself. "The symptoms weren't right. Besides, I'd have smelled it."

"So would Dad." Kathy pushed a pillow behind her and sat back. "I'd never be dumb enough to smoke here at home, he's got a nose like a bloodhound. What went on last — Oh!" As she twisted to push the pillow into a more comfortable shape she saw something that made the healthy flush fade from her cheeks. "Oh, I'm beginning to remember. . . ."

She was looking at the lamp on the bedside table.

"It wasn't a dream," Kathy said slowly. "That hand — that awful, bony hand . . . It threw the lamp at me."

# *Three*

The hands of Pat's wristwatch pointed to seven thirty when she inserted her key in her door, congratulating herself on being in time to destroy the note before Mark got up. His first class was at nine A.M., and he saw no reason to rise before eight thirty. After all, it was only a twenty-minute drive to campus.

She had felt compelled to leave a note, in case some uncharacteristic quirk roused Mark earlier than normal, but Pat was thankful he wouldn't see it. She didn't want to tell him the truth and she was too tired to think up a good lie.

But as she opened the door she realized that the fate that hates mothers had dealt her another low blow. Leaving the door ajar, she made a dash for the kitchen.

Unfortunately for her, Mark was already on the stairs, and the hall was long. It never entered his head to wonder why his mother was racing through the house in the early morning hours; he entered into the game with youthful enthusiasm, and naturally beat Pat to the kitchen door by at least six feet.

"The winnah and still champeen!" he shouted, blocking the doorway and foiling Pat's efforts to pass him. "Don't you know when you're defeated? Can't run the way you used to, old lady; sit down and rest those aged bones."

He swept Pat off her feet and deposited her in a chair with a thud. He loved to carry her around the house; she suspected it was an unconscious revenge for all the years she had dragged him from place to place against his will. Or maybe it wasn't unconscious. . . . Rubbing her posterior, she made a hideous face, trying to hold Mark's attention. It was in vain. His first move, after a long starving night, was always toward the refrigerator.

After a moment fraught with suspense, Mark looked up from the paper. His smile had vanished.

"Kathy or her old man?"

"What do you —"

"Which of 'em is it? How sick? Is she all right?"

"How did you know?"

Mark handed her the note. For the first time Pat saw what was on the other side of the paper. She cursed her own good manners. If she had folded it, instead of trying to show Josef she trusted him. . . . Kathy had begun a theme on economic theory. Her name was neatly inscribed in the upper-right-hand corner.

"Oh, damn," Pat said, and then took pity on her distraught son. "She's fine, Mark. Really."

"I'll cook breakfast," Mark said. "You talk."

So she told him. She and Jerry had lied to Mark often enough, when he was too young to bear pain lightly — when a neighbor's dog, adored by Mark, had been hit by a car, when a pet hamster had been devoured by Albert in an absentminded moment. But, as Jerry had always said, never lie if there's a chance you'll get caught.

Mark almost burned the bacon as he listened. He interrupted only once, when she mentioned drugs.

"No," he said flatly. "Not Kathy."

"How can you be so sure?"

"I'm sure. Nobody but high-school kids takes LSD these days, and. . . ." Mark stopped, giving his mother a wary look. They had had this discussion before, and it always ended in a fight, because Mark maintained no one over forty knew anything about drugs, and then Pat would demand how he knew so much. This time they were both too preoccupied with other issues to pursue a minor one. Mark went on indignantly, "Damn it, Mom, how can you suggest theories like that when it's obvious what happened?"

"You mean —"

"Freidrichs. I knew that old pervert was —"

"No." It was Pat's turn to be positive. "I know. Wait, you haven't heard the rest of it."

She left out only one thing — her own dream, which had so oddly echoed Kathy's nightmare. When she finished, Mark's eyes were shining and his face had the queerest look, half excitement, half wonder.

"She was awake, when she saw it?"

"Of course she wasn't," Pat snapped. "She dreamed she woke up. I've had that happen in dreams, so have you."

"So she dreamed she woke up. Tell me again what she dreamed she saw when she dreamed she was awake."

"Now, see here, Mark —"

"Please, Mom. In detail."

Pat sighed. "Oh, all right. I haven't got the strength to argue with you.

"Kathy said she was lying on her side facing the window." Pat spoke slowly, trying to reproduce, if not the girl's exact words, the mood and the atmosphere. "She wakened with a start, the way you

107

wake when some loud, unexpected noise jars you out of sleep. She said she could feel her heart beating. It was a frightening sensation. She lay still for a moment, wondering what had awakened her and why she felt so alarmed. She saw the curtains — filmy white dacron — moving in the night breeze, like ghostly figures. But she knew that wasn't what had frightened her."

"Go on," Mark said urgently.

"My scrambled eggs are getting cold," Pat said, taking a bite. "Besides, I'm trying to remember exactly. . . . She was cold, horribly cold. The window was open only a few inches, but she felt icy air envelop her body, as if it slid under the blanket to get at her. With the cold came a mindless terror, and a conviction that something was in the room."

"Something or someone?"

"She said 'something,' " Pat admitted. "She couldn't see clearly, but she imagined a kind of curdled shape in the shadows. She was afraid to call out. If a thief had sneaked into the room, an outcry might alarm him and cause him to attack her. She said she and her friends had discussed what they would do in such cases, and had decided the safest course was to pretend to be asleep. Thieves don't usually attack people unless they —"

"Never mind the crime lecture," Mark interrupted. "We've discussed it ourselves; what defenseless citizen hadn't, these days? It wasn't a burglar that woke Kathy."

"I don't know that and neither do you," Pat said. "She did decide to remain still — which wasn't a difficult decision, because she couldn't have moved if she had wanted to. Then . . . then the objects in the room began to move around."

This was the part of the story that bothered her most. All the rest could be explained away. So could this, of course, as a product of dreaming; but . . .

"Small objects at first," Pat went on reluctantly. "Papers on the desk lifted and scattered. That could have been the wind. But wind couldn't have shifted a pair of china figurines or pulled books from the shelves — or moved the lamp on the bedside table. It . . . it's a rather heavy lamp, with a bronze base. She had chosen one of that type because the dainty porcelain types fall over easily, and don't give enough light to read in bed."

Mark paled visibly. Pat knew he was thinking of Kathy's lovely little face, with its fragile bones and delicate skin. The lamp had been lying on her pillow, where her head had rested. At best, it would have bruised and cut her.

"It didn't hit her," she reassured him again. "She moved when it started to topple. She remembers running and screaming, nothing more; not even her father grabbing her."

Mark started to speak; then he closed his mouth and cocked his head. Pat knew the look, and was on guard when he said craftily, "She's probably lying, to protect her father."

"You don't believe that any more than I do. You're trying to distract me, and I only wish I knew what from. Homework? Did you finish that paper?

Is that why you're up so early, hoping to get it done before class? If you think I'm going to type it for you, at this hour —"

"The paper has been turned in," Mark said, in injured tones. "I have to get to school early, that's all. I told Jim I'd help him with his math before class."

"You mean Jim told you you could copy his homework. Get going, then. I'm so tired I can hardly keep my eyes open. I'm going to bed."

Mark insisted on helping her upstairs, as if she were a hundred years old. She sank into dreamless slumber the minute her head hit the pillow.

## II

It was late afternoon before she woke, and she probably would have slept longer if Albert had not settled down on her stomach. He did that when he decided it was time for his slothful humans to arise and feed him.

Pat heaved the cat off, and got up. The house was quiet, so she knew Mark wasn't in it. He had returned from school, however. The dishes piled in the sink and the splashes of spaghetti sauce on the stove told her that. She got herself a cup of coffee and drank it, glancing through the paper as she did so. Then she went outside.

The first thing she saw was her son's back. He was sitting on top of the fence that separated their house from that of the Friedrichs'. She was too far away to hear what he was saying, but she could see that he was talking; his head bobbed up and down, and once he waved both arms in an eloquent gesture that almost sent him toppling off the fence.

The grass needed cutting again. Pat waded through it toward the fence, her mouth set. She moved silently, but some sixth sense warned Mark of her approach. He turned a tousled brown head toward her, and before she could speak he said in dulcet tones, "I'm not breaking the rules, Mommy. My feet aren't touching the forbidden ground."

"Smart mouth," Pat said.

There was a giggle from the other side

of the fence, and a voice said, "Hi, Mrs. Robbins. Isn't it a pretty day?"

"Hello, Kathy. How are you feeling?"

"Fine." A wide blue eye appeared in a crack between two boards. "Dad said I didn't have to go to school. But I feel great. I wanted to thank you for what you did last night."

"That's quite all right." Pat felt peculiar talking to an eye. She came closer to the fence. "Is your father there?"

"No, ma'am. He went to work."

"I've been thinking perhaps you ought to see a doctor, Kathy. Just to be on the safe side."

"Oh, that's not necessary, Mrs. Robbins. Really. Mark just explained everything to me." The eye narrowed in an expression only too familiar to Pat, who grimaced disgustedly as Kathy continued in adoring tones, "He knows all about it. I mean, I really appreciate him telling me. It's not so scary when I know it was a ghost, not me going crazy or anything like that."

Even after years of exposure to that

curious phenomenon that passes for reasoning among the young of the human species, Pat was left speechless by this comment. She glanced up at her son, who was regarding her with what could only be described as a superior smirk. Then he looked away, and his expression changed to one of guilt and alarm. If Pat hadn't been so angry she would have laughed. She didn't need Kathy's cry of greeting to know who was approaching.

"Hi, Dad. You're home early."

"One of my meetings was canceled," said Josef's deep voice. "We have a date for dinner, Kathy, remember? If you're sure you feel up to it."

Pat leaned against the fence, folded her arms, and prepared to enjoy the conversation — if it was going to be a conversation and not a dialogue. Would Josef acknowledge Mark's presence? It would be difficult to ignore the lanky figure atop the fence, but if anyone could do it, Josef was the man.

Kathy foiled her attempt to remain a detached spectator.

"Mrs. Robbins is there on the other side of the fence, Dad," she said gaily. "Aren't you going to say hello?"

"Hello," Josef said.

Feeling like a fool, Pat responded.

"You'll excuse us," Josef said smoothly, "but we've a long drive and I don't want to be late. Kathy?"

"Yes, all right. Good-bye, Mrs. Robbins, and thanks again. So long, Mark. See you."

Pat scuttled toward the house. What a fool she must have looked, lurking behind the fence. But there was no gate in it. Jerry had made sure of that.

Later, she was to call herself bad names for ignoring the vital clue in that conversation. But she was thinking of other things, such as Josef's successful attempt to squelch Mark by pretending he was invisible, and when she reached the house she found another distraction. She had condemned Josef for bad manners — he might at least have thanked her for her all-night vigil — but as soon as she walked in the back door she heard a knock at the front. When she answered it she saw a messenger carrying a long white box. It contained a sheaf of exquisite, long-stemmed yellow roses. The card was particularly eloquent, it read simply. "Thank you," and his name. But how had he known that yellow roses were her favorites?

She was looking for a vase tall enough to contain such elegance when Mark came in. With cool effrontery he picked up the card and read it aloud.

" 'Thank you, Josef.' Where does he get off using his first name?"

Rummaging in seldom-used cabinets high above her head, Pat found a tall crystal pitcher.

"We spent the night together, after all," she said.

"Hmph," said Mark.

Pat put the flowers on the table between the brown plastic bowl and the chipped cream pitcher.

"Classy," Mark said. "Inappropriate, but classy."

"You've been seeing Kathy, haven't you?"

Mark dropped the spoon he had been

playing with, and dived under the table in pursuit of it. When he came up his face was red, but that might have been explained by his upside-down position. However, one look at his mother's face told him the futility of denials.

"Two hundred years ago they'd have burned you as a witch," he muttered.

"Don't flatter yourself, you aren't that enigmatic," his mother said cruelly. "I should have known you were up to something; you've been so cheerful lately. Today's conversation with Kathy was just a little too fluent if you had seen as little of her as you claimed.

"And?" Mark raised his eyebrows."

"And, while I was searching her room last night I found a note — don't sneer at me like that, I had to do it, Mark! It was under the blotter on her desk and it said, 'Meet me at the usual place, midnight.' It wasn't signed; but I thought at the time the writing looked familiar. If I hadn't been concerned with more important things I'd have put two and two together long before this."

"We only met a couple of times,"

Mark mumbled.

"Where?"

"That old oak tree at the back of their yard. The branches go down almost to the ground on one side, and — uh —"

"I don't know what to say."

"That's a change," Mark said cheekily. "Hey, Mom, take it easy. I'm not doing anything you need to be ashamed of."

"The note had one other word. I didn't quote it because I didn't want to embarrass you."

Mark's eyes fell. "You sign letters that way even to people you hate. Great-Aunt Martha —"

"I do not meet Great-Aunt Martha under the oak tree at midnight. Mark, let's not play games. You know what I'm talking about."

"Yeah, I do, and I think I'm being insulted. Mom, let me handle it. I know what I'm doing."

"Do you?"

They ate in cold, unhappy silence. The velvety roses mocked Pat with their serene beauty and their promise of friendship. If Josef Friedrichs found out Mark and Kathy had met clandestinely — and in such a stupidly romantic, potentially dangerous place. . . . Why couldn't they get together at a local pizza place or even a bar? But Pat knew why. Kathy was so closely supervised she could only elude her father late at night, after she was supposed to be in bed. Josef was wrong to treat a girl that age like a baby or a criminal, but his folly did not excuse Mark's.

## III

Winston Churchill, it is said, conducted World War II on three hours of sleep a night, augmented by frequent naps. Pat was not one of the napping kind; her afternoon sleep always left her cross and groggy, fit only for an early night. She went to bed at ten. Mark's light was still on. He had been at his desk since seven, and when she glanced in to say a rather cool good-night she was softened by the evidences of scholarly industry. His desk was piled high with books and he was taking notes with furious energy.

But instinct prevails. Pat woke in the post-midnight dark fully alert and vibrant with apprehension. At first she could not account for her feeling of impending danger. The house was quiet except for the usual creaking of shutters and thumping of radiators. Albert lay at the foot of the bed snoring and twitching, dreaming of mice.

Jud usually slept with Mark — in his bed, if he could get away with it. As Pat lay wide-eyed in the dark, listening, she heard the faint metallic jingle that accompanied the dog's movements — the rattle of his license, ID, and rabies tags. She knew, however, that this noise had not awakened her. Jud sometimes walked in the night, looking for food, water, or entertainment, especially if Mark had roused enough to kick him out of the bed. Her sleeping mind had long since learned to ignore this familiar sound.

With a sigh she swung her feet onto the floor and padded down the hall to Mark's room. Somehow she knew what she was going to find: a smooth, unrumpled bed, the spread as neat as it had been that afternoon when she made it.

She went to the window. The foliage had filled out, and it was difficult to see the house next door, but a faint gleam from the window of the master bedroom cut through the night. Kathy's window was dark. Moonlight traced the shape of the flowering apple tree at the back corner, turning it into a pale cloud of whiteness.

Pat swore, using some of the words she had learned from Mark. Muttering to herself, she went back to her room and dressed quickly in jeans and shirt, slipping her feet into a pair of worn sneakers. The hall light was on, as it always was at night. The rest of the house was dark. Pat pressed the switches as she proceeded, down the stairs and along the passage to the kitchen, remembering how the lights had moved through Halcyon House on the previous night. She hoped Josef wouldn't see her lights and come rushing to the rescue.

That could be disastrous, if what she was beginning to fear was true.

There was no one in the kitchen except Jud, sitting hopefully by the back door. When he saw Pat his tail switched and his mouth opened, emitting a long moist pink tongue. The chain on the kitchen door dangled.

Pat left the door on the latch, shoving Jud back inside with a peremptory foot when he would have accompanied her. One hurt, irritated yelp followed her; then came silence. Jud was not much of a barker.

As soon as she stepped off the path into the long grass, her shoes were soaked with dew. She had to go around to the front gate. There was no other way through to the next house. A streetlight some distance away sent long shadows wavering eerily across the sidewalk. Pat thought of going back for a flashlight, and decided that on this occasion she had better not risk it.

The night was abnormally still. The click of the latch on the gate as she closed it behind her echoed like a gunshot. She went through the Friedrichs' gate, leaving it open. Shuffling in the darkness, she tripped over a loose brick in the sidewalk and caught at a tree trunk to keep herself from falling.

The backyard was huge, over two acres in extent, spotted by old trees that spread great pools of dark shadow across the moonlit grass. Some were fruit trees; the pale blossoms looked ghostly in the dimness. Pat went toward the apple tree by Kathy's window. She was beginning to feel a little foolish. Perhaps her hunch had been wrong. But when she put her hand on the tree trunk her fingers recoiled from a clammy lump of some wet, sticky substance. Mud. A large chunk of it, lodged in the wedge between the trunk and the first low-set, spreading branch. Someone had climbed that tree, so recently that the earth left by his shoes was still wet. Pat had no doubt whatever as to the identity of the climber.

She wiped her muddy fingers on the seat of her jeans and tried to think what she should do. Kathy's window was wide open. A wisp of white curtain moved in the night breeze. Had there been a screen in that window? She couldn't remember. If there had been, it had been removed; the end of the curtain flailed out through the opening and then blew back.

She couldn't call out. That would really create a crisis. Josef was still awake. The light from his window cut a wide swath across the darkness, touching the edge of the apple tree. She was sure, with the unerring instinct of infuriated maternity, that her son was up there in Kathy's room, and she had no idea what to do about it.

She had little time to debate. As she stood, raging and uncertain, her hand absentmindedly rubbing the rough bark of the tree, she realized that something was happening up above. The window of the girl's room, which had been as black as a cave mouth, began to lighten. The light was not that of any normal lamp; it was a sickly blue-green glow, phosphorescent and ugly. No sooner had she observed it than she heard a muffled crash from the interior of the room; then the light was obscured by a dark shape, and she heard voices. They were mere whispers of sound; but she recognized both of them.

"The branch is there by your foot," muttered her son. "I've got hold of you, don't worry. . . . Quick. It's coming."

"I'm all right. Hurry, Mark, please hurry . . ."

The second voice was Kathy's. Staring up, Pat saw a slim dark shape squirm out of the window, attach itself to the tree, and move downward. Her heart was thudding in her breast. As the light above strengthened, turning the open window into a square of unspeakable, nameless color, the sounds from within increased — crashes, thuds. . . . And Mark was in there, with — whatever it was.

Even as her lips parted, prepared to scream a warning, Mark scrambled onto the tree limb. The light was strong enough to illumine his face, giving his skin a livid, corpselike hue.

Kathy slid down practically into Pat's arms, and the older woman clutched at her. Kathy let out a squeal. Then she recognized Pat, in spite of the darkness. "Goodness, you scared me," she said.

"Mark," Pat gurgled.

"He's here," Kathy said coolly, reaching out an arm to touch Mark as he jumped the last few feet, landing with a squashy thud.

"Hi, Mom. What are you doing here? You ought to be in bed."

For the second time that day Pat's voice failed her. It was not only indignation that rendered her speechless. Something other than light flowed from the open window; a finger of sickening cold touched her, weakening her knees, so that she had to grab at the tree for support. And the smell . . . No, not a smell; it was no phenomenon that could be identified by any normal sense. Its strangeness assaulted all the senses, making her skin crawl and her nose wrinkle, offending even vision by the noncolor of that ghastly light. The very sounds affronted reason, for they were the sounds of objects moving without anything to make them move.

A particularly appalling crash came from the window. It was followed by footsteps, muffled by distance, but clearly audible — running footsteps, and a cry, cut off almost as soon as it began by another crash.

Pat caught her son's foot as he started back up the tree.

"Not that way," she gasped. "For God's sake, Mark!"

The horrid, sickly light was fading, but the aura of foul cold still wafted in weakening waves from the open window. For once Mark yielded to her demand without argument or delay. He slid back down the trunk.

"That was Mr. Friedrichs," he said. "We've got to get in the house. Kathy, how —"

"The front door," Kathy said. She began to run.

She ran like Atalanta, driven by terror. When Pat caught up with her she was on the porch, groping with frantic fingers along the ledge over the door.

"Here it is," she gasped. "We keep a key there in case —"

Mark snatched it from her shaking fingers and inserted it in the lock. But they had forgotten the extra precautions taken by nervous householders. The door yielded only a few inches and then was held by the chain.

"Get back," Mark said. He flung his full weight against the door.

With a crack the chain snapped and the door flew open. Mark plunged in.

The hall was in darkness, but a light shone down the stairs from the corridor above. With the two women in close pursuit, Mark ran up.

They found Josef Friedrichs in the hall outside Kathy's door. He lay face down on the floor, his arms outflung as if he had tried to snatch at something — or ward it off. All around him were the sparkling, glowing shards of what had once been a tall Chinese vase. Pat had noticed it the night before, the exquisite curving shape of it, and the magnificent reds and pinks and greens of a pattern of chrysanthemums and feeding birds. Its carved teak stand was empty.

Kathy's bedroom door was closed; but Pat was aware that the sounds and the breath of sickly cold air had stopped. Thank God for that, she thought; if he's fractured his skull or broken any bones, it would be dangerous to move him . . . but not as dangerous as to leave him within the range of the unknown force that had invaded Kathy's room.

She brushed the sobbing girl out of the way and knelt by Josef, her skilled hands searching for signs that would tell her what she needed to know. Some of the broken shards, melancholy in their reminder of broken beauty, lay on Josef's back. Automatically Pat brushed them off.

The vase had struck him on the side of the head, behind his right ear. A lump was already rising, and a thin trail of blood snaked down his neck and under the collar of his shirt. Minor cuts marked his right hand and forearm. But his pulse was steady, and his breathing regular.

Kathy, held in the protective circle of Mark's arm, struggled to control herself.

She brushed pathetically at the tears on her cheek with the back of her hand, leaving a streak of mud across her smooth skin.

"He's all right," Mark assured her, stroking her hair. He was obviously more concerned with Kathy's feelings than with her father's wounds; and his mother shot him a look of active dislike before adding her own words of reassurance.

"There's no fracture, Kathy, just a nasty lump. Unless he has a concussion —"

Josef interrupted the diagnosis by groaning. His eyes opened and stared blankly at Pat. He struggled to a sitting position.

"Kathy," he muttered.

"I'm right here, Dad. I'm fine."

She threw her arms around him, so enthusiastically that he fell back against the wall, giving his head another nasty bump. The Robbinses, mother and son, watched the touching tableau with mixed emotions. Pat wasn't sure what Mark was thinking; her own feelings, a blend of relief, bewilderment, and fright, included a sudden awareness of the fact that she was wearing the jeans she usually used for painting, and that she had neglected to take the curlers out of her hair.

Friedrichs insisted he didn't have to go to the hospital.

"I am well aware of the symptoms of concussion," he told Pat brusquely. "If I start seeing double, I'll tell you."

Pat knew a stubborn man when she met one. She didn't argue. But she did prevail in one thing: that the Friedrichs spend what remained of the night at her house. Josef agreed for his daughter's sake. The sight of Kathy's room, a disaster area of broken glass, scattered papers, and toppled furniture, turned all of them a little sick. It wasn't so much the mess as the suggestion of malevolence behind such destruction that was frightening.

Reassured about her father, Kathy responded with enthusiasm when Mark suggested they all have a snack and talk things over. The adults were not so eager.

"Tomorrow is Saturday," Pat pointed out. "We can talk after we've had some sleep. I don't think any of us is in condition to think sensibly just now."

Mark, about to remonstrate, caught Josef's eye, and subsided. It was obvious even to him that among the things that would have to be discussed was his presence in Kathy's bedroom at one o'clock in the morning. He didn't need Kathy's warning nudge to know that his excuses would have to be very convincing and his audience very kindly disposed toward him.

Although it was Pat who had insisted on going to bed, she was the only one who failed to woo slumber successfully. The big old house had plenty of bedrooms, it was no problem to find room for two guests. The young people dropped off immediately; and when she peeked into Josef's room he was lying quietly. But she was keyed up and worried; despite Josef's disclaimers she felt she ought to keep an eye on him. On her third visit to his room a voice came out of the dark as she hovered

132

distractedly in the doorway.

"For God's sake, Pat, will you go to bed? Every time you tiptoe in here, that damned dog follows you. He jingles so loud he wakes me up."

Pat crept away, aiming a backward kick at Jud as she did so. He eluded it easily, being accustomed to such signs of disapproval, and jingled down the hall after her. She had been more active than Mark that evening, and Jud had hopes of further activity. But this time Pat disappointed him by falling asleep.

It was well past noon when she was awakened by her son, who was looking revoltingly healthy and alert. He had at least had the tact to bring her a cup of coffee. That cheered her briefly, but then the events of the previous night came back in a flood of horrible memories. She told Mark he was a rude, inconsiderate brat, and tried to put the pillow over her head.

"Everybody else is up," Mark said. "I'm making brunch. Shake a leg."

Pat spent considerable time getting

dressed. The memory of her curlers and dirty jeans still rankled, so she put on a new blouse and checked skirt and made up her face with particular care. As she might have expected, Mark greeted her entrance into the kitchen with a piercing whistle and the question, "Where's the party?"

"I always dress in my best for a round-table discussion about burglars," Pat said disagreeably.

Kathy was sitting at the kitchen table, looking sleepy and adorable in Pat's favorite robe, the pale-blue chiffon she had bought on sale at Saks, and saved for special occasions. The girl was watching Mark with wide-eyed admiration as he moved efficiently from the sink to the stove. When Pat appeared she jumped up — the tribute of youth to age — and Pat noticed in passing that the gown was several inches too long for her. No doubt the hem would be ripped, and dirty.

"Thanks," she muttered, as Kathy pulled out a chair. "Where's your father?"

The back door opened and Josef came in. He was freshly shaved and was dressed neatly in tan slacks and plaid sports shirt, but his expression was grim.

"All quiet on the home front," he said. "I think it's safe for us to go back. We won't intrude on your hospitality any longer."

"You can't run away from it," Mark said, placing a platter of scrambled eggs and sausage on the table. "You can't pretend it didn't happen. Kathy can't go back to that house, Mr. Friedrichs."

"Now just a minute, young man," Pat began. Josef shook his head.

"He's right, Pat. We do have a few things to discuss. First and foremost, I think, is the question of what you were doing in my daughter's room last night . . ."

"Mark," said that young man helpfully. "The name is Mark, Mr. Friedrichs. Have some scrambled eggs."

"He makes wonderful scrambled eggs," Kathy said. "How many heroes can also cook?"

She smiled broadly at her father. After

135

a moment he smiled back at her. Pat blinked. She had never imagined that a smile could do so much for a man's looks. He was really quite handsome when his eyes lost their steely coldness.

"Mark won't defend himself, so I will," Kathy said. Mark's mother wondered where she had gotten this idea, but did not contradict it; and Kathy went on, "We planned it yesterday afternoon, Dad. He suspected what might happen. And he was right, wasn't he? If he hadn't been there . . ."

A shiver ran through her body, and Friedrichs' smile faded.

"What precisely did happen?" he asked.

"Well, *it* came back," Kathy said simply. "We were sitting in the dark, just talking, in whispers. . . . And then it came. First the light. It was kind of a sickly glow, faint at first; then it got stronger. And things started to move around. You know what it was like, Dad? Like somebody very weak, trying to move after lying for a long time in bed. First it just blew the papers on the desk.

Then it got stronger. The mirror lifted up off the wall and broke. A chair fell over. Mark helped me out the window —"

"Why didn't you go out the door?" Pat asked.

"It was between us and the door," Mark said.

He spoke through a mouthful of eggs, and his voice was muffled; but instead of sounding funny, the statement sent a chill up Pat's spine.

"I was outside the window," she said. "I saw it. At least, I saw the light, and felt . . . It was indescribably bad. All the same —"

"Come on, Mom," Mark exclaimed. "You're not going to insist that it was burglars, are you? Damn it, you were down below, but I was *there*. I never felt anything like that in my life. It was fascinating."

Josef choked on a mouthful of food. When he had recovered himself he looked at Mark and said thoughtfully, "I have a feeling, Mark, that you are going to be one of the greater trials I have encountered in a lifetime not entirely free of aggravation. All the same, I can't help admiring your attitude. Fascinating?''

''Well, you know,'' Mark mumbled around a sausage. ''I never believed in that stuff before, not really. Ghost stories are fun, but in real life . . . When Kathy and I talked it over yesterday afternoon, I was ninety percent convinced, but it was intellectual conviction, you know what I mean? Not a real gut belief. Then the damned thing began — and it was like, well, like Saint Theresa describing her meeting with God. It can't be described, it has to be experienced; and when you do experience it, you have no doubts at all.''

Pat had not been to church for years, but she had once been a good Presbyterian. She was about to protest Mark's comments, which smacked of one of the lesser heresies, when Josef said calmy, ''That's not a bad analogy. Poorly expressed, of course — your generation is barely literate, Mark — but the comparison is valid."

"Josef!" Pat exclaimed.

"He's right, Pat. I experienced it. I'm sure you and all the good ladies of the neighborhood are aware of the fact that I am a lawyer. That doesn't mean I'm not a fool; but the legal profession does give one some regard for evidence." His hand went to the back of his head, where the lump was rising to spectacular proportions. "That's evidence, Pat. I wasn't drunk, or drugged, last night. I was dozing; after what had happened the previous night I was a little apprehensive about Kathy, and I meant to stay awake, but I was pretty tired. I didn't hear the trouble begin. One particularly loud crash woke me, and I went tearing toward her room. I was almost there when the vase — that Chinese vase that stood on a pedestal in the hall — rose up off its base and flew at me."

Pat stared, her eyes wide. Josef nodded.

"Yes, I saw it. Out of the corner of my eye, admittedly; but I couldn't be mistaken. There was no one there. The vase didn't fall, it lifted up into the air before it came at me. I had just time enough to turn and shield my head with my right arm. My hand deflected it somewhat, I think, or I'd be in worse shape than I am. It was quite heavy."

"Poltergeist," Mark said.

"Well . . ." Again the glance Josef gave Mark was mingled with unwilling respect. "I suppose you're right. I hadn't thought of it in quite those terms."

"What is a poltergeist?" Pat asked, hoping it wasn't quite as unacceptable to common sense as an ordinary ghost.

Apparently she was the only one unfamiliar with the term. The others all spoke at once. As was to be expected, Mark's voice dominated.

"It's a mischievous spirit, or malicious ghost. It makes rapping noises and throws stones and things. The classic case — the one that marks the beginning of the Spiritualist movement — was that of the Fox sisters, in 1848 —"

"Not a good example, Mark," Josef interrupted. "Margaret Fox confessed, forty years later, that she produced the rappings by cracking the joint of her big toe."

"But —" Mark began.

"Let me finish." Josef turned to Pat. "I became interested in the subject because I once had a case that involved a supposed poltergeist. A family had bought a house that proved to be virtually uninhabitable. The bedclothes were pulled off the beds while people were sleeping in them, the walls reverberated with knocking and rapping all night long, stones and rocks fell, apparently out of empty air. The family sued my client, claiming that he knew when he sold them the house that it was haunted. There was no denying that disturbances had occurred; several unimpeachable outside witnesses had observed them."

"You never told me about that case," Kathy said.

"It was ten years ago, Kathy; and God knows I never imagined we'd have any personal interest in haunted houses. At any rate, I did some research on poltergeists and learned a few facts that saved my client from an expensive settlement.

"In almost every reported case, as in that one, there was an adolescent child living in the disturbed house. Often psychic investigators were able to prove that the child had caused the disturbances by the same sort of trickery practiced by stage magicians. The hand is faster than the eye, in fact, and these kids were amazingly adept at twitching strings, pushing objects with their toes, and so on."

"Wait a minute," Mark said. "Not all the cases could be explained that way. I remember reading —"

"A book by some quack ghost hunter, probably. People of that ilk are either cynical professional writers, willing to report anything that will sell, or they are incredibly gullible. The investigators of the Society for Psychic Research aren't so naïve. When a thorough, controlled investigation of a poltergeist was made, trickery was almost always found."

Mark's face was getting red. Pat knew he was controlling himself with an effort; he would have interrupted anyone but Kathy's father long since.

"Aren't you being inconsistent, Josef?" she asked. "You say you saw the vase move, but you maintain that all poltergeist cases are faked. Or are you accusing Kathy?"

"Certainly not! Besides, if Mark's evidence can be trusted, she was outside the house when the vase moved."

It was Mark's turn to choke with indignation.

"If that's what legal training does for you, I don't want it. You can't clear your own daughter of trying to brain you unless she's got an alibi? What kind of —"

"That's the only way we can approach this mess," Josef said angrily. "By being rigorously logical. If we make exceptions —"

"Well, dammit, I don't suspect the people I love of —"

"You young jackass, it isn't a question —"

Pat banged her hand down on the table. Plates rattled, and the debaters

143

stopped shouting.

"That's enough," she said severely. "You're behaving like spoiled brats — both of you. Mark, is there any more coffee?"

Mark got up and went to the stove. Even the back of his neck was red.

"You are quite right," Josef said, his flush subsiding. "I apologize for shouting. All the same —"

Mark returned with the coffeepot and poured, rather sloppily. Being younger, he was not as well disciplined as Josef; his cheekbones still showed bright spots of temper, but when he spoke he was obviously trying to be conciliatory.

"I — uh — guess I should apologize too. But if you'd just let me say something . . ."

"He's right, Dad, it's his turn," Kathy said. "You aren't conversing, you're lecturing."

Josef turned impetuously to his daughter.

"Kathy, you know I didn't mean —"

"I know." She patted his hand. "It's

144

that blasted legal training. Now listen to Mark."

A lesser personage might have been intimidated by the glare Josef turned upon him, but Mark was not the most modest of men. His chest expanded visibly as the others sat waiting for him to speak, and he took his time about beginning, measuring sugar into his coffee and clearing his throat several times.

"You left out one thing about poltergeists, Mr. Friedrichs. Sure, some of them are out-and-out fakes. But there is another theory. Some psychologists claim that a young person, especially a female entering puberty, is sort of . . . well . . . overflowing with psychic and sexual energy. Sometimes, especially if the adolescent personality is disturbed to begin with, this energy finds an outlet in poltergeist-type manifestations."

Despite Mark's pompous language, his meaning was clear. Pat half expected Kathy to throw something at him. Instead she laughed, freely and delightfully.

"That's the silliest thing I ever heard of."

"It certainly couldn't apply to Kathy," Pat agreed. She smiled at the girl, ready to forgive even the ruination of her favorite negligee. "I've never seen a less disturbed adolescent personality. Besides, if you are talking about puberty —"

"I went through *that* six years ago," Kathy said scornfully. "It's just *silly,* Mark. I mean, back in the nineteenth century maybe it was a shock to a girl, but these days . . ."

"Oh, I don't believe it," Mark said. "I just mentioned it to clear the air. I don't think what we've got is a poltergeist, anyway."

Josef followed the exchange interestedly, his elbows on the table, his fingers buried in his hair.

"Then what you believe," he said precisely, "is that there is an active, malevolent personality behind this — not just some vague, undefined burst of psychic energy."

"Good," Mark said patronizingly. "Right on. What we have got, ladies and sir, is a ghost."

Silence followed this statement. The refrigerator turned itself on with a click. Sunlight streamed through the windows, brightening the faded, flowery chintz of the curtains and setting sparks flaring off the coppery molds that adorned the walls. In the center of the kitchen table the yellow roses had spread their petals wide.

"This is unreal," Pat said.

Three pairs of eyes turned toward her. Josef's were a deep brown, almost black. She hadn't noticed their color before.

"I know how you feel," he said gently. "But I'm afraid it's a possibility. At least I'm willing to listen to Mark's statement." His voice sharpened as he turned to Mark. "I assume he has a statement — a long one."

"Not as long as I'd like it to be," Mark said, with unusual humility. "However, I will start with the fact that this isn't the first time your house has seen manifestations. Old Hiram —"

"Yes, I've heard of old Hiram," Josef said. "Go on."

"He wasn't crazy," Mark said. "I guess you could call him eccentric, although Dad used to say any man had the right to live the way he wanted, so long as he wasn't hurting anybody else."

"Did old Hiram hurt anybody else?" Josef asked.

Mark grinned. The chipped front tooth, damaged in a hard fall on the basketball court, gave his smile a gamin look.

"He threw rocks at us," he said. "Looking back on it, I don't think he really meant to hit anybody, any more than we meant to hassle him. Well, maybe we did, a little, he was such an old grouch. But mostly it was the place — all overgrown and weedy, a swell place to play war games and spies. And there were the buried-treasure stories. But then old Hiram complained, and Dad made me build that fence. Wow. That really hurt. Spending three Saturdays working, when I could have been playing baseball. Anyhow, after that we didn't bug Hiram; but he kind of liked Dad. . . ."

"You are wandering from the subject," Pat said.

"What?" Mark gave her a startled look. "Oh. I guess I was. Anyhow, Hiram told Dad that when he first moved into the house some funny things happened. Lights, and objects moving around. He said he figured it was a ghost, so he stood in the middle of the hall and yelled out that he was a stranger, and he wouldn't bother it if it didn't bother him."

" 'Eccentric' is hardly the word for Hiram," Josef said drily. "Did that stop the manifestations?"

"I guess so. He said he never had no more trouble —"

"Mark, your grammar," Pat said.

"I'm quoting," Mark said blandly. "But Dad said it was an interesting story. He believed it, not because old Hiram wasn't peculiar, but because his peculiarities wouldn't take that form."

He looked at the others as if hoping they would understand what he meant. Surprisingly, it was Friedrichs who nodded.

"Yes, I see. Old Hiram might have delusions of persecution from Russians or Martians or vicious small boys, but not from poltergeists. Nor would he have mentioned the subject to your father, who was only a casual acquaintance, unless —"

"Yeah, that was it. He didn't want us hanging around anyway; he hated everybody, especially kids. But he told Dad he was afraid we'd start the ghost up again. Things were nice and quiet, he said, and he liked them that way."

"He wasn't so crazy," Josef muttered. "All right, Mark, I'll accept your first point. The — er — trouble did not originate with us. Are you suggesting I stand in the hall and shout reassurances, as he did, to our racketing spirit?"

"No, look — you don't get what I'm driving at. It isn't just a random effect. It woke up, like, when Hiram moved in. But he wasn't . . . what it wanted."

"Ugh," Kathy said violently. "I don't like that idea."

"Neither do I," Pat said. "Stop beating around the bush, Mark. You insinuated that you and — and your father had looked into the ghost theory. What are you driving at?"

"It sounds so unconvincing when you just state it flat out, without explaining —"

"State it flat out," Pat said firmly.

"Okay, okay. I think there is a ghost . . . spirit . . . whatever you want to call it. I think it dates from the period just after these houses were built. Now wait — do any of you know anything about the history of these two houses?"

He knew they didn't. Pat glowered at him, and Josef froze him with a cold legal stare; but Mark was basking in the warmth of Kathy's admiration and ignored the adult disdain.

"They are twin houses, as you know," he said, addressing all of them, though he continued to look at Kathy. "They were built in 1843, by a Mr. Peters, for his twin daughters. . . ."

# *Four*

If the midwife hadn't sworn to the fact,
people would not have believed that
Lavinia and Louisa Peters were sisters,
much less twins. They were both fair-
haired and blue-eyed, but with that the
resemblance ceased. Lavinia was a fairy
child, fragile and exquisite; Louisa was
chubby and stolid, regarding the world
with cool detachment from behind the
thumb that was usually in her mouth. As
they grew to young ladyhood, Louisa lost
her baby fat, but she was never as slim
as her sister, whose waist attained the
fabulous seventeen-inch span so desired
by Southern belles. Her blue eyes kept
their look of calm appraisal, while
Lavinia's danced coquettishly, flirting
long lashes at her dozens of beaux.

("I've seen old photographs of the two," Mark said. "They didn't even look alike. They were older when the pictures were taken, but one was still the professional Southern lady; the other had a placid, motherly sort of face.")

They were devoted to one another, and that was odd; for although the term "sibling rivalry" had not yet been coined, the reality had existed for centuries, and many sisters have a healthy detestation for one another. Not Louisa and Lavinia. It was not surprising that they should fall in love and marry at the same age, for they did everything together. Nor was it really surprising, considering how different they were, that their husbands should be such opposites.

Albert Turnbull was a widower, almost twenty years older than Lavinia, but every other factor was in his favor. He was a neighbor, a planter, an aristocrat; his estate, adjoining the Peters' tobacco plantation, included fifty slaves and four hundred acres.

("And he was a good-looking guy," Mark said. "I mean, if you like the type

— mustache, high cheekbones, the deliberate aristocratic sneer. I don't know why he and Lavinia didn't move into his house. Maybe she refused to live with the relics of his first wife, or maybe the ancestral mansion was falling apart. . . .")

Whatever the reason, Turnbull moved into the handsome new house built as a wedding gift by his father-in-law. The name he gave it, Halcyon House, was not especially original, but it indicated an optimistic hope for happiness with his new bride. He may not have been so pleased about his new brother-in-law.

His name was Bates — John Bates. It was a flat, thumping, monosyllabic name, and the pictures of him that have survived show a face that suits the name — expressionless, dour, dark. A New Englander by birth and a schoolteacher by trade, he had somehow found his way to Maryland and the headmastership of one of the new private schools in the area.

("I don't know how Louisa met him," Mark admitted. "Schoolteachers weren't gentry, not exactly. . . . But they weren't lower-class types either, so I guess she could have run into him at some social function. It must have been a genuine love match. To a girl of her background, Bates had nothing in particular to recommend him. He looked like a sour-faced, sanctimonious old —'')

He wasn't old, though; he was only twenty-six when he married the eighteen-year-old Louisa, more than ten years younger than his brother-in-law, Turnbull. Peters, one of the wealthier landowners of Maryland, endowed his adored daughters with wide acres, and built them each a house. It seems reasonable to suppose that the mutual affection of the sisters dictated the relative proximity of the houses, for western Maryland in those days had plenty of empty space — and the odd fact that they were duplicates. One might have expected the placid Louisa and her stolid New England husband to prefer a more classic style. But old Mr. Peters was providing the money, and perhaps it was he who demanded the very latest mode in architecture — the bizarre mixture of Tudor and castellated medieval styles known as American Gothic revival.

Some students of local architecture suspect that the twin houses were designed by the same man who built Tudor Hall, the boyhood home of the Booth brothers — Edwin the actor, John Wilkes, the assassin. The red brick walls boasted mullioned windows and diamond-pane casements. The great bay windows in the drawing rooms had Gothic tracery. Wooden curlicues and curls hung like icicles from the porches, roofs, and gables.

("Most of the wooden wedding-cake trim is gone now," Mark said. "It was too expensive to paint and repair. The houses aren't exact duplicates anymore because over the years people added things like bathrooms and kitchens. But the floor plans are the same.")

The name the Turnbulls gave their home was typically pretentious, but names were not pure affectation, they were a convenient form of identification before street names and route numbers.

The Bateses also named their house.

("It's funny," Mark said. "Most of the old names are remembered. Not that one. It's mentioned in one old book, and nowhere else. Freedom Hall. You could reasonably assume a New England schoolteacher would be an abolitionist. The name he gave his house makes it certain.")

The slave owner and the antislavery schoolteacher might not have been the best of friends, but the two families lived side by side in apparent amity for almost fifteen years. Turnbull had one daughter from his previous marriage. Lavinia presented him with another child, a son, born in 1844. Louisa was more prolific than her sister, but not much more fortunate. Her first child was also born in 1844, but it did not survive infancy. She became pregnant again almost at once, producing twins in 1845 — a boy and a girl. She had other children, but only one of them lived as long as eight years. By 1860 the pattern of duplication still prevailed, with two members of the younger generation in each of the twin houses. Lavinia's stepdaughter, Mary Jane, was twenty-six. Her son Peter was sixteen. The Bates cousins, Edward and Susan, were a year younger than Peter. In that year the war clouds were gathering, hanging low and dark over divided border states such as Maryland.

## II

They had agreed not to interrupt Mark. No one did, but Pat was amused at the effort it cost Josef Friedrichs to keep his mouth shut. Every now and then a particularly questionable statement or undefended assumption would produce a visible contortion in the older man's face, his cheek muscles twitching as he struggled not to speak. When Mark ended with his dramatic metaphor Josef could contain himself no longer.

"You'd be a great trial lawyer," he said caustically. "Eloquent, florid, and full of hot air. How much of that is factual?"

"There's a genealogy," Mark said.

158

"Deeds, architect's plans —"

"I assumed you had those. Where did you get all that about Bates's abolitionist beliefs?"

"But, Dad, it's obvious," Kathy exclaimed. "Can't you see the conflict building between the two families? Maryland was a border state. It almost seceded. It probably would have if the federal government hadn't occupied Baltimore and thrown a lot of Southern sympathizers in jail. There were Maryland regiments in both the Confederate and Union armies —"

"I'm glad you're learning a little history in that expensive school," Josef said. "Oddly enough, my dear, I knew all that. But you haven't proved that the two families who lived in these houses were divided in their sentiments, or that, if they were, there is any connection whatever with the presumed apparition that —"

"I'll prove it," Mark said. His lips set in a stubborn line, his dark brows drew together. "I've just started to look. But, damn it, I know I'm right. I'll do it myself if I have to, but it would go a lot faster if I could get some help from you guys."

"I'll help," Kathy said.

Josef looked at his daughter as if seeing her for the first time that morning. His eyes widened.

"Where did you get that — that garment?"

"It belongs to Mrs. Robbins." Kathy contemplated a splash of coffee with some dismay. "Gosh, Mrs. Robbins, I'm sorry. I guess I'm getting it dirty. I'll wash it —"

"The time is midafternoon and you are sitting around in a bathrobe," Josef said indignantly. "Get dressed immediately."

Kathy made a mutinous face, but obeyed. She had barely left the room when the front-door bell rang.

"It's probably one of your friends," Pat said to Mark. "Tell him to come back later. I don't think we want the whole town to know Kathy spent the night here."

"Okay, okay." Mark went out.

Josef rose. His face had fallen back into its rigid lines.

"I appreciate your thoughtfulness, Pat. I did not intend —"

"Oh, stop being so pompous," Pat said. "We can't go back to the old formality, can we? I don't know what to say about Mark's crazy theory, but one thing is certain: you two can't sleep in that house until we figure out what went on there."

Before Josef could answer, the swinging door to the kitchen burst open and Mark entered.

"It's Mrs. Groft," he hissed, like a stage villain. "She says you were supposed to go antiquing with her. She's in the living room, but you know her, she's got the biggest mouth in town, and she'll be coming out here any minute. . . ."

"Darn, I forgot," Pat exclaimed. "Of all the people we don't want to know about this —"

Josef's eyes opened wide. Through terror, distress, and even unconsciousness he had maintained a

161

certain dignity; this threat reduced him to quivering, unconcealed cowardice.

"I know that woman. She's been driving me crazy ever since I moved in. For God's sake, Pat, head her off. Mark, keep Kathy out of sight. If she sees —"

Nancy's not so dulcet voice reverberated, even through a closed door and a long stretch of hall. "Pa-a-at! Aren't you ready?"

Josef made a brief, vulgar comment and bolted, leaving the back door ajar. Mark fled in the other direction, up the back stairs. Pat leaned against the sink and laughed.

## III

She caught Nancy before that inquisitive lady reached the kitchen. The piled-up dishes would have been a dead giveaway. She could imagine Nancy's delighted inuendos: "My, my, what class — brunch at one P.M., and with whom, my dear? Not, by any chance . . ." Fortunately Pat was already dressed to go out; she had only to snatch up her purse and propel her friend from the house. Upstairs Mark was thundering around like a herd of demented moose, presumably in order to cover any sounds Kathy might make.

The antique show was in Gaithersburg, a fast half hour's drive away. Fortunately it was a good show, and Nancy, who collected everything from old silver to antique duck decoys, was sufficiently absorbed to leave Pat alone. Nancy was known to, and hated by, most of the dealers, since her method of bargaining consisted of making derogatory remarks about the merchandise. Pat wandered off, leaving Nancy arguing with a gray-haired woman who was selling old glass.

In the cold light of day she found it harder and harder to believe what had happened the previous night. Surely — surely! — there must be some sensible explanation. Mark was young and given to strange enthusiasms . . . but he was just plain nuts if he really believed this ghost theory. Kathy was also young, and so infatuated with Mark she would believe the sun set in the east if he told her it did.

Pat couldn't dismiss Josef's experience so easily. She tried, though; and as her eyes moved unseeingly over displays of medicine bottles, postcards, Victorian chamber sets, and other dubious treasures, she finally came up with a hypothesis — not a wholly satisfactory hypothesis, but one that was easier to accept than Mark's ghost. The Chinese vase was tall and top-heavy, tapering down from swelling sides to a relatively narrow base. If Josef, running to his daughter's aid, had tripped and started to fall, his outflung arm, or even the vibration of his footsteps, might have toppled the vase. In his overwrought state, he might fancy the object had moved of its own accord. The whole thing was self-hypnotism, autosuggestion. . . . And that same convenient diagnosis would explain her own sensations as she stood in horrified suspense under Kathy's window.

Pat grimaced. The theory was unconvincing, even to her. It was hard for her to dismiss her sensations of loathing as sheer imagination.

There was another explanation. Pat let it emerge into her conscious mind, from the depths where it had been simmering, and looked at it dispassionately.

Josef Friedrichs had engineered the whole thing. He had, in fact, attacked his daughter on the first occasion, and had stage-managed a second "supernatural" attack in order to conceal his guilt.

"No," Pat said aloud. She shook her head violently.

"I'll make it nine hundred," said the dealer, who had been showing her a piecrust table, in the fond belief that her fixed stare indicated interest.

"What?" Pat started, and blushed as she realized she had been talking to herself. "Oh — no, thank you, I'm sorry."

She turned into the next aisle. Nancy was nowhere in sight, but Pat fancied she heard the familiar tones raised in hoarse triumph somewhere in the distance.

The next booth featured old books. One of the titles caught Pat's eye, and she stopped to examine the volume. It was a battered, cheaply bound cloth edition of a history of Maryland, and she turned to the chapters on the Civil War. She was familiar with some of the material. Jerry had talked about it. But the story proved unexpectedly interesting, in the light of Mark's comments, and she was deeply absorbed when the dealer's voice cut into her reading.

"Let you have it cheap, lady. A bargain. First edition, rare book. . . ."

He was a sharp-faced man with graying brown hair and tobacco stains on his teeth. At least his tone had been courteous; Pat wouldn't have blamed him for pointing out that he was not running a library.

At five dollars the book wasn't really a bargain. It was certainly a first edition, but Pat suspected that was because it had not been popular enough to rate more than one printing. Nancy would have offered three dollars, and probably would have gotten the book for that price. Pat paid five.

"Do you have anything else on local history?" she asked.

The dealer shook his head.

"Not my field. Try Blake."

"Is he here?"

"Not him. He's got a shop in New Market. He's an independent old — er — cuss; won't do shows. But he's the man for Maryland history, if that's your bag."

Pat thanked him, and went to look for Nancy. She was suddenly anxious to get home. For one thing, it would be a good idea to find out whether or not she might expect overnight guests. She had planned to get Chinese food, or pizza, or something of that sort for herself and Mark. But if the Friedrichs were going to be there for supper. . . .

Nancy was also ready to leave. Flushed with triumph, she clutched an armful of bargains even more hideous than her usual spoils — a battered oil lamp, its glass base chipped; a crocheted bedspread, spotted with ambiguous stains; a large china figure of a puppy and two repulsive kittens.

167

"That's the third bedspread you've bought in a month," Pat exclaimed.

"But this was a real buy. I bargained the woman down to thirty bucks. The stains will come out, with bleach."

Pat doubted that, but she didn't say so. When they were in the car, on their way home, Nancy stopped gloating over her buys and said accusingly, "Didn't you get anything?"

"Just a book." Pat displayed it. admitted that she had paid five dollars for it, and listened amiably while Nancy told her that she should have bargained over the price.

"I thought Jerry was the book addict," Nancy said. "Are you going in for that now?"

"Not really. It's just that Mark and I were talking about history the other day, and I decided I'd like to know more about my house. Jerry always meant to do some research."

"Mmm." Nancy swerved to avoid a child on a bicycle. Putting her head out the window, she yelled, "You're going to get killed if you don't stay off main roads, young man." Then she went on, "You ought to talk to Jay Rankin, Pat."

"Who's he?"

"You have become such a recluse it is unbelievable," Nancy said severely. "If I've told you once, I've told you a dozen times. . . . He's the curator of the county historical association. Bachelor. . . . Not your type, though. He's one of those weedy-looking kids with long hair and a beard." She chuckled as Pat made a wordless noise of negation and disapproval. "Anyhow, he's too young. He and a couple of other boys moved into the Jenkins house at the end of the street last year. The Jenkinses wanted to rent to a couple, but they were in a hurry to get the house off their hands, and at least these young fellows have jobs — I mean, if you could see some of the communes, or whatever they call them, that have moved into some of the houses in the county. . . ."

Pat smothered a grin as Nancy went on with her diatribe. Nancy's own four sons were amiably disorganized, as frankly disinterested in work as the types she was so vigorously castigating. At least the topic kept Nancy busy for the rest of the drive. She came to a crashing halt — her driving was like her personality, vigorous and decisive — in front of Pat's house and asked, "Do you want Jay's number?"

"I expect he's in the book." Pat opened the car door. "Thanks, Nancy, I enjoyed it."

"There's a show in Columbia next week."

"I'll see. If I'm not busy . . ."

Nancy did not reply. She was staring out the window at the house next door. Through a gap in the hedge Pat saw what had caught Nancy's attention: a bright-golden head and a flutter of pink.

"She's out," Nancy announced, leaning out the window in order to see better. "Hey — somebody is with her. A boy, as I live and breathe. I wonder who."

Mark was wearing the same horrible jeans and dirty T-shirt all the local boys wore, but there was no hiding his gangling height. Nancy knew his appearance almost as well as she knew that of her own sons. She turned a bright, speculative gaze on Pat and let her lips curl in an expression her neighbor knew only too well.

"How long has that been going on?"

"I can't see that much is going on," Pat said. "It's late, Nancy. I'll call you —"

"Wait till I tell Ron," Nancy said. Ron was her oldest son, Mark's buddy and rival. "He's been trying to date that girl for weeks. Of course Mark has the advantage of proximity."

Pat finally made good her escape. Peeking through the curtains of the Gothic bay, she saw that Nancy's car remained parked in front of her house for ten more minutes. But the young people had disappeared, and finally Nancy gave up and drove away, with the usual squeal of tires.

A few moments later Pat heard the kitchen door open and went to investigate. She found Mark foraging in the refrigerator. Kathy, slim as a pencil in her faded jeans and pink shirt, her fair hair windblown, leaned against the stove.

"Hi," she said blithely. "I hope you don't mind, Mrs. Robbins. Mark offered me a Coke."

"Nancy saw you," Pat said. "What were you two doing next door?"

Mark filled two glasses, spilling liquid all over the counter and spraying fragments of ice hither and yon.

"You want one, Mom?"

"I'll have coffee," Pat said, turning on the burner under the kettle. "Mark, why were you and Kathy over there?"

"What difference does it make?" Mark asked.

"Well . . . none, I guess. I just don't want Nancy to know Kathy is sleeping here."

"Naturally." Mark rolled his eyes and flung a muscular, oil-stained arm aloft in a theatrical gesture. "She'll never learn the truth from me."

Kathy giggled appreciatively. She had a pretty laugh, light and bubbly as champagne — one of the sweeter, cheaper California varieties, Pat thought sourly. She had spent the entire afternoon worrying, while these two tiptoed through the tulips.

"Where is your father?" she asked.

"Working. But," Kathy added gaily, "He's going to take us out to dinner tonight."

"I don't think that is a good idea," Pat said.

"Why not?"

"We still have some decisions to make, Kathy. I think we could talk more freely here. I'll cook some — uh — something."

"I'll call Dad, then," Kathy said. "It's time he stopped working, anyhow." As she went toward the phone, she added, "I'll just write our number in your little book, Mrs. Robbins. We're not listed, and you just might want to call sometimes."

"Yes, I might," Pat said drily. "If your father insists on going out, let me talk to him, please."

Apparently Josef was not in an intransigent mood. Kathy hung up after a brief exchange.

"He's coming right over," she announced.

The teakettle began to shriek. Pat made herself a cup of coffee. When Josef appeared at the back door, she waved the kettle at him.

"Coffee?"

"I'd rather have a drink." He was wearing a sports coat and tie; the pale-blue coat was an unexpectedly frivolous touch, but it set off his dark eyes and graying hair. From behind his back he produced two bottles. "Scotch and gin. If I had four hands I could offer more variety."

"Help yourself," Pat said. "I'll stick to coffee."

Josef made himself a Scotch and water, while Pat watched.

"Kathy says you don't want to go out," he said. "Why not?"

"Oh, this is ridiculous," Pat exclaimed. "We stand around here acting like any normal . . ." She cut off the word she had almost said, but it hung in the air as if it had a palpable shape of its own. "Family." Hardly, Pat thought angrily. She went on, with rising heat. "It's getting late, and we don't even know where you two are going to spend the night. We left everything hanging. It's driving me crazy, not knowing —"

"That's the trouble with your generation," Mark said, slurping his Coke. "You haven't learned to relax. You've got to hang loose, and let things —"

"Quiet," Josef said. "Your mother is right. The trouble with *your* generation is that you never plan in advance. And who gets stuck with the chaotic results of your lack of foresight? Your despised parents, that's who. I have had so many cases —"

"Okay, okay," Pat said hastily. She had seen the bright spots of temper form on Mark's cheekbones, and wanted to avert an argument. "You're both right. I am too uptight. On the other hand, we could stand a little advance planning. For instance, what happens tonight?"

"I wanted to take you out," Josef said. "As a token of appreciation, if nothing more. But if you don't want to go —"

"I want to talk. I want to plan. I want to know where the hell everybody is going to sleep tonight!"

Kathy giggled.

"You're a very cool mother, Mrs. Robbins."

"Oh, damn," Pat said.

"I agree with Mom," Mark said. "I mean, I think we'd be more relaxed here than in some restaurant. But we have to eat."

"I can't imagine you going without nourishment for more than two hours," Pat agreed. "Why don't you and Kathy go to the Oriental and get some Chinese food to bring home?"

"I'll go," Josef said. "Where is the place?"

He was obviously unfamiliar with the routine, and so was Kathy. Watching the girl's pleased amusement as they bickered over what to order, and then placed the call so that the food would be ready to be picked up, Pat wondered how the Friedrichs had lived B.P. — before Poolesville. Had they always dined formally at the best French restaurants? Had Mrs. Friedrichs been a gourmet cook? And what business was it of hers anyway?

Josef went to get the food, the two young people vanished into the upper regions, and Pat set about cleaning up the breakfast dishes, which were, as she might have expected, still squatting in the sink. It might have occurred to someone to wash them, she thought, scrubbing at encrusted egg and wondering why someone hadn't thought to make cement with that as a base. Cleaning up the kitchen took longer than anyone might have reasonably supposed. Twilight was well advanced and she was setting the table when Josef returned, walking into the kitchen without knocking, as if he lived there.

"Where are —" he began.

"Upstairs," Pat said. She hated washing dishes. That may have been one of the reasons why she was in a bad mood. "They are not in bed together," she said nastily. "But I suppose you will want to go and check."

"Now why should you suppose —"

"Oh, forget it."

"I'd rather not, if you don't mind. That abominably conceited son of yours is right about one thing: we've all been forced by circumstances beyond our control into a situation which, if nothing else, demands some degree of honest communication." He unloaded the cartons of food as he spoke; his expression, as he peered uncertainly at a bag of egg rolls before putting it on the table, was comically at variance with his sober, precise voice. "Believe me," he went on, "I regret the intrusion into your life as much as you must resent it. But —"

"I don't resent it," Pat said.

"You don't?"

Pat felt herself flushing.

"Not in the way you mean. I'd pitch in and help any neighbor who was in trouble — although God knows I've never encountered anything like your problem! I like Kathy. I like her . . . very much. I think we could all be . . . well, friendly, without getting into anything. . . . I mean, I've no interest in and no intention of . . ."

She had begun fluently enough. Now to her annoyance she felt her cheeks burn more hotly as she began to stutter and stumble over the words.

Josef came to her rescue.

"You needn't go on. Pat. We have not known one another long, but as you say, the circumstances are extraordinary. I think I know you well enough to realize . . ."

He stopped speaking. Pat realized he was as embarrassed as she was.

"This is silly," she said, her own self-confidence rising as his declined. "Two middle-aged adults ought to be able to talk without blushing or stammering. We understand one another, I think. Now let's get to the heart of the problem. It's not me you're worried about; it's Mark. You think he is using this situation as an excuse to — well, to get closer to Kathy."

"And you're going to assure me he would never dream of doing such a thing."

"Good heavens, no. He'll use it. But that doesn't mean he is not genuinely concerned, or that he is stupid. And you must accept the fact that Kathy is going to be interested in young men. She could do worse than Mark. I'm not claiming he is a paragon, but —"

The thud of approaching footsteps — unquestionably Mark's — made her break off. Josef looked mutinous. Pat knew she hadn't gotten through to him. It had been naïve of her to assume that reasoning could cure him of his prejudice against Mark, even if she had been allowed to finish her arguments.

The kitchen door opened. Mark held the door for Kathy and followed her, his nostrils quivering.

"Let's eat," he said.

"What about a drink before dinner?" Josef suggested, eyeing the white cartons without enthusiasm.

He made himself a drink; no one else joined him. Mark seated his ladies with a flourish. He was obviously in a euphoric mood. Pat wished she could say the same for Josef. Conversation was almost nonexistent until Mark had satisfied the first pangs of hunger.

"Any luck on your research?" Pat asked.

"Not much," Mark answered. "We've pretty well exhausted what the library had to offer. The historical association was closed today; but I thought maybe we'd stop by Jay's place tonight."

"Jay?" Josef asked.

"He's the curator of the historical association," Pat answered for her son, whose mouth was full. "He lives down the street. I didn't realize you knew him, Mark."

"I know him slightly," Mark said, reaching for another egg roll. His mother gave him a sharp look. It had not dawned on her until that moment that the bachelor pad on the street might offer attractions to other young males in the neighborhood. She sent forth a silent prayer to whatever powers-might-be that Jay was neither gay nor in trouble with the police, and said moderately, "Then you still cling to your — excuse me — nutty idea that we have a historical ghost?''

"Nicely put," Mark said. "Now as I see it, what we have to do is find out more about the families who lived here. There are all kinds of things we can try. I made a list." He tilted to one side so that he could reach his hip pocket, and flourished a grubby piece of paper. "First Jay and the local historical association. Then the state association in Baltimore, and the Library of Congress manuscript division. Genealogical societies, like the DAR and the Daughters of the Confederacy. I want to track down the descendants, if any, of the Bateses and the Turnbulls. There might be family records — diaries, old photo albums, letters. They wrote diaries like crazy in those days, especially the women. Some of 'em have even been published. We ought to check the Library of Congress card catalog, just in case Louisa or Lavinia got their memoirs into print. Old army records, too. I also want to search both houses."

"What on earth for?" Pat demanded. "I can assure you, Mark, that when we moved in, there were no mysterious trunks or boxes of books lying around. Your father stripped the wallpaper down to the plaster, and —"

"I know, I know," Mark said impatiently. "We did that here. But what about Halcyon House? Have you looked in the attic and the basement, Mr. Friedrichs? People sometimes pack things away and stick them in corners and they remain there for years."

"I went over the house from top to bottom," Josef said shortly. "I cannot remember seeing anything of the sort you are thinking of. What the hell *are* you thinking of, Mark?"

His tone, Pat felt, was deliberately offensive.Before Mark could answer, Kathy, who had been demurely silent, spoke up.

"We don't know, Dad, we're just investigating every possibility. There could be a secret room or something, where people kept money or records —"

"Fantasy," Josef snapped. "Where do you kids get these ideas? I thought the younger generation had stopped reading books like *The Count of Monte Cristo.* I suppose it's TV."

"I've read *The Count of Monte Cristo,*" Mark said. "But we're talking about fact, not fiction, Mr. Friedrichs. The Civil War was the last romantic war. People actually did do things like that. And if you don't like my ideas, what do you propose — to let Kathy sleep in that room again tonight?"

Josef's eyes were as dark and cold as basalt.

"I propose to sleep there myself," he said.

There was a brief pause.

"Wait just one moment," Pat said. "After what happened last night —"

Josef turned to her. His cold stare might have softened infinitesimally, but Pat wasn't sure.

"There are two ways of going at this, Pat. One is to delve into the background; and at the risk of being rude I must say that I find Mark's theories poorly based on fact. The other is the pragmatic approach. I admit that something decidedly abnormal is occurring in my house. Mark has suggested that it is purposeful — directed by a conscious intelligence. All right. One way of testing that is to see what it — if it exists — does want. Mark has implied that it wants Kathy." Mark started to object at that point, and Kathy let out a gasp. Josef waved them both to silence and went on. "That is certainly a possibility. So we'll test it. I will stay in her room tonight; I don't claim I'll be able to sleep. If the . . . presence is sentient and directed at Kathy, it will not disturb me. If nothing happens tonight —"

"Then we try Kathy again, tomorrow night, just to make sure?" Pat demanded angrily. "Josef, do you realize what you are saying?"

"We try Mark tomorrow night," Josef said.

This time the silence lasted longer.

Night had fallen. Through the open kitchen windows the soft scent of spring filled the room. The noise of rushing traffic, voices raised in Saturday-night social activities, all these sounds were muted by distance. Across the table the eyes of the two men met and locked. Mark had accepted, and approved, the challenge. His response enraged Pat even more than Josef's original suggestion.

"You are crazy," she said. "If you think I'll stand for —"

"Right on," Kathy exclaimed. "Dad, you're nuts."

"Quiet," Mark said. "He's right. Only tonight I stay in Kathy's room."

"What about me?" Pat shouted. "You two male chauvinists . . . If you think you can keep the women safe behind the lines of battle —"

She had not realized Josef could speak so loudly. His voice overrode hers, and Mark's reply to her suggestion.

"The problem began when we moved in — never mind old Hiram, Mark, his ramblings are not evidence. We need not risk Kathy again. It obviously reacts to her. I am the most logical person to try next. As for the charge of chauvinism —"

"I'm bigger than you are," Mark said, glowering at his mother. "You just try."

"Your father would have let me

try," Pat said.

It was dirty pool, and she knew it. Mark's face went white. Pat was only dimly aware of the reactions of the other two; she was concerned with Mark.

"You're bigger and stronger and younger and tougher than I am," she said. "If any material danger comes along, I'll gladly let you rush to my defense. But this is not a physical danger."

For once, Mark was incapable of speech. It was Josef who replied.

"You're crossing bridges too far in advance, Pat," he said mildly. "The first attempt is mine, that's only fair. If nothing happens tonight, we'll discuss the next step. Okay?"

Pat could only nod. The sight of Mark's hurt face made it impossible for her to pursue the discussion, which had to do with basic issues far more important than the trivial question of ghosts or no ghosts. Some day it would have to be settled, but she couldn't push her son any farther now. At any rate, her argument had stupefied Mark to the point where he was not battling with Josef for the honor of being next in line for the poltergeist's attentions.

"That's settled," Josef went on. "You can all perch on the tree outside and watch, if you like; I'm not so stupid or heroic as to refuse help. But if you plan to spend the night on guard, you might consider having a nap this evening."

Mark, recovering, shook his head.

"I'll be perching in the tree, Mr. Friedrichs, don't worry. But I want to talk to Jay tonight."

"You aren't going to tell him what happened, are you?" Pat asked.

"Out of the question," Josef said.

"Why?" Mark demanded. "We'll get more help from him if he knows all about it."

"Oh, Mark, no," Pat said. "We can't have this spread all over the neighborhood."

"Especially," Josef added. "if I have to sell the house. It would certainly have an adverse effect on the price."

"What?"Mark stared at him.

"Surely you must realize that that is

the final solution," Josef said. "If nothing else works, and the manifestations continue, I have no alternative."

Obviously the alternative had not occurred to Mark, or to Kathy. Her blue eyes opened wide in distress, and then turned to Mark. Their glances met, touching as palpably as a handclasp, reflecting the same consternation. Josef was aware of the intensity of their speechless communication. His lips pinched together.

"I'll sell the damned place," he repeated. "It may be the only way out of this."

Pat knew he was right. She also knew he had failed to consider one consequence of this threat — for so it would be regarded by Kathy and Mark. Faced with such a challenge, and such a loss, Mark would stop at nothing to find another solution.

# Five

Pat had known Norma Jenkins well enough to exchange greetings when they met in the grocery store, but she had never been in the Jenkins house. Slight as her acquaintance with Norma had been, Pat suspected the elegant, well-groomed woman would have keeled over in a faint if she ever saw what her renters had done to her neat split-level house. It had been rented unfurnished. It was still unfurnished, by normal middle-class standards. One disheveled sofa, its fabric fraying, a number of large squashy pillows, bookcases built of boards and bricks, and a few tables were the only pieces of furniture in the living room. But the wall-to-wall carpeting — which probably served as bedding for transient

190

guests — was fairly clean, and the dog, industriously scratching on the sofa, looked healthy and bright-eyed, except for its hypothetical fleas. After all, Pat thought charitably, it might just have an allergy.

Her host did. He apologized, thickly, as he blew his red nose for the third time.

"It's the damned flora," he complained. "My sinuses clog up when anything blooms, even dandelions."

He had drooping mustaches and a scraggling black beard. Small dark eyes blinked at Pat through reddened lids and very thick glasses. He wore the inevitable jeans and a torn blue T-shirt with "Arizona State" printed on the front. Pat liked him. He had a nice smile and a firm handclasp, and he had had the courtesy to put out his cigarette when she came in, though the room still reeked with the sickly, cloying smell of marijuana.

"I didn't realize you were having a party," she said apologetically. "You should have told Mark."

Jay looked blankly at the other guests, a round dozen or more, who were disporting themselves on the pillows in various uncouth poses. One young man, his dirty blond hair streaming down his back, was trying to coax music out of a battered guitar.

"It's no party," Jay said, "Just . . . you know. Sit down, Mrs. Robbins. Uh, wait a minute." One hand swept the dog off the sofa; the other gestured at the vacated seat, with a grace worthy of a Spanish don. Pat sat down and Jay continued hospitably, "Let me get you something. Uh . . ." From his facial contortions Pat deduced that he was rapidly and despairingly running through a mental list of available refreshments.

"Beer?" she suggested, picking what she assumed to be the least evil of the possibilities. Jay's face brightened. "Right," he said.

Kathy and Mark were sitting on the floor listening to the guitarist. Mark had given her a lecture on how she was to behave as they walked down the street; she could have done without it, but she

192

was doing her best to present the proper image.

Josef had refused to come. He had work to do, if nobody else did, he had remarked austerely. At least he had agreed to work at her house, instead of returning to his own. She wasn't quite sure she could trust him, but she intended to return long before the witching hour.

It took Jay some time to bring her beer, and when she saw the damp glass he proffered with naïve pride she knew he had had to search for a glass, and wash it. His usual guests probably drank from the can. She sipped the beer and tried not to shudder. She didn't really like beer, and this was not a good brand.

"It's nice you could come," Jay said, squatting on the floor beside her. The dog had returned to the sofa and was sprawled beside Pat. "I've been trying to get up nerve enough to visit you; I mean, your house is really fascinating. But I didn't want, you know . . ."

"That was thoughtful."

"Oh, well, like, you know —" Jay

waved his can of beer. Some liquid slopped over onto the dog, which roused itself and licked its stomach appreciatively.

"I meant to visit the historical association too," Pat said. "You know how it is; when you live in a town, you never see the important sights."

"Well, I wouldn't say the building is that much of a historic landmark," Jay said. "It isn't as old as some of the houses in town. But it was donated and, well, you know how it is. You should have seen the place when I took it over. What a mess! The old guy who had been curator for like a hundred years had good intentions, like, but he was just too old for the job — lately, I mean. I've been working my — I mean, I've been putting in fourteen hours a day since I started, just getting the library more or less in order."

Pat realized that for all his uncouth appearance Jay was interested in his subject and was probably good at it. She made encouraging noises, and Jay went on, "You really ought to come over and look at some of the material on your house. It's interesting. And up till six months ago you couldn't have even found it. I mean, like, it was buried."

"What kind of material?" Pat asked. This was almost too easy. But her house was one of the genuine historic landmarks, and it was not surprising that Jay should be intrigued by it.

"Odds and ends," Jay said vaguely. "You know the family that owned your place was named Bates. Old Miss Betsy Bates, she was the last; she lived there till she was, like, eighty years old. Wouldn't sell or rent, and the place was falling down around her ears. Her relatives, they were some kind of cousins, tried to get her to move out and go to an old folks' home, but she wouldn't do it. Not that they cared whether she lived or died, they wanted to sell the house while it was still in one piece. They even tried to get her declared incompetent. But the judge, he was the son of an old boyfriend of hers, and he wouldn't do it."

"The house was in bad shape when we

bought it," Pat said.

"So I was told. I hear you and your husband did a great job of restoration."

"Jerry did it, not I. You must come and see it."

"Hey, could I?" His eyes shone with genuine antiquarian fervor. "I'll show you some of the Bates family stuff. Miss Betsy left it to the historical association instead of to her relatives. They were pretty mad. Tell you what, I'll let you borrow the family papers. They're not supposed to leave the library, but what the hell, you'd take good care of them."

"I would, of course; but maybe you shouldn't —"

"There's an old photo album that will give you a real charge," Jay went on, warming to his subject. "You know Mr. Bates, the first owner, was some kind of government official during the Civil War."

"Was he?"

"Uh-huh. Kind of unusual, because he wasn't especially important locally. Maybe Lincoln was trying to get in good with the abolitionists."

"Are you sure Bates was an abolitionist?" Pat asked. Mark had insisted on this very point, but she had shared Josef's skepticism. The confirmation of Mark's hunch made her vaguely uneasy.

Jay nodded vigorously.

"Yeah, I'm sure. And his son was in the Union army. Got a bunch of medals."

"What regiment?" asked a voice. Pat turned and saw that her son had crawled across the floor to join them. He was listening avidly.

"I forget. You could look it up."

"I'll come over tomorrow," Mark said.

"But tomorrow is Sunday," Pat protested.

"Yeah, I can't tomorrow; I've got a date to go sailing," Jay said.

"Come over for a drink afterwards," Mark said. "Maybe you could bring the Bates records with you."

"You're as subtle as a sledgehammer," Jay said, without rancor. "If you're that anxious, I just might be persuaded to lend you the stuff, before I take off. . . . If you'll tell me why this sudden passion for history.''

''Term paper,'' Mark said. ''It's already overdue.''

This was no explanation and no excuse, and Pat knew it as well as the two men, who exchanged looks of mutual suspicion.

''We really would like to have you drop in, Jay,'' she said, feeling embarrassed, though why she should be she did not know; she had had ample evidence of the strange manners of the youth subculture, and it was clear that Jay had not taken offense. With a genuinely charming smile he patted her hand.

''Look, Mrs. Robbins, you're a nice lady and someday I would like to see your house. But not tomorrow. I won't be back till late, and I can see Mark is putting you on the spot. How about another beer?''

She accepted, out of appreciation of his thoughtfulness, and Jay swiveled on his haunches, preparing to rise. As he did so he caught sight of Kathy, who had been sitting modestly behind Mark. His eyes narrowed.

"I've seen you someplace before," he said. "I thought when you came in you looked familiar, but . . . Damn, I almost had it."

"You probably have seen me around," Kathy said. "I live in Halcyon House, next door to Mrs. Robbins."

"Speaking of houses I'd like to see . . ." Jay's voice trailed off and his brow furrowed as hc continued to pursue the elusive memory. Eventually he shrugged. "No, I can't remember. But I've seen you somewhere — and it wasn't on Magnolia Drive."

The room was filling up as more and more people arrived at the non-party. Jay returned with Pat's beer but he was soon occupied with the newcomers, and before long Pat was able to make her excuses and depart. She had expected some argument from Mark, but he seemed even more anxious than she to leave. As the three of them walked down the dark, spring-scented street, Mark betrayed himself.

"Of all the worn-out lines," he said bitterly. " 'Where have I seen you before, chick?' I thought that one went out with high-buttoned shoes."

Pat paid no attention to this adolescent outburst. It was later than she had thought; she quickened her steps, letting the young people fall behind. Surely Josef wouldn't be foolish enough to take up his position earlier than they had agreed, before there was someone to stand guard. . . .

He was in the parlor, in the big chair that had been Jerry's favorite, a squashy, almost shapeless object of indeterminate color, which Jerry had laughingly defended from all Pat's redecorating plans. The table beside the chair held a stack of books, and Josef was so absorbed in his reading that he didn't look up immediately. His dark head, bent over the book, was utterly unlike Jerry's sandy mop, but the familiarity of the tableau stabbed Pat with a new pang of pain.

Josef looked up and saw her. He rose, politely.

"Did you have a nice time?"

His tone was not without sarcasm. Pat took the chair on the opposite side of the table — her chair. . . .

"I've acquired a headache from drinking beer, which I detest. But I think it was a sacrifice in a good cause. The young man is more capable than he appears. He has offered to lend us some of the Bates papers."

Josef's eyes strayed from her face toward the front door.

"Where are the kids?" he asked.

"In the kitchen," Pat snapped. "That's where they always go first — contrary to what you may be thinking."

"It was a perfectly harmless question. I didn't mean to imply anything."

The parlor was dark and shadowy except for the circle of light cast by Josef's reading lamp. It shone full on his face, the harsh, unflattering illumination bringing out every line and wrinkle. It occurred to Pat that he might not be looking forward to another encounter with the unknown force that had already attacked him once before.

"I'm sorry," she muttered. "I found out something tonight that bothers me — though I'm not sure why it should. Mr. Bates *was* an abolitionist. His son served with distinction in the Union army."

Josef's eyebrows lifted alertly.

"I know why it disturbs you. You're wondering where your son has been getting such accurate information. And so am I. At the risk of adding to your perturbation I must tell you I've found another fact that substantiates Mark's wild theory. Mr. Turnbull was a Confederate officer, as was his son, Peter." He held out the book he had been reading. Pat recognized it as one of Jerry's — a history of Maryland military units during the Civil War.

The tramp of feet heralded the appearance of Mark, carrying a tray.

"I thought we might have a little snack," he announced.

Josef eyed the heaped-up tray with consternation. "Does he eat like that all the time?" he asked Pat.

"My food bills are unbelievable," Pat admitted. "But his friends are just as bad. I suppose the girls are always on diets, aren't they?"

Mark, absorbing a piece of chocolate cake, saw the book Josef was holding.

"Oh, you found it. I left some of my books for you, in case you finished your work before we got home."

His voice was bland, his face innocent; but the older man caught the implication.

"You mean you knew I would want to check your facts," he said. "You were correct. Is this where you got the information you gave us this morning?"

"Some of it," Mark said cautiously. "That book was my source for Turnbull's Southern sympathies." He took another bite, and added thickly, "You can tell Mom and Kathy about it if you want. I'll bet they never even heard of Captain 'Lige White."

"I haven't," Pat said. Mark was manipulating his rival very nicely. She wondered if Josef was aware of being manipulated. From his severe expression she suspected that he was, but he responded as he was meant to.

"White was one of Maryland's most famous Confederate officers. Born not far from here, as a matter of fact. He formed his own cavalry troop, mostly of Poolesville men. They called themselves White's Rangers. They became part of the Thirty-fifth Virginia Battalion and fought all the way through the war until Appomattox."

"They didn't surrender, even then," Mark said. "They broke through the Union lines and —"

"Turned themselves in later on," Josef said, eyeing Mark without favor. "Don't romanticize a group of killers. These men even raided their home county. In December of 1862 a group of them stole horses and supplies from their former neighbors. Among those present was Captain Albert Turnbull."

"Our Turnbull?" Pat asked.

"Yes. The author of this book seems to share Mark's weakness for stupid violence; he mentions, admiringly, that Turnbull was almost sixty at the time, but 'as straight in the saddle as his own young son, who served as his aide.' "

He dropped the book contemptuously on the table. Seeing battle in the eyes of her own son, Pat said hastily, "But young Turnbull — Peter — must have been barely sixteen. How could he —"

"In 1862 he was eighteen," Mark said. "Some of them were a lot younger than that."

He reached a long arm out and selected another book from the pile on the table, flipped through the pages, and handed the volume, open, to his mother.

It was a large, handsomely illustrated picture history of the Civil War. So remote and so romantic does that era seem that many forget that photography was well advanced. The faded photos reproduced well — too well. The crumpled bodies of the dead struck Pat no more painfully than the faces of the living, most of whom would also die violently in battle. Some were boys younger than her own son, standing as tall as they could in their too-large uniforms, their rounded faces set in expressions meant to be grim.

"Such a waste," she murmured.

"War always wastes the young first," Josef said. "And back then boys grew up to adult responsibilities earlier than they do today."

Pat looked at him suspiciously, wondering if this was meant as a slur on Mark, but Josef's face was serious, without visible malice, as he went on, "The same thing happened in this century, in World War Two; toward the end our men were fighting boys of fourteen and fifteen — the Hitler Youth. And, my dear, lest you take it too hard, I might add that the young ones are sometimes the most vicious and intolerant of all soldiers."

Leafing through the pages, Pat came upon photographs of survivors of the prison camps, Northern and Southern. They reminded her of World War Two atrocity pictures. She closed the book.

"Horrible. Why do men —"

"This is no time for a debate on ethics," Mark said impatiently. "Don't you see what it means? The two families were divided — violently divided. Can you imagine what it must have been like, living right next door to each other — two sisters, once devoted — and their sons fighting on opposite sides? Don't tell me that wasn't a tragedy."

He and Josef continued to talk. Pat paid no attention. The faces of the long-dead children in uniform — they were no more than children, some of them — had given the case a human immediacy it had never had before. The idea of the two women waiting for news from the battlefield, news of beloved young sons, wrenched her heart. They could not even console one another; loyalty to their husbands and the causes they espoused would alienate them. The gun aimed at one boy might be held by the other's hands. . . .

"Did they survive?" she asked.

"Who?" Interrupted in midsentence, Mark blinked at her.

"The boys. Peter Turnbull and the Bates boy."

"Edward," Mark said. "You mean did they survive the war? Edward did.

According to the genealogy he died in nineteen-something." He reached for another book, a thin, limp volume bound pretentiously in brown calf. Pat caught a glimpse of the title. *"Morton Genealogy,"* she said, in surprise, "I thought —"

"Morton was the name of the man Susan Bates married," Mark explained. "This was written, and privately printed, by her son. He was more interested in the Morton family, so there isn't much about the Bateses."

"I wonder," Pat began, and then stopped. No need to wonder where the book had come from; Jerry was always picking up used books in secondhand bookstores, or sending away for them. He had received a small box of books a few days before he died.

"Here it is," Mark said, leafing through the genealogy. "Edward Bates, born 1845, died 1915. A ripe old age. And here is a picture of his father, John Bates."

The portrait, waist-length, showed a man wearing a dark suit, his hands folded. The stiff points of his white collar, which was encircled by a broad neckcloth, jabbed into his cheeks. Heavy horizontal creases disfigured his forehead, but all the other lines in his face were severely vertical, even to the cleft in his protruding, prominent chin. The dark hair, which had retreated from his brow, stuck out in luxuriant tufts on either side of his face. It was an uncompromising face, Pat thought, and yet there was something rather attractive about the steady dark eyes, and the shape of the full lips belied the rigidity of their setting.

Pat reached out and turned the page. Mark had mentioned seeing portraits of the two Peters girls, and here they were: arms around each other's waists, simpering at the camera. They must have been in their early thirties when the picture was taken, for if the families had indeed split over political issues it was unlikely that the sisters would have been shown together in such amity after the late 1850's. In truth they did not look much like sisters; Louisa was at least thirty pounds heavier than Lavinia, but it was not only extra weight that broadened her cheeks and gave her face the gentle, maternal look Mark had described. Lavinia was more elaborately dressed and bedecked with jewelry — heavy earrings, bracelets, brooches, and chains. Her hairstyle was a bit too girlish for a face that was already slightly haggard.

Pat handed the book to Josef, who waved it away.

"I've seen it — and the other books as well. This is fine, Mark, as far as it goes; but it doesn't really go very far. All you've proved is that the families disagreed. What the hell have you got that ties this situation, potentially tragic as it may have been, to our poltergeist?"

Before his critical stare Mark's eyes fell. He scraped up chocolate icing with his forefinger, and licked it.

"Just a hunch," he muttered. "But give me time. I'll prove it."

# II

At midnight they took up their positions, but not until after there had been a heated argument. Kathy wanted to be near her father. Why couldn't she stay in another room of the house, or at least in the apple tree outside the window? The others unanimously rejected both suggestions, arguing that Kathy's proximity would negate the experiment. To Pat the discussion had an element of sick humor. How did one calculate the geographical limitations of a ghost? Eventually Kathy agreed to remain inside the Robbins house, provided Pat stayed with her.

As soon as the men left, Kathy bolted for the stairs. Pat was right behind her. She lost ground as she climbed — Kathy was younger and in better condition — but reached Mark's window in time to see her son and Josef pass through the gate of the house next door.

Since the houses were mirror images of one another, Mark's corner room directly faced the windows of Kathy's bedroom. From that height they could see over the fence and into the backyard. Kneeling, her forehead pressed against the screen, Kathy gripped the sill with clenched hands.

"You can't stay in that position for an hour," Pat said. "Pull up a chair and make yourself comfortable."

Kathy ignored her; so, with a shrug, Pat followed her own advice. However, her heart was beating fast and her stomach felt queasy. Her view of the two tall figures had been both comical and touching; the slight suggestion of bravado in the swaggering walks, the false implication of comaraderie in the face of danger. . . . They had known that their womenfolk would be watching.

The sound of distant revelry, from neighbors entertaining and being entertained, came faintly to Pat's ears. However, the noise was not loud enough to cover the sound of the front door in the neighboring house when it opened and closed again. Mark came around the corner of the house and disappeared behind the shrubbery. Then they saw him again at the base of the apple tree. The blossoms were fading, and the leaves were young; it was possible to follow his progress as he climbed. When he reached the branch nearest to Kathy's window he was clearly visible, though only in outline. The black shape shot out an arm which waved vigorously; then it settled down, its back against the tree trunk, and remained motionless.

''How much longer?'' Kathy whispered.

Pat answered in the same low tone, though there was really no need for quiet. ''About fifty minutes.''

They had agreed on the time, if on nothing else. It had been a few minutes after one A.M. when Pat burst into the house in response to Kathy's shrieks. Mark had been careful to note the time of the next demonstration. One of the strongest points in favor of his theory was the coincidence in time — one A.M., almost to the minute.

The wait seemed a good deal longer than fifty minutes. For someone who paid little attention to the dictates of time and schedules, Mark had a passion for clocks. Several of them shone in the dark. The two women followed the crawling progress of the faint green streaks of the hands with disbelief. Long before they came close together, at the top of the dials, Pat was kneeling on the floor beside Kathy.

She had almost decided nothing was going to happen, and that Mark had fallen asleep on his perilous perch, when the boy's dark outline jerked forward. The window of Kathy's room, which had been a black square between the white-painted shutters, began to glow.

Pat's hand clamped on Kathy's forearm as the girl started to rise.

"No — wait! We promised."

Kathy subsided, with a moan of distress. Pat continued to clutch her arm. It was almost more than she could bear to remain where she was; on the other hand, she was reluctant to lose sight of what was happening. By the time she got down the stairs and out of the house it would be too late to render assistance, even assuming there was anything she could do to help.

In spite of her self-control she let out a yelp when Mark started crawling along the branch toward the window. He did not try to enter, but remained in a crouching position. He stayed there for an interminable period — almost a minute, in real time — and then Pat realized, with indescribable relief, that the light was not growing stronger. Between one breath and the next — and she was breathing quickly — it vanished altogether, as if a door had slammed between one world and another.

"Where's Dad?" Kathy demanded. "Where is he? I'm going over there!"

"No," Pat said again. "It's gone . . . I think. It's all right. Look, Mark is waving."

He waved both arms, then slid down from his perch and went toward the front of the house. When he came back into sight, on the walk, Josef was with him.

Pat realized then that her anxiety had not been solely for her son. Josef also turned and waved reassuringly. Then the two men stood by the gate talking. Pat saw Mark's arms move; he always gesticulated when he was excited.

"Men!" She exclaimed angrily. "They know we're dying to hear what happened; why don't they come? I'm going out to the gate and make rude gestures at them."

"I . . . I think I'll go and wash my face," Kathy said.

Her voice betrayed that she had been crying. Well, Pat thought, naturally she was nervous about her father, but all the same. . . . Then she remembered how she had felt as she stood on the outer fringes of the unspeakable aura. Kathy had been in the thick of it, not once, but twice.

"Good idea," she said, and patted the girl on the back.

She went quickly down the stairs. After the darkness of the bedroom the lamplit hall looked warm and serene. However, she must have left a window open somewhere; there was a draft of cold air blowing. . . .

Pat stopped in midstride, her nose

wrinkling. Without quite knowing how she had gotten there, she found herself backed up against the kitchen door, staring down the length of the hall. Both doors were closed. How could there be a draft? There had been none on the stairs. And . . . no, surely not; surely it was her imagination. It must have been imagination, for it was gone now — the faintest possible suggestion of that foul, well-remembered odor she had sensed under Kathy's window.

# Six

The brown cardboard carton was medium-sized — two feet square by about a foot and a half high. Pat stared blearily at it, wondering how her fogged brain had been able to produce even that approximation of dimensions. She turned an even less enthusiastic gaze on her son. He was at the stove. The smell of bacon, usually so appetizing, did not improve Pat's disposition that morning.

She had taken a sleeping pill the night before, the first time she had done so for over six months. It had left her groggy and cross. She would still be asleep, and glad of it, if Mark had not shaken her awake. He had given her time to put on a bathrobe, but she was groping under the bed for her slippers

218

when Mark had snatched her up and carried her downstairs, showing off for Kathy, who followed them giggling and making admiring comments.

The bathrobe was an old green terrycloth garment, snagged by Albert's claws, and not very clean. It added at least fifteen pounds to Pat's apparent weight. She had not been able to find her good robe; probably it was still in Kathy's closet, or, if she knew teenagers, crumpled on the floor of Kathy's room. She had not had time to comb her hair or wash her face or put on makeup, and she hated Mark. Kathy too.

She added Josef to the list as he entered, neatly dressed, freshly shaved, every hair in place. If the lines on his face were perhaps a little deeper than they had been when she first met him, that didn't count for much when weighed against the snagged old bathrobe and the straggly hair.

"Good morning," he said brightly.

Pat lifted her lip in a silent snarl and snatched at the coffee Kathy put in front of her.

"Is that it?" Josef transferred his attention from Pat to the carton. Not that she blamed him. Even a worn, battered cardboard box looked better than she did this morning.

"That's it." Mark turned, waving his spatula. "I barely caught Jay; he was ready to take off when I got there, and I had to bribe him before he would let me have the material."

"What with?" Pat demanded. Even her voice sounded rusty and antique. She cleared her throat. "An invitation to dinner tonight?"

"I mentioned your name," Mark said innocently. "He really thinks you're a cool lady, Mom."

An eloquent, ancient Anglo-Saxon four-letter word leaped into Pat's mind. She managed not to say it.

"I hope you didn't give anything away," Josef said. He seated himself at the table. "You have asked this young man to violate the rules by loaning out such material; you must have given him a pressing reason."

"I just told him Mom wanted

it," Mark said.

Pat, who was fairly familiar with the moral codes of the younger generation, knew that to Jay and to Mark this was a perfectly adequate reason. They were all so hostile to rules and regulations; they took a perverse delight in breaking the rules, especially for someone they liked.

She felt no need to explain this to Josef, even if she had been capable of rational conversation. She drank her coffee.

"We'll have breakfast and then open the carton," Mark went on. He flipped an egg. Grease spattered, followed by a horrible smell of burning oil.

"Can I help?" Kathy asked.

"You could set the table," Mark answered, turning. Their eyes met; for a long moment Mark stood still, his spatula poised, dripping grease onto the kitchen floor.

"The eggs," Pat said.

"Oh." Mark turned back to his cooking while Kathy set the table. Pat knew Josef was looking at her, but she refused to meet his gaze. She kept her eyes fixed on her coffee cup.

It wasn't only lack of sleep or the sleeping pill or even her awareness of how she looked that made her silent and sullen. Convinced, and yet unwilling to believe, her mind raged against the events of the previous night.

The two men had entered swaggering, as they had left; but Josef admitted he needed a drink, and Pat had observed that his hands were not completely steady when he poured it. All the same, he had insisted, he was not completely converted to Mark's theory of a sentient, conscious intelligence as the agent behind the manifestations.

"But it came and went without completely materializing," Mark had argued. "Damn it — excuse me — Mr. Friedrichs, you must have felt it. I was outside the room, and I felt it. Something came — realized you were not what it was after — and left."

"It was bad enough, even half formed," Friedrichs muttered.

"Compared to what Kathy and I encountered, that was nothing," Mark insisted. "We saw it, and felt it. It hit every sense."

Josef had the last word.

"If your ideas are correct, Mark, we'll see the proof of them tonight. Your hypothetical entity will come, dismiss you as it dismissed me — or it will have learned, from tonight's experience, that Kathy has left the house, and it will not return."

Remembering this conversation, Pat felt a surge of panic. Did they really intend to risk Mark tonight, as Josef had risked himself the night before? Both men insisted there had never been any danger; the manifestation had started to fade almost as soon as it began, leaving the victim sickened but unharmed.

Even if that was true, it was not proof that the thing wouldn't react as violently to Mark as it had to Kathy. Had not Josef said that poltergeists were activated by youth? Besides — Pat went on with her silent argument — even if Kathy was the sole catalyst, where did that leave them? It left them with the conclusion that Kathy could never again enter her

223

father's house.

"A nice thing that would be," she said suddenly. The others, who had been tactfully ignoring her bad mood, looked at her in surprise.

"Ah, she is showing signs of life," Mark said. "Eat your eggs like a good girl. As soon as you finish we'll open the carton."

"That fails to inspire me," Pat said. "What do you expect to find, Mark? A magic formula for exorcising demons?"

"Facts," Mark said.

After all, he was too impatient to wait for her to finish a meal for which she had little appetite. Kathy helped him clear away the dishes. Then he began to unload the box.

It was a motley and rather unsavory collection that appeared. The books and papers were spotted with damp and smelled sour, as if they had been permeated with mold.

"Jay figured Miss Betsy must have kept this stuff in the basement," Mark explained as his mother withdrew, her nose wrinkling fastidiously. "Some of it is in bad shape."

"And of the wrong period," Josef said, examining a long thin volume whose covers were held in place only by tatters of cloth. "This is someone's book of recipes — some handwritten, some cut out of newspapers and magazines. The type is too modern to be nineteenth century."

Kathy pounced on a packet of letters.

"These are dated 1934," she said, disappointed.

"I never promised you guys a rose garden," Mark said. "Did you think we'd find a document entitled 'The Family Ghost and what it wants out of life'?"

"Empty the carton," Josef suggested. "We'll put the irrelevant materials back into it."

The kitchen table was heaped with miscellany by the time Mark reached the bottom of the box. The last thing he took out was an elaborately bound book some eighteen inches long and several inches thick. Its padded covers, banded in brass, were of velvet turned green with age.

"Here we go," Mark said, his face brightening. "This must be the family photograph album."

The others discarded the unproductive documents they were investigating. By returning most of these to the carton they cleared enough space for the album, and Mark opened it to the first page.

It was like meeting, if not an old friend, at the least a familiar acquaintance. They had seen a reproduction of John Bates's photograph in the Morton genealogy; here was the original, and its impact was just as strong on the second viewing — even stronger, perhaps, because the reproduction had been slightly blurred. John Bates's dark eyes looked straight out at the viewer, as if demanding an answer to some vital, if unexpressed, question.

Mark turned the page. Again familiar faces — those of Louisa and Lavinia, née Peters, caught for posterity, so long as paper and chemicals would survive. The stilted, simpering smiles seemed unbearably poignant to Pat. Could they have manufactured even a pretense at happiness if they had known what the next few years would bring?

"Mr. Morton must have had this album," she said.

"Or copies of the same photos," Mark said. "Louisa was his grandmother, and Mr. Bates was his grandfather. He didn't go farther back with the Bateses; I guess they weren't distinguished enough. No Revolutionary War heroes, or anything."

They were clustered close around Mark, who had taken upon himself the position of master of ceremonies and official turner of pages. Kathy, too polite to elbow her elders aside, stood on tiptoe to see over Mark's shoulder. Mark lifted his arm and pulled her close to the table, so that she was in front of him instead of behind him. His arm remained draped casually around her shoulders. Pat glanced at Josef. His lips had tightened, but Mark's gesture had been made so smoothly and so naturally that he could hardly complain without sounding foolish.

Mark turned the page.

There were two photographs, one facing the other. The first was that of a young man standing straight and proud in the dark of a Union uniform, his face stiff under the unbecoming short-brimmed forage cap. But the audience paid that photograph little heed. Three pairs of eyes focused, aghast and unbelieving, on the picture on the opposite page.

The girl wore her prettiest party dress, dotted with tiny flowers, ruffles framing her white shoulders, billowing skirts reducing her waist to ridiculous proportions. Ringlets tied with ribbon framed a smiling girlish face . . . Kathy's face.

Pat's eyes moved from the yellowing photograph to the living features of the girl who stood sheltered by Mark's arm.

Kathy had heard the gasps of surprise but she alone, of them all, seemed unaware of what she saw. Naturally, Pat thought, her mind reeling; people don't really know how they look to others, they see only a mirror image, reversed. . . .

Kathy let out a yelp of pain. Mark's fingers, which had been resting lightly on her arm, crooked like claws.

"What's the matter?" she demanded shrilly. Her eyes moved from Pat to her father.

"They aren't the same," Pat said. Her own voice sounded strange in her ears.

It was true, though; the pictured face was not identical with Kathy's. It was plumper, fuller of cheek. Kathy's exquisite coloring was not reproduced by the brownish tints of the old daguerreotype. Indeed, as Pat continued to stare, she found less and less to marvel at. The face in the photograph was that of a girl about Kathy's age, her inexperienced charm the same; the clustered curls were obviously blond. But the resemblance ended there.

Mark's taut hand relaxed its hold, but he was still incapable of speech, an almost unheard-of situation.

"Who is she?" Pat asked. "The pictures aren't labeled. I don't know why people assume their descendants will know Great-Aunt Mabel and Cousin

229

George. . . ."

"That's not Cousin George," Mark said. "That's Susan Bates. Don't deny it, Mom; who else could it be? The costume is right for the period, the age is right. . . . And that must be her brother Edward, opposite. He was a Union officer, we know that."

Now Pat was able to wrench her eyes away from Susan (Mark was right, it had to be Susan) to look at her brother. The cool, direct dark gaze was his father's, but the resemblance between Edward and his sister was just as plain.

"He's so proud of that uniform," Kathy murmered. "You can see it in his face. Actually, he's kind of cute,"

Pat realized that the girl was still unaware of the resemblance that had struck the others. Looking up, she saw that Mark and Josef were both staring at her, radiating the same silent, imperative message. As if I would tell the child, she thought indignantly. The whole thing is moonshine anyway; pure imagination and nerves.

"They were a handsome family," she

said, in response to Kathy's comment.

"The men were," Kathy said. "I don't know; I think Susan is stupid-looking."

"Oh, yeah?" Mark had recovered himself. "I think she's foxy. Cute figure."

"How can you tell?" Kathy demanded. "All those skirts . . ."

Mark put on a convincing leer.

"What shows is very nice, very nice indeed. Girls in those days used to brag about having waists so small a man could span it with his two hands. I'll bet yours isn't —"

Kathy giggled and wriggled as he put his hands around her waist. With only a little squeezing, his fingers met. The gesture, meant — in part, at least — as an attempt to amuse and distract, was not such a bright idea. It only reinforced an identity the others were struggling to deny.

"Go on, Mark," Josef snapped. "Turn the page."

Considerably subdued, Mark obeyed.

The next photo was a family group. The father stood, stern in muttonchop whiskers, his hand placed in a proprietary grasp on his wife's shoulder. She was seated — probably, Pat thought, because she was holding a baby. Otherwise she would have stood behind her seated lord and master. Five other children clustered around the mother's skirts. The youngest was a toddler. Held erect by his brother's ruthless grip on his collar, he looked as if he were choking.

"Good heavens," Pat said, half amused, half horrified. "Look at that lot! Six . . . Considering the infant mortality rate, even among the well-to-do, she must have had several other pregnancies. No wonder the poor woman looks exhausted. I wonder who she is."

"Don't you know?" Mark said. "Look at her again."

Perhaps she caught the truth from Mark's mind. She was almost ready to admit the feasibility of such a relatively sane idea as thought transference. Or perhaps it was some other sense that forced the knowledge into her mind.

"It can't be," she exclaimed.

"The man is Henry Morton," Mark

said inexorably. "His picture is in the Morton genealogy, that's how I know. He was Susan's husband."

And the woman was Susan. There was no doubt about it when one looked closely. And yet it was no wonder Pat hadn't recognized her. Kathy had said Susan was stupid looking. In truth the young girl's face had lacked character; it was unformed, as young faces often are. But instead of gaining distinction or hardness with maturity, Susan's face had lost what little identity it had ever possessed. The very outlines were curiously blurred.

"No," Kathy said. "Oh, no, Mark. She's . . . old."

The word was an epithet, a condemnation. Pat shivered.

"Not old," Josef said. "Beaten. That is the face of a woman who has given up hope. How old was she when this photograph was taken?"

"She died at the age of thirty," Mark said.

"Six children," Pat muttered. "Depending on when she

married. . . . A baby every eighteen months?"

"She died in childbirth," Mark said. "With number nine. Two had died in infancy. That's Henry, Junior, the man who wrote the genealogy."

His finger jabbed at the page, indicating the smug-looking lad in the sailor suit who had a stranglehold on his little brother.

The rest of the photographs were anticlimactic. There were no more pictures of Susan, although her children appeared now and then in pictures of family gatherings, as the century wound down toward 1900. By 1890 the stripling Lieutenant Edward Bates had become a portly patriarch, beaming paternally at his increasing progeny and their offspring. Not only had he survived the war, but he had prospered, if prosperity was measurable in inches of girth and increasing children. Pat felt some sympathy for Kathy's obvious disappointment and disgust; no doubt it was distressing to see slim youth buried in fat and complacency. But she had no difficulty in recognizing Edward Bates. His eyebrows whitened and thickened as time went on, but the eyes below them were his father's eyes — steady, dark, demanding, belying the easy geniality of his plump cheeks.

As Mark turned pages the costumes changed, from the hoop skirts and tight dark suits of the midnineteenth century, through bustles and frock coats, into the middy blouses and straw hats of the turn of the century. The only constant face was that of Edward Bates, who occupied the honored center of every family grouping. Pat found herself searching for Susan's features. Often resemblances reappeared in new generations. But the Bateses were all dark, like their father and the rather plain, sallow girl Edward had married.

"That's it," Mark said, closing the album.

"What a disappointment," Kathy said. "I hate seeing people get old. I mean, when it's a real person it happens gradually, so you get used to it."

The others eyed one another, for once

in complete, if silent, accord. All were aching to comment on the resemblance, and what it implied; all were equally reluctant to mention it to Kathy.

"I'm going to get dressed," Pat said, rising. "I hope somebody is going to volunteer to do the dishes."

"I will," Kathy said. "Mark did the cooking, it's the least I can do."

She obviously expected that Mark would offer to help her. Instead he mumbled, "Be back in a minute, Kath. I've got to — got to — er —"

Josef followed Pat and Mark upstairs, into her room. He closed the door after them.

"There's your connection," Mark burst out, before either of the others could speak. "Susan. You saw —"

"A pretty blond young girl," Josef interrupted. "Not really like Kathy at all."

"It's not so much a physical resemblance, It's — uh — psychic," Mark argued. "You both saw it too. Don't tell me you didn't."

"Damn it, you're jumping to

conclusions again!'' Josef's fists clenched. ''Stop trying to push ideas into my mind.''

''I don't have to push hard, do I?''

''All right, Mark,'' Pat said. ''You've made a point; don't belabor it. Now will you two get out of here so I can get dressed?''

They left, eyeing one another like two strange dogs. Pat shook her head. The antagonism between them was growing; sooner or later it might erupt into open violence. Mark must realize that any such action would end his hopes of friendship with the Friedrichs; so far he had done well, but he was young, and he had his father's quick temper. . . .

Pat had planned to take a nice long hot bath. Instead she showered quickly and threw on the first clothes that came to hand — an old brown cotton skirt and matching print blouse. Somehow, against her conscious will, Mark had made a convert of her. The evidence was accumulating, slowly, inconclusively; and yet each new detail fit uncannily with the theory Mark had formulated at the very beginning. Knowing her son as she did, Pat would not have been willing to swear that Mark had told them everything he knew. He must have evidence beyond what he had shared with them, otherwise how could he have gotten the idea in the first place? At the start there had been nothing to indicate what Mark obviously believed: that Kathy was the object of a conscious attack, based on some spiritual identity between her and the long-dead Susan Bates.

Pat paused in the act of putting on makeup. Her face stared back at her from the mirror, her hazel eyes wide and shadowed with incredulity, her lips twisted in a wry grimace. Her hair needed cutting — or styling — or something; the dark locks had lost their usual luster, and surely she had more gray hairs than she had had a week ago.

Pat turned from the mirror. She didn't like what she had seen. The face of a blithering idiot, she told herself savagely.

When she started downstairs she heard the voices, raised in angry comment and counterretort. With a sigh she quickened her steps. How long she could keep those two from each other's throats was anybody's guess.

"What's the problem now?" she demanded, entering the kitchen.

Josef turned toward her, his face flushed.

"Your insane son wants to tear my house apart. I told him I won't have Kathy there —"

"It's perfectly safe in the daytime," Mark said.

"How the hell do you know that?"

"One A.M., on the dot, three nights running. . . . Don't you see that points to a specific event?"

This was a new thought to Pat and, obviously, to Josef also. They considered the suggestion for a moment and Mark took advantage of their silence to make another point.

"See, Mom, it occurred to me that maybe Kathy isn't the only catalyst. Maybe it's the room itself. I'd like to know who slept in that bedroom in 1860."

"Your mind jumps around like a

grasshopper," Pat said irritably. "I can't keep up with you. Are you suggesting that something happened at the witching hour of one in the morning, in that room? Murder and sudden death? It wasn't Susan's room, Mark. This was her home."

"I'd like to know whose room it was," Mark insisted.

"And how do you propose to find out?" Josef demanded.

Mark's eyelids dropped. He had long, thick lashes, and with his bright eyes concealed, his face took on a look of youthful charm that seldom failed to melt his mother.

"I've got an idea," he said sweetly.

## II

After two days of unoccupancy Kathy's bedroom had acquired a hotel-room feeling. Pat went to the windows and threw them open.

Mark prowled, peering behind bookcases and bureaus, mounting a chair to stare at a corner of the ceiling.

"You really did a job on this place," he said to Josef, who was standing with his hands on his hips, watching. "Stripped off all the old paper, repainted, scraped woodwork —"

"I didn't do it; Joe Bilkins, contractor, did. At least I trust he did, that was what I paid him for."

"You shouldn't have," Mark said.

"I suppose we should have lived with the rotted wallpaper and flaking plaster."

"I mean, you should have kept records of what you found," Mark said. "Mom, remember when Dad was working on our house? Remember, he had a scrapbook, describing the color of the original paint, and structural details? He even pasted in pieces of old wallpaper."

"I remember," Pat said.

"See, Dad always said that every little bit of the past should be preserved," Mark explained, turning to Kathy; she was a much more appreciative audience than the others. "He said that the history of mankind is a long story of destruction, and he didn't want to be one of the destroyers.''

Pat had packed the scrapbook away. Its reminder of frustrated enthusiasm and unfulfilled plans had been too much to bear.

"He said that if we ever got enough money he'd like to have someone duplicate the old wallpaper," she said. "Of course we never did have enough. . . ."

After one quick glance Josef had turned away and was pretending to watch birds outside the window. She appreciated his tact.

"That is interesting, Mark," he said, over his shoulder. "But I don't see its relevance here. And perhaps your mother —"

"No, that's okay," Pat said. Mark was speaking of his father freely, fondly, without hurt. That was the way she wanted it.

"But it is relevant," Mark said. "Mom, remember the day we were working in the closet of my room? I was helping Dad strip off the paper in there. Remember when we found the name written on the wall?"

"Good heavens, I had forgotten," Pat exclaimed. "I'm surprised you remember, Mark, it was so long ago. You weren't more than —"

"I was twelve," Mark said indignantly. "And I had good reasons to remember it. It struck me as a neat idea, so I wrote my name on the walls too. When Dad found out he made me spend all day Saturday scrubbing."

"What else did you write, Mark?" Kathy asked, smiling. "Just your name?"

"And the date. That was what we found — 'Edward Bates, aged twelve, 1857.' It seemed so funny to me then, that some kid, just about my age, had written that, over a hundred years ago. I thought, wow, it would be cool if a hundred years from now some other kid would find my name." Mark grinned. "Dad never did find them all. I put one in the back of my closet, next to Edward's."

"So you concluded your room was once Edward's." Josef's quick intelligence was learning to follow the curious leaps and twists of Mark's mind. "But perhaps he wrote his name elsewhere, just as you did."

"He wouldn't write it in anybody else's closet," Mark argued.

"Hmmm. Possibly. And you think the Turnbull boy did the same here? That's pretty farfetched, Mark."

"No, it's not. Look, you keep thinking about these people as grown-ups. Soldiers, mothers, like that. I think of them as kids. I mean, they grew up together — Peter Turnbull and his cousins, right next door. They must have played together, they were only a year apart in age. There were no other houses close by. Peter was the oldest. He was also an only child; I bet he was spoiled rotten, not only by his parents but by his big sister —"

"It's much more likely that she detested him," Pat said drily, remembering youthful battles with her own elder siblings.

"Boy, are you a cynic," Mark said. "I don't agree. Mary Jane was ten years older than Peter, just the age to appreciate a nice live baby doll. Girls in those days were trained to be *motherly.* I mean, all this Women's Lib —"

"Get on with it," Josef interrupted. "What are you driving at, Mark? As if I didn't know . . ."

"Well, it's obvious, isn't it? Peter would be the leader of the gang. Edward would imitate *him,* not the other way around. I suspect this was his room, as the corresponding room in the other house belonged to Edward, because it's the best bedroom next to the master bedroom in the front. And I'm hoping to find written proof."

His shining enthusiasm and unconsciously arrogant voice carried conviction. Kathy was an immediate convert.

"Of course! It would be in the closet, wouldn't it?"

She dropped to her hands and knees and began throwing out shoes, clearing the closet floor. Josef, contemplating his daughter's shapely bottom with dismay, exclaimed, "That is the wildest idea you've come up with yet, Mark. I gave orders that this place was to be stripped down to the bare plaster. Nothing like that would survive, even if —"

"We need a flashlight," Kathy's muffled voice remarked from the depths of the closet.

"It's worth a look, isn't it?" Mark said. "The Edward Bates name was written in indelible ink, in the corner near the door. That's the kind of place a painter won't concentrate on — not these days, anyhow."

With a muttered imprecation Josef left the room, returning almost at once with a flashlight.

"I keep one in my bureau drawer, in case of a power failure," he explained. "But I would like to go on record as stating —"

"I know, I know," Mark said. "Get out of the way, Kath, and let me in there."

Pat sat down on the bed. Her conscious mind agreed with Josef; this was the craziest idea Mark had advanced yet. But somehow another part of her brain twitched with surprise when, after a prolonged search, Kathy said, "I don't see anything, Mark."

"It doesn't seem to be down here," Mark admitted. He stood up and, with one grand sweep, shoved Kathy's wardrobe into a mashed confusion at one end of the rod.

"Here it is," he said.

Pat was the last to get a look. The others crowded in before her. And there it was, just as Mark had predicted — faded, barely visible under the shrouding paint, but unmistakable. No modest, secret scrawl, this one; inscribed in the very center of the wall, the bold, spiky letters were over two inches high: "Peter Turnbull, aged thirteen, 1857."

Pat knew the suspicion that had crossed Josef's mind. Yet he must have dismissed it immediately, for the thing was impossible. The name had been painted over, and the paint was uniform. There was no way Mark could have written the name himself, at least not within the last few days.

Yet the survival of the name for over

a century seemed almost equally incredible. Patches of the old plaster had fallen and had been replaced; by a strange trick of time (or was it merely a trick?) this particular section had remained firm. The twentieth-century workmen had patched only where necessary and had slapped a quick coat of paint over the whole. It was only a closet, after all. No one wasted time on a closet.

Mark was the least excited of them all. It was as if he had known what he would find.

"He was tall for his age," was his first comment.

Pat started to ask how he knew, and then refrained. People had a tendency to write at their own eye level, she had read that somewhere. No doubt Mark, who thought he knew everything, had calculated the average size of thirteen-year-olds, and could deduce Peter's height to the inch.

"A big, arrogant guy," Mark continued. "A bully."

"Now really, Mark," his exasperated

mother exclaimed.

"No, look where he wrote his name. Edward's was stuck away in a corner."

"Like he was shy," Kathy contributed, getting into the spirit of the thing.

"Not necessarily." Mark frowned thoughtfully. "He figured like I did — he wanted his name to survive, so he put it in a place where people wouldn't be so apt to notice it. He was more . . . calculating. Sensible. But Turnbull stood straight up and splashed his name for the world to see — daring them to obliterate it."

"Mark, what are you trying to say?" Pat demanded.

"It's clear enough, I think," Josef replied, before Mark could speak. "Mark thinks he has identified the ghost."

His voice was rich with sarcasm.

"Yes, I do," Mark said defiantly. "It was his room. He probably died in battle, fighting for a losing cause — a cause his cousins despised. Cocky, arrogant, still hating. . . . Peter Turnbull has come back."

# III

For the sake of peace Pat concluded it would be best to separate Josef and Mark for a few hours. She had intended to go to New Market to look for the secondhand bookstore the antique dealer had mentioned, and she managed to persuade Josef to go with her.

It was a gray, cloudy day; the close, muggy air was a foretaste of a Washington summer. Like everything else in her aged Volkswagen, the air-conditioning was functioning erratically. Slumped in the seat beside her, his long legs bent at an uncomfortable angle, Josef was silent for the first few miles. Pat let him sulk.

Finally he sighed deeply and straightened up, with a sudden movement that brought his head into abrupt contact with the roof.

"I'm sorry," Pat said. "This car isn't built for tall people. That's why I bought it; to keep Mark from driving it."

"I should have offered to take my car." Josef rubbed his head and tried to find a place to put his feet. "I was preoccupied. Your son has gotten me to a point where I'm forgetting my manners."

"I guess we'd better have it out," Pat said.

"Wasn't that the purpose of this expedition?"

"Partly. But I really do want to see what we can find in that bookstore."

"You don't mean you really believe all this — this —"

"Well, at least I'm not dismissing it out of hand because of my personal prejudices."

"What prejudices are those?" Josef asked, his voice chill.

"Against Mark. What did you think I meant?" He started to answer, but Pat, aghast at the direction in which they were going, cut him off. She had no more desire than he to go into the other emotional problems that distorted their friendship. "I don't blame you for being skeptical. You can slap Mark down as often as you like when his theories get out of hand; he's young, and he gets carried away. But if you think he's inventing all this in order to — well, to get closer to Kathy —"

" 'Invent' is not the word. I do think he is capitalizing on a most unpleasant situation."

"That's honest." Pat kept her eyes on the road. For a moment they were silent. She could have left it there, and she was tempted to do so. But things rankled in her mind, and she had learned that this was not a healthy situation. "One thing you said," she went on. "About Mark going to the local college —"

"I think I understand that now. I was unjust, and I apologize."

"Schools like that fill a need, and fill it well. Just because a boy or girl goes to a junior college doesn't mean they aren't —"

"I said I was sorry."

"Did you say that to Mark?"

"Damn it, Pat, there is a limit!"

"To what? Justice?" Pat gave him a sidelong look. His profile resembled the stony contours of a Toltec statue — lower lip protruding, brows lowering.

"All I'm saying is that Mark is no monster. He isn't trying to — er —"

"Seduce my daughter?" Unexpectedly, Josef's rigid features relaxed. "I'd think he was abnormal if he didn't."

"Then it must be Kathy you don't trust," Pat said.

Immediately she knew she had made a grave misstep. His whole body went rigid.

Oh, damn, Pat thought wretchedly. So that's it. I guess I should have known. Why would a woman leave a man like him — attractive, intelligent, comfortably well off — unless she fell in love with someone else? Well, but there are other reasons, lots of them. He's also arrogant, dogmatic, something of a snob — not easy to live with. Damn, why did I have to say that? Shall I drop the subject, or try to explain? . . .

"What is it you hope to find in New Market?" Josef asked.

He had raised the No Trespassing sign; and there was no way she could bypass it. Her own position was too vulnerable.

"Nothing in particular," she answered. "I thought we might find some books on local history."

"It's worth a try. I confess I'm becoming curious about the Turnbulls. The people I bought the house from were named Stanton. Does that imply, perhaps, that the Turnbull family died out?"

"Maybe they just sold the house. Or . . . Wasn't there an older sister? She could have married a man named Stanton."

They continued to speculate — fruitless speculation, since they had so little evidence, but it got them over the bad moment. By the time they reached New Market they were conversing without strain. However, Pat had not forgotten her faux pas.

New Market, advertised as the antiques capital of Maryland, has a single street lined with lovely old houses. The majority of them have been converted into antique shops. Since this particular trade caters to the weekend shopper, the town was crowded, and Pat had to go some distance before she found a parking space. They walked back toward the center of town and the bookstore.

The building was constructed of pale, rough stone. The front door stood open; from the interior came the musty smell of old paper and worn leather bindings.

Josef went immediately to the nearest shelf and began browsing. His absorbed expression told Pat that he belonged to the same breed as Jerry — the book fanatics. Not being of that breed herself, she looked around the dusty room. Shelves lined the walls, stretching all the way to the ceiling. Books filled the shelves and overflowed into untidy heaps on the floor. A desk in the middle of the room was also piled high. The shop was very quiet. A few other browsers stood like statues, pouring over one esoteric volume or another.

Then a head appeared behind the heaped-up desk in the center of the room. Pat stared, amazed, as it rose, and rose, and rose. The man must have been over six and a half feet tall. Drooping white cavalry-style mustache, long white hair, and an old-fashioned string tie and high collar converted him into an image out of the past: a gentleman of the Old South. She was not at all surprised when he addressed her in courtly terms.

"May Ah be of some assistance, ma'am?"

"Uh — thank you. I'm looking for books about the Civil War."

The mustache quivered.

"You refer, ma'am, to the War Between the States?"

Josef, who was behind the irate Confederate, turned to stare. His mouth curved into a grin. Pat resisted the impulse to shake a fist at him.

"Yes," she said meekly.

"Two of the rooms of this h'yere house, ma'am, are filled with volumes on that subject. Mah more rare and expensive volumes repose behind glass on shelves in the regions above stairs. May Ah ask what partic'lar aspect of that epic struggle interests you?"

Josef had abandoned all pretense of interest in his book. Pat felt sure that without his malicious enjoyment of her discomfiture she would never have been able to reply.

"Maryland," she said. "The Poolesville area in particular."

"Not much goin' on there," said the relic of the Old South. "Unless it's Captain 'Lige White. . . ."

"The Turnbulls," Pat said. "And the Bateses. I live in the old Bates house."

The white mustache vibrated, and a spark of interest lit the faded blue eyes.

"Most interestin', ma'am. If you-all will wait a moment, till Ah deal with this gentleman . . ."

With lordly condescension he accepted a ten-dollar bill from a waiting customer and retreated into the back regions, presumably to get change. The buyer, a middle-aged man wearing a sports shirt and horn-rimmed glasses, grinned at Pat and said in a conspiratorial whisper, "Don't let Bill get to you, lady. He was born in Hartford, Connecticut. It's all an act. He —"

He broke off as Bill returned with a few limp dollar bills. With a last, amused wink at Pat, he departed with his book.

"Now, then," said Bill. "What was it you were sayin', ma'am?"

The mystique, alas, was gone; the accent was palpably false.

"I said, 'I live in the old Bates house,'" Pat said.

"And I," said Josef, advancing, "have purchased the Turnbull house. We are interested in the history of the families."

"Nat'chrally." Bill stroked his mustache and eyed them speculatively. "But o' course you wouldn't hope to find any personal memoirs or reminiscences, now would you? That would be too great a stroke of luck."

"Well," Josef began.

"Aha." Bill leaned forward. "And what would you-all say if Ah told you that Ah happen to posses one o' the few remainin' copies of Miss Mary Jane Turnbull's memoirs? Privately printed in Richmond after war" — he pronounced it "wo-ah" — "in an edition of only two hundred copies, excellent condition, pages uncut. . . ."

"Mary Jane?" Pat turned to Josef.

"Peter's older sister? Do you suppose —"

Josef jabbed her in the ribs; she took the hint, and stopped speaking. She had sounded far too eager. Bill's blue eyes had taken on the gleam of a good businessman encountering a prospective buyer.

"We might be interested," Josef said. "Could we have a look at the book, please?"

"Certainly, mah dear sir." Bill trotted off. The memoirs were obviously one of his choicer volumes, kept under glass in the chambers above.

"How much is this book worth to us?" Josef asked softly.

"Why — a few dollars, I suppose."

"It won't be a few dollars. I know this routine; it always means large sums of money. Let me handle it, will you? You are obviously lousy at bargaining."

When Bill returned he carried the book balanced on both hands. It lacked only a silver salver. Its appearance did not justify Bill's tender care. Bound in faded green cloth, the gilt-lettered title equally faded, it was not an imposing object.

Pat's intention of skimming through the pages was frustrated from the start by the fact that there were no separate pages, only the thick bundles of the uncut fascicles. Opening the book at random, she came upon the following paragraph:

The more we learn of the victory last Sunday the greater it seems to be. They say the Yankee dead lay upon the field like a blue blanket. The arrogant ladies and gentlemen of Washington had anticipated triumph; coming in carriages to view the annihilation of our hopes, they carried picnic baskets and bottles of French champagne, all of which they were forced to abandon in their precipitate flight when their army was overwhelmed. Hurrah! We expect momentarily to hear of the arrival of our men in the enemy capital.

"Wednesday, July 24, 1861." Pat read

the date aloud.

"Bull Run," said Josef, who had been reading over her shoulder. "First Manassas, as the Confederates called it. They might indeed have taken Washington then, if they had pressed on."

"It's all so impersonal," Pat complained. "Nothing about the family."

"An invaluable record, suh and ma'am." Bill saw a prospective customer losing interest, and increased the pressure. "There is considerable information there, as you will discover when you cut the pages. Naturally Ah would not do so until the book is sold. It is in mint condition and therefore much more valuable uncut."

Josef closed the book.

"How much?" he asked.

## IV

"You didn't buy it?" Mark's voice rose to a squeal of outrage.

"For two hundred and fifty dollars?"

Pat imitated his tone. Yet she felt defensive, and that angered her. "You act as if we had all the money in the world," she exclaimed. "From what we could see the book didn't have any personal material; it was written for publication, after all, so it must have been edited —"

"All right, I'm sorry," Mark muttered. He ran his fingers through his hair.

"I bought these," Pat said, proffering them like a propitiatory offering to an outraged deity. "This ragged little pamphlet cost me fifteen bucks. I mean, really, Mark —"

"I said I was sorry." Mark took the stack of books, like Jehovah accepting a less-than-perfect lamb. He tossed most of them aside with contempt, but the sight of the expensive pamphlet made his face brighten. "Hey, this looks good. 'Montgomery County Families of Distinction, and the War Between the States.' Maybe it mentions the Turnbulls."

"It does," Josef said. "We wouldn't

have bought it otherwise. Your friend Peter . . .''

Mark wasn't listening. He had subsided onto the floor, cross-legged, his head bent over the little book. Kathy knelt beside him, her fair hair brushing his shoulder.

''Here it is,'' he said. '' 'The Extinction of an old and honored family . . .' The old man was killed in 1863. In a cavalry skirmish, 'somewhere in Maryland.' His body was returned to his grieving family and interred with military honors in . . . Hey. Did you know you had a family graveyard, Mr. Friedrichs?''

''Forget it,'' Josef said promptly. ''You are not going to excavate my backyard.''

''Would you object if I just looked around for tombstones or —''

''Yes.''

''Oh. Well, okay. The old man isn't the problem, anyway. It's Peter we . . . Oh, wow. Here it is. He was killed too.''

Pat felt the same shock she would have felt at the news of the death of a personal acquaintance. In spite of Mark's conviction that Peter Turnbull was an arrogant, unpleasant young man who had become an even more unpleasant ghost, she found his death, at nineteen, tragic and disturbing.

Josef's reaction was less sentimental.

"So he did die violently in battle," he said. "Mark, how do you know these things, before we find written evidence? Are you holding out on us?"

Mark pretended not to hear the question. Perhaps it was not all pretense; he appeared to be genuinely puzzled as he read on.

"One of his men saw him fall. He was shot. . . . It doesn't say where. But he fell over his horse's neck, and there was a lot of blood, and . . . That's it. The trooper who saw it was wounded too, he lost track of what was going on. He — the trooper — was picked up when reinforcements arrived and drove the Federal troops away." Mark stared raptly at the ceiling. "I wonder if his bones are still lying there, in the underbrush near White's Ferry. . . ."

Pat let out an exclamation of disgust,

but Kathy obviously found the idea more romantic than repulsive.

"Maybe that's what he wants," she suggested. "Burial in sanctified ground, with the rites of the church."

"You've been reading too many horror stories," her father said disagreeably. "I refuse to dig up half of Montgomery County looking for the remains of Peter Turnbull."

Rain pattered against the window. Pat reached up to turn on a lamp. It was already dark outside. An involuntary shiver ran through her. What would happen at one o'clock? Was Mark really determined to go through with the insane plan they had formulated earlier? She didn't want to ask. She was afraid of the answer.

"Food, anyone?" she asked.

"I made spaghetti sauce," Mark answered, his eyes still fixed on outer space, his expression remote.

"It smells as if it were burning," Josef said maliciously.

With an exclamation of distress Kathy leaped to her feet and ran out.

"What about a drink?" Josef asked.

Pat bit her lip. She had been about to suggest that this was no time for alcohol. But Josef's habits were none of her business. She revised her comment.

"What about some wine? I think there is some Chianti downstairs, in the wine bin —"

Mark snapped to attention.

"Wait, Mom, don't go down there. I mean — I'll get the wine. I mean —"

"I knew you were up to something," Pat said wearily. "What did you do this afternoon, Mark?"

Mark tried to look innocent.

"Now, Mom, what makes you think —"

"You're too clean," Pat said, inspecting his unspotted T-shirt and neatly creased jeans. "You changed your clothes before we got home. You wouldn't do that unless —"

"Ah, so that's your secret." Mark smiled at her, and her treacherous heart softened. "I'll know better after this."

Kathy came running back.

"It's all right," she announced

266

cheerfully. "I turned it down and added some water. Was that all right, Mark?"

"Never mind the damned spaghetti sauce," Josef snapped. "What *did* you two do this afternoon? You've changed your clothes too, Kathy. What —"

Mark caught the implication and — to the surprise of his mother, who had thought him impervious to innuendos of that nature — turned bright red.

"It isn't what you think," he said angrily. "We got dirty, that's all. Cobwebs and mud and . . . We opened up the tunnel."

"Tunnel," Pat repeated blankly. "What tunnel?"

"The doorway Dad uncovered in the basement," Mark answered. His angry color had not subsided, and he avoided Josef's gaze. "He walled it up again, remember? The ceiling looked as if it were about to collapse, and you said it was dangerous, and —"

"That wasn't a tunnel, it was a room, a root cellar or —"

"It was a tunnel. The ceiling had fallen in, that's why we couldn't see how far it extended. Don't you get it, Mom? This house was a station on the Underground Railway. 'Freedom Hall,' Mr. Bates's abolitionist sympathies. . . .''

"Show me," Josef said.

Pat never went into the cellar if she could help it. Unlike modern structures bearing the same name, or the more euphonious appellation of basement, the substructure of her house had never been designed for conversion into family rooms or game rooms. It was almost wholly subterranean, dank-smelling and dismal. The whitewashed stone walls had smears of green lichen, and water often oozed from the floor. Jerry had converted an old enclosed porch off the kitchen into a laundry room, so there was seldom any reason for Pat to go belowstairs. Though she was barely conscious of the fact, her dislike of the area was not based solely on its physical unattractiveness. Its unpleasant atmosphere went beyond damp and darkness.

Now, as she descended the wooden

steps, she saw a gaping hole in the wall behind the furnace. The floor was littered with bits of mortar.

"What a mess!" she exclaimed angrily. "Mark, how could you?"

"I'll clean it up," Mark said. His voice sounded distant, muffled.

"What were you looking for?" Josef demanded, ducking to avoid braining himself on the pipes that traversed the low ceiling.

"I don't know. I just thought maybe . . . ."

Pat started forward, picking her way delicately through the debris. A low, eerie moan made her stop and turn. She saw Jud squatting on the top step. His bulbous eyes were fixed on the dark hole in the wall. He looked perturbed. But then, Pat thought, he often did.

"He sat there and whined all the time we were working," Mark said, indicating the dog. "That must mean something."

"It means he doesn't like damp, cool places," Pat said. "He's always hated the cellar."

Yet as she approached the gap in the

wall she was conscious of a chill that transcended the normal dampness of the place. Cool, wet air wafted out of the darkness, like a draft. But there could be no passage of air through the earth that filled the far end of the hole. . . .

Mark had brought a flashlight. He switched it on and turned the beam into the darkness.

Brick walls, green with mold, framed a narrow rectangle barely two feet wide. The floor was of beaten earth, shiny with damp. The low ceiling was supported by planks now gray and cellular, like elongated wasps' nests: the evidence of industrious termite colonies. Beyond the gap in the wall the open space was barely six feet long. It ended in a sloping wall of dirt.

"I remember this," Pat said. "Jerry found it the first year we lived here. We assumed it was just another room. What makes you think it was a tunnel?"

"I'm afraid he's right," Josef said, before Mark could answer. "It's too narrow to have been a room. Given Mr. Bates's abolitionist sentiments. . . ."

For a moment no one spoke. The only sound was the heavy panting of the dog, so magnified and distorted by the low ceiling that it seemed to come, not from the stairs behind, but out of the darkness of the collapsed tunnel. Pat's scalp prickled. Surely more than one pair of lungs were emitting that agonized breathing. She seemed to hear gasps, low moans of effort and distress. . . . How many weary, frightened men and women had crawled through that dark space, laboring toward freedom?

"Mark, you don't think . . . ." Kathy began. She did not finish her sentence, but her gesture, toward the fallen earth, expressed the horrified surmise they all shared.

"No, no," Mark said reassuringly. "They would have dug the dirt out if the tunnel had collapsed while it was still in use. I think it gave way later, long after there was any reason for its existence."

"No ghosts here, then," Pat said. "You didn't find anything, did you, Mark?"

"No."

"Then let's go."

Their retreat was not dignified. If there were no ghosts in the buried tunnel, there was the memory of old cruelty and injustice. Pat recalled a friend of hers, an Army wife who had spent several years in Germany, describing a visit she had made to the former concentration camp at Dachau, now a memorial to the tortured victims. "I stalled at the gate," her friend had admitted. "I couldn't go in. I was sick at my stomach, unable to breathe." There was nothing supernatural or psychic about such impressions; they were simply a physical expression of the impact of tragedy on a sensitive mind.

All the same, she breathed more easily when they were upstairs, with the cellar door closed. Darkness was complete outside, and the rain hissed drearily against the windowpanes. After searching, Pat found a bottle of wine in the kitchen cabinet. No one volunteered to go downstairs again.

Josef drank most of the wine. He had had two drinks before dinner, and when they returned to the parlor, after eating, he went straight to the liquor cabinet. When he asked Pat to join him she shook her head, not trusting herself to speak. She could not see that he was visibly affected by what he had drunk. But she didn't like it. Her feelings must have shown on her face; Josef returned her unconsciously critical glance with a look of sullen defiance, and poured a sizable jolt of Scotch into his glass.

Mark settled down on the floor with the photograph album.

"I promised Jay we'd return this tomorrow," he said. "Mom, you better come with me."

"I have to work tomorrow," Pat protested.

"How can you think of work at a time like this? I'll call in for you, tell them you're sick."

"I can't do that!"

"Well, you can't sit up half the night and expect to work."

It had been expressed, the thought she had dreaded. Pat let her breath out in a long sigh.

"Mark, are you really going to go over there tonight?"

"We agreed," Mark said. "Nothing's going to happen, Mom. I promise."

Pat turned away with a helpless gesture, and met Josef's gaze. She knew what he was thinking as clearly as if he had spoken aloud. Mark was so sure. He had been unnervingly accurate so far, in all his guesses and hypotheses. What source of information was he tapping? A possible answer occurred to her, and the very idea turned her cold with apprehension.

# Seven

It was still raining at twelve thirty, when the men left the house. Without star- or moonlight, the night was as black as pitch. From Mark's bedroom window the house next door was a darker shadow in the darkness, eerily distorted by the water streaming down the windowpane.

Her forehead pressed against the glass, Pat strained her eyes.

"Your father is going to get soaked, squatting in that tree like a pigeon," she muttered.

The inane comment scarcely deserved a reply. Kathy made none. She knelt beside Pat, her face also pressed against the glass, and Pat felt the tension that held the girl rigid. She herself was ready to shriek with nerves. It must be the

275

weather, she thought. There's no reason to be nervous. Nothing much happened last night; if Mark is right, tonight should be without incident.

The weather was certainly responsible for Jud's state of nerves, and no doubt the dog's misery was affecting her. Jud hated rain. No fool he, he knew that thunder and lightning often accompanied that atmospheric disturbance, and he was deathly afraid of thunder. He had been on Pat's heels all evening. Mark was a lot of fun, but when danger threatened, Pat was more dependable. He had accompanied them up the stairs and was now lying on the floor by the bed, his head under it. His agitated panting scratched Pat's nerves like a fingernail on a blackboard.

Something is coming.

The words flashed across her mind with the impact of a hot brand pressed against flesh. So keen was the mental anguish that Pat fell backward, landing with an ignominious thump, her legs doubled up under her. The dog was no longer panting, but whimpering — a

276

craven, abject sound, as if Jud were so terrified he could not even express his feelings in a long howl of woe. Turning, with some difficulty, Pat saw the bed shudder as Jud forced himself under it, well-padded rump and all.

Even then she did not understand. She assumed the danger would come from the house next door, the house where her son and Kathy's father waited. She tried to get back to the window so she could see, and found her limbs so stiff she could barely move.

Then the smell reached her nostrils. The same foul, indescribable stench she had smelled twice before. And it came from behind her.

Squatting, awkward and ungainly, Pat managed to turn.

It filled the doorway. A thin, spinning column of luminescence, taller by several feet than she herself, the color of . . . But there was no word for that shade. It was part of the infernal aura the thing gave off, a deadly miasma compounded of parts the normal senses could not absorb. It was not heat or cold, not light or color or smell. But because the human sensory organs were limited, they had to translate it into terms they could transmit. So . . . her nostrils flared and her stomach heaved at the odor; her eyes winced away from the cold, pale burning; the hairs on her arms rose, as a current of . . . something . . . filled the room like smoke, acrid, choking.

The feeble remnants of reason left in her flailed helplessly, seeking escape. But she knew she could not allow herself the luxury of fainting; bad as it was to face the thing, it would be much worse to lie powerless before it. It was not after her. She knew that as surely as she knew her name, her age, the color of her hair. . . . It wanted Kathy.

She was fond of this girl; perhaps more than fond. But the strength that came into her body did not come from love or from any hypothetical maternal instinct. It came from without. Not in a great, overwhelming flood; it was more like — the incongruous simile occurred to her — more like liquid from a leaky faucet, slow and trickling. But it was strong enough to raise her, first to her knees, then, swaying, to her feet. With something like horror she felt her knees bend and saw her foot slide forward.

As she moved, one unsteady, reeling step after another, the thing in the doorway changed, in response to her advance. It thickened and shrank in height, as if condensing; and if its former amorphous contours had been hard to contemplate, this was worse, for there was in it a dreadful suggestion of human form. In the crown of the burning column two spots formed, like the low blue flames of a dying fire.

Through the pounding of her pulse, Pat heard a distant sound and recognized it: the door downstairs crashing back against the wall, as it did when Mark was in a hurry. The cold flame in the doorway flared and was gone, as suddenly as if air had first sparked and then overwhelmed its burning.

She was still on her feet when Mark burst into the room. He hit the light switch as he passed it, without pausing. Pat's eyes closed against the brilliance.

279

She felt her son's arm around her, and pushed feebly at him.

"I'm all right," she said. Her voice gurgled idiotically. "I'm . . . How is Kathy?"

"She's just been sick," said Mark. "Hey, Kath, hang in there, will you? At least wait till I can get you into the bathroom."

The voice came from behind her. Pat opened her eyes.

Not Mark's arms — Josef's. She recognized the blue-and-brown plaid of his shirt. That was all she could see; her face was mashed against his chest and his arms were squeezing the breath out of her.

"I'm all right," she repeated. "I'm —"

"All right?" Josef held her out at arm's length. His voice was quizzical, his expression calm; only the fact that he was paler than the white background of his shirt betrayed his feelings. "Sit down," he said.

"No, I don't want . . ." Pat glanced around the room. It was unbelievably normal. There ought to be some traces of that incredible presence — the marks of scorching or destruction. From the bathroom she heard gulping sounds, and Mark's voice, forced to calm: "Atta girl, you're okay now. Cool it, love; gotta get back and see how Mom is doing."

Pat pulled away from the hands that held her.

"Where is Jud?" she demanded.

"Under the bed," Mark answered. "Some watchdog!"

He stood in the door, his arm around Kathy. She looked very small and pathetic; her hair hung in dripping strands, darkened by the water she had splashed on her face. She pulled away from Mark and ran to Pat.

"I told him how wonderful you were," she whispered, her head against Pat's shoulder. "I was petrified. And you were so brave. I don't know how you did it."

"Neither do I," Pat said honestly. "It wasn't me. Something . . . came into me."

She patted Kathy's shaking shoulders.

"You mean that?" Mark demanded. "Tell me what happened, Mom. Exactly. It's very important."

Pat was tempted to swear at her best-beloved son. She didn't blame Kathy for being sick. Her own stomach felt unsteady. She wanted to lie down and have a cold cloth on her head, and someone holding her hand, telling her how wonderful she was . . . and a sleeping pill, a very large, very strong sleeping pill that would knock her out for about a year. And maybe when she woke up it would turn out that the whole thing was a nightmare, some neurosis from early childhood. . . .

"Leave your mother alone," Josef said. "She's had enough."

Pat turned on him, pushing Kathy out of her way.

"Don't talk to him that way!"

"I'll talk to him any way I like. He is a . . . Get your things, Kathy. We're spending the rest of the night at a motel. Tomorrow I'll put that damned house on the market."

"You're not serious," Pat said.

"I have never been more serious." He took her hand, his fingers curling around her wrist like manacles. "You're coming too. Pack a bag."

"Wait a minute." Mark advanced on them, his pallor gone, his cheeks flaming with anger. "Who the hell do you think you are? That's my mother you're talking to."

"You seem to have lost sight of that fact." Josef glared at him.

Mark put his arm around Pat's waist. For a moment she was literally pulled between the two of them, for Josef did not release his hold on her wrist.

"Cut it out," she said. "You are both acting like —"

"Let go of her," Mark said.

"You let go. She's an adult, with a life of her own to live. She can't spend the rest of it coddling some lazy —"

Mark's clenched fist interrupted the tirade. The old man staggered back, his hand covering his face.

For a few seconds they all froze. Mark's arms fell to his sides.

"Cripes," he said, his voice squeaking

like that of a twelve-year-old. "Oh, God. I didn't mean —"

Josef lowered his hand. The austere lines of his mouth were blurred with blood.

"Kathy," he said.

"Oh, Daddy, please —"

"Get your things."

Kathy gave Mark an anguished glance. He was still staring in horror at his victim, and did not respond. She lowered her head and ran out of the room. Josef followed.

Mother and son contemplated one another. After a moment of internal struggle Pat held out her arms.

"You goofed, bud," she said.

"I know." Mark gathered her up, buried his head against her shoulder. "Oh, God, Mom — do I know."

## II

After an encounter with a visitant from beyond the grave one does not worry about mundane matters, such as a job. Pat fell into bed as if she had been hit over the head with a rock, and did not stir until late the following morning.

Memory flooded back, in all its dreadful detail. Pat couldn't decide which depressed her more, the fear that her house was haunted by a particularly malevolent spirit, or the recollection of Mark's attack on Josef Friedrichs.

Normally when she overslept she was awakened by Albert, demanding his breakfast; but today the cat was nowhere to be seen. Pat got out of bed. She glanced at the clock and then at the telephone, and shook her head disgustedly. No use calling the office. If Mark hadn't already phoned to say she was sick, she was in trouble; and she was in no mood to invent symptoms or listen to reprimands.

She stood in the shower for a long time and dressed slowly, trying not to think about anything. The house was quiet. Perhaps, wonder of wonders, Mark had gone to class. After what had happened he would hardly have the gall to seek Kathy's company.

Sighing Pat trudged down the stairs,

feeling as if the descent took her back into a world of complex troubles. She had no idea what, if anything, she could do to solve even the smallest of them.

The sink was piled with dirty dishes. Pat sighed again, louder, and with more feeling. That was all she needed to start her day. She turned on the burner under the teakettle as she passed the stove and started to take the dishes out of the sink. As she did so her eyes went to the window, and what she saw made her drop a glass.

Not what she saw — what she did not see. The fence was gone.

Pat ran to the back door. The fence was still there, but it was in fragments. Mark had piled some of the wood into a rough heap. He was squatting on top of it like a gargoyle on a cathedral, his back to his mother, his attitude one of profound meditation.

He turned his head as Pat came squelching across the lawn. It was still wet with the rain of the previous night. Her sneakers were soaked before she had taken three steps.

"Hi," he said.

"What the hell —" Words failed his mother.

"Did I wake you? I'm sorry. I tried to be quiet."

"Quiet! What — how — *why*, Mark?"

"It's our wall." Mark's eyes were steady. He mopped his perspiring brow with his forearm. "Dad put it up; I guess we can take it down if we want."

"Yes, but —"

Mark dismissed her objection with a wave of his hand. Hand and forearm were streaked with bloody scratches, and his shirt — one of his best new shirts, Pat saw — had a jagged tear across the right sleeve.

"They're home," he said, and she didn't need to ask whom he meant. "I saw the car pull in ten minutes ago. I guess they'll be over pretty soon. Sit down."

Pat looked at the seat he indicated — a heap of scrap studded with splinters and rusty nails.

"I certainly will not. Get down from there, Mark, before you sit on a nail or something. You'd better get a tetanus shot this afternoon."

"I had one a couple of years ago."

"Yes, but —" Pat stopped herself. She recognized Mark's technique; he excelled at it, having had years of practice. Get the old lady off on some trivial point and let her rave

"Come in the house," she ordered.

"Nope. That would look like I was scared, or ashamed. I'll wait for him here. You can go in if you want."

Swearing under her breath, Pat retreated, but only long enough to take the screaming teakettle from the stove and make herself a cup of coffee. She was just in time. As she crossed the yard, carrying her cup, she saw the Friedrichs family emerge from their back door and advance on Mark.

Kathy looked like a brand-new china doll, her sweep of shining hair tied back by a blue ribbon, her complexion perfect as plastic. She wore a blue-and-white-checked dress with a wide ruffle around the bottom of the skirt, and white sandals. Her father was dressed as impeccably, his brown slacks creased to knife sharpness, his dark hair brushed back from his high forehead. They looked like a family paying a polite social call on friendly neighbors.

Mark, still squatting, his scarred hands dangling, appeared much cooler than Pat felt. Josef's dark eyes met hers. His face was quite impassive, but his lower lip was definitely out of kilter.

He came to a stop a few feet from Mark and looked up at the tottering pyramid of wood and the boy atop it.

" 'Something there is,' " he asked, " 'that doesn't love a wall?' "

His tone was neutral. That was better than Pat had expected, and she relaxed a little.

"I thought," Mark answered, "that it was time for walls to come down."

He meant every word of it, but he had enough ham in his soul to let the statement stand, in its theatrical glory, for the admiration of the hearers. Then he went on, more prosaically, but quite as intensely: "Mr. Friedrichs, if I said I was sorry about last night, that would be the understatement of the year. If you want to slug me, go ahead. You've got it coming.''

Friedrichs' lip twitched.

''No, thank you. But I'll take a rain check. There may — no, there undoubtedly will — be occasions in the near future when I will feel like hitting you. Why don't you get down off that heap of trash and clean up? I'm taking your mother to lunch. You can come along if you wash.''

Mark obeyed, sliding down the stack amid a clatter of collapsing scraps. Pat suspected the boy's movement had not been planned. She had seen his breath go out in a vehement whoosh of relief when Josef accepted his apology; his relaxation had probably destroyed his balance.

''I'll cook lunch,'' he offered, grinning from ear to ear. ''We can talk better here.''

''We can talk anywhere,'' Josef said. ''I refuse to eat any more of your cooking, thanks just the same. Get moving.''

Mark ran off, one hand clapped to the seat of his pants — to hide a rip or soothe a puncture, Pat wasn't sure which. After a half-defiant glance at her father, Kathy followed.

"What made you change your mind?" Pat asked. It was a beautiful day. A warm breeze brushed her cheek, the sun shone . . . and Josef was smiling. The expression was not as symmetrical as it had once been, but it was still pleasant.

"The wall, in part," he answered, glancing at the heaps of debris. "One can't help admiring the idea, and the energy. But there were other things Kathy told me about last night. I can't thank you —"

"If she told you I flung myself into the breach to defend her she's not entirely accurate," Pat admitted. "My impulse was to crawl under the bed with Jud. I don't know what made me move, but it certainly wasn't heroism."

"I won't argue with you. I'll even admit that your disgusting son is right again. Running away won't solve the problem."

"Come in and have some coffee while I change," Pat said.

"Why change? You look fine."

Pat looked down at her wet, dirty sneakers. Who was she to argue with him?

As they walked side by side, Josef matching his stride to hers, she knew the real reason for his change of heart. He was facing the same unpalatable fact she had already recognized: that physical removal from the scene of earlier attacks might not be enough to save Kathy. If the thing could cross eighty feet of ground, why not eight miles, or eight hundred?

# III

Monday was not a popular day for lunching out. The Inn in Poolesville was almost empty, so they were able to talk without reserve. Not that Mark was bothered by eavesdroppers; his mother had to keep reminding him to lower his voice, and once or twice the waitress, overhearing a fragment of conversation, gave Mark a startled glance.

He came close to another fight with Josef when he insisted that Pat and Kathy recapitulate their experience, in harrowing detail. However, the majority consensus overruled Josef's objections. Mark cross-questioned the women mercilessly.

"You felt it too?" he asked Kathy. "The second ghost?"

"Sssh." Pat indicated the waitress, who had stopped dead in her tracks, balancing two bowls of soup.

Mark subsided until the woman had left, but then he returned to the question.

"Well, Kath?"

"I don't know," Kathy said uncertainly. "I felt something. Like a — a breath of cool air in a hot, closed-up place. I thought it was you." Her wide blue eyes admired Pat, who realized, with somewhat cynical amusement, that Kathy had added her to her list of Robbins heroes,

"It didn't feel like me," Pat admitted. "I was horrified when I realized I was actually walking toward the damned thing."

"Damned is right," Mark said. "Why are you all looking so depressed? Don't you realize this is the most encouraging thing that has happened?"

Pat looked at him in surprise. "I don't see why."

"I'm afraid I do." Josef put down his fork. "Mark is implying that some other entity has come to our aid. Hell," he added, with a flash of irritation, "it worries me, the way I can read your tricky little mind. If I thought my own mental processes resembled yours . . ."

"Jeez." The idea obviously appalled Mark as much as it did Josef. They gazed at one another in mutual consternation. Pat was tempted to laugh.

"Anyhow, you're right," Mark went on. "I think somebody else was there — somebody hostile to Peter, somebody who wants to help."

"We will now take a poll on the identity of that somebody," Josef said sarcastically. "Pat?"

"How on earth should I know?"

"The brother, maybe," Kathy offered. "Eddie."

"You're just saying that because you think he's kind of cute," Mark said crushingly. "It wasn't Edward."

"You know what makes this whole thing unreal?" Pat demanded. "It isn't the idea of spirits or supernatural attack; it's the way you all bicker and quarrel, like twelve-year-olds."

"You mean we ought to take it with deadly seriousness?" Josef smiled at her. "That isn't the way people behave, Pat. Only Socrates could conduct a dialogue on the subject of his own death. Besides, the whole situation is so unbelievable I find myself relapsing into trivia as a release from intolerable stress. One can't live at the height of tension without some break now and then."

"Hmph," Pat said.

"You're avoiding the question," Mark said. "Who do you think the second —"

Pat waved him to silence in time to spare the sensibilities of the waitress, who was bringing their entrees. When the woman had retreated, rather more

295

hastily than she had come, Pat said,

"You obviously think you know, Mark. Who?"

"Mrs. Bates, of course. Louisa,"

They considered the suggestion — if Mark's dogmatic statement could be called that. As was to be expected, Kathy was the first convert.

"Sure, that makes sense," she exclaimed.

"A nice, motherly ghost," Pat murmured. "I suppose one aging mom would attract another's spirit. . . ."

The irony with which she infused this comment was lost on Mark — and on Kathy, who nodded approvingly. Pat realized that they were now taking for granted a point that had appalled them when it first arose — the identification of Kathy with Susan Bates. Apparently Mark had discussed this with the girl, and helped her to accept it without distress.

"It's too facile," Josef complained.

"Go ahead, sneer." Mark took a bite of steak. He added, "Who would you expect to come to a girl's rescue? All the men in her family look like cold fish. They're probably too busy flapping their angelic wings in their nice Calvinist heaven."

"I can't stand this tottering tower of illogic," Josef shouted. The waitress turned to stare; Kathy giggled; Josef flushed slightly and went on in a more subdued voice, "You pile one unwarranted assumption on top of another, Mark. You are the only one who's convinced that Peter Turnbull is ghost number one —"

"It had blue eyes," Kathy said.

"No," Pat said vehemently.

"You saw it too, Mrs. Robbins."

"I know, but . . ." Pat was unable to continue. She was not denying the color, she was denying the suggestion of humanity. The worst part of the entire episode had been those moments at the end, when the alien shape had begun to assume the dimensions of a human body.

The reminder took away what remained of Pat's appetite. Mark was the only one of the group who ate with relish. Watching him demolish a piece of lemon-meringue pie, his mother entertained herself by trying to conceive of a situation in which Mark would be unable to eat. She failed

Cramming the last bite into his mouth, he announced thickly, "Better get moving. We've got a lot to do."

Josef, who had been lost in some abstruse speculation of his own, gave Mark a suspicious look. "Where are we going now?"

"The historical association, of course. I've got to return that Bates material. It closes at three, so we'll have to hurry."

"It's barely two o'clock," Josef said.

Mark rose to his feet.

"We are going to go through that place with a fine-tooth-comb," he announced. "Old newspapers, military records, anything we can find. Time is passing."

And that, Pat thought, was another of Mark's understatements. Less than twelve hours until the next manifestation. . . . And God only knew what form that might take.

Although she had lived in the town for almost ten years, Pat had never visited the old red brick house that sheltered the historical association. She had never even seen it, since it was on a side street, away from the highway and the shops. Almost unconsciously she had absorbed some knowledge of architecture from Jerry, so she was able to date the building to a period at least fifty years older than that of her own house.

It was, in fact, one of the oldest houses in the county. So Jay informed them, after he had greeted them.

"The oldest part was built in 1757, a regular log cabin. The Peabodys made it into a kitchen when they built the central part in —"

"We'll take the tour some other time," Mark interrupted. "Today we — er — I have some work to do in the library. Okay if we go on up?"

"Sure." Jay glanced disparagingly at a family group — father, mother, and two small girls — who were waiting meekly by the door. "Wouldn't you know — I usually don't get more than five, six people a week. I'll join you as soon as I get rid of this lot."

They climbed the graceful curving stairs. Pat felt the handrail shift when she touched it. The house was neat and fairly clean, but it was clear that the association had no money to spare for anything more than basic repairs. The walls needed painting and the shallow stairs were bare of carpeting.

The library occupied the whole of the third floor. No doubt the room had once been a ballroom; it had long windows along one wall and a hardwood floor that was still beautiful despite its scuffed surface. Bookshelves covered the wall opposite the windows; there were rows of filing cabinets on the short walls, and a heaped desk in one corner. Three long library tables took up part of the floor space. One held a card index and a microfilm reader. Pat drew her finger along the nearest shelf and saw a miniature dust pile build before it.

"You don't know what this place looked like before Jay arrived," Mark said, as she made a fastidious face.

"He's done a helluva lot."

"There is still a great deal to be done," Pat retorted.

"If people like you would donate some time, and people like our neighbors would donate some money, it might get done. Do you know how much Jay makes a year?"

"Stop arguing with your mother," Josef said. "Weren't you the lad who said we had a lot to do?"

Giving him a sour look, Mark jerked open one of the filing cabinets.

"The local newspaper," he said, taking out a roll of microfilm. "We'll start with 1858. Here, Kath, look for any mention of the Turnbulls or the Bateses, and let me know when you're ready for the next roll."

He turned to Josef.

"Tax records," he said curtly, indicating a nearby shelf. "Census reports, other legal garbage. That's your specialty, Mr. Friedrichs."

"How about me?" Pat asked, as Josef, without comment, began scanning the dusty volumes Mark had pointed out.

"You get the dirty job," Mark said, his frown relaxing. "The books have been catalogued, but only roughly, and they aren't well arranged. Read the shelves. Look for anything that might apply to our families. I don't think I could have missed a genealogy or a family history, but the Turnbulls might be mentioned in any of the contemporary memoirs. Don't waste time on modern histories," he added, as Pat approached the nearest shelf. "I've read most of them."

He opened a file drawer. Pat saw that it was filled with folders all jammed with papers and apparently unlabeled.

"What is that?" she asked.

"Miscellaneous," Mark replied, with a wry smile. "I told you we'd leave no stone unturned. Get to it, lady."

For half an hour there was silence as all four worked steadily. Out of the corner of her eye Pat saw that both Kathy and Josef paused from time to time to take notes. So far she hadn't found anything worth noting down. As Mark had said, hers was the dirty job, and not only because of the vagueness of her assignment; her hands were dark gray by the time she had worked her way through the top shelves of the first section. Abandoning all hope of staying clean, she sat down on the floor and began on the lower shelves.

Almost immediately she came upon a group of books that promised more than the zero she had scored so far. They were memoirs and collected letters. In style and in appearance they reminded her of the book by Mary Jane Turnbull, and she marveled at the prolific literary habits of the ladies of the nineteenth century. However, it was not surprising that they should have written so much; the dramatic events that led to secession and its bloody aftermath must have prompted many a young girl to start a diary. And they had time, lots of it. Perhaps not the hard-working mistresses of large plantations, glamorized by writers like Margaret Mitchell, but well-to-do women of the urban upper classes had few demands on their leisure and plenty of slaves and servants.

The memoirs gave her less than she hoped. Few were from the area that interested her. And, she realized, even if one of the authors had been acquainted with the Turnbulls, she would have to go through the books page by page to find such references.

Then she came upon a volume entitled *My Imprisonment and the First Year of Abolition Rule in Washington,* and her interest revived. Obviously the author had been Southern in sympathy, and she had lived in the capital, not all that far from Poolesville.

After the first few pages Pat forgot that she was supposed to be looking for the Turnbulls, and became involved in the fantastic narrative. Mrs. Greenhow had not only been a Confederate sympathizer in a hostile city, she had been one of the most skilled and effective spies of the time. She had sent coded messages to General Beauregard, across the river in Virginia, telling him of Northern military plans, and she had finally been arrested by Allan Pinkerton, the famous detective, when her plots were uncovered. Sentenced at first to house arrest, she was able to elude her guards long enough to sneak into the library and destroy damaging papers. Later she was moved to the grim confines of the Old Capital Prison. No place for a lady, Pat thought, fascinated; but then spying was no game for a lady either, or so she would have thought.

She was deeply absorbed in the troubles of Mrs Greenhow when the door opened and Jay entered.

"History buffs," he announced, with a contemptuous wave of the hand in the general direction of the lower regions, whence, one was to assume, the tourists had departed. "How are you doing? Need any help?"

He might have meant the offer for all of them, but he came straight to Pat and prepared to join her on the floor.

"I'm going to stand up," she told him. "My joints are stiffening. I should have known better than to sit crosslegged, at my age."

Jay took her hand and hoisted her up with such energy that her feet missed the floor altogether. He put one long arm around her waist and kept her from falling.

"There you go," he said genially. "What are you reading? Oh, Mrs. Greenhow. You shouldn't sit on that dirty floor. Take the book home if you want."

"But I thought books weren't supposed to go —"

"Oh, hell, rules don't apply to my friends." Jay gave her a friendly squeeze.

"Found something?" a voice inquired. Josef had come up behind them, unheard until then. Jay removed his arm, looking faintly embarrassed, and Josef scowled at him.

"We really must go," Pat said. "We don't want Jay to work overtime, not at his salary."

Jay hastened to assure them that he was willing to stick around. Josef insisted that they wouldn't hear of troubling him. After a further exchange of courtesies they took their departure. As they went along the brick walk, Josef's hand possessive on her arm, Pat glanced back. A pensive figure leaned against the door, staring after them.

"I should have asked him over for a drink," Pat said.

Josef muttered something, in which Pat thought she caught the word "hairy," affixed to a pejorative noun. She did not ask him to repeat the comment.

They were using Josef's car, a dark-blue Mercedes which managed to look ostentatious in spite of its modest lines and subdued color. Mark put his hand on the hood, as gently as if he touched living flesh.

"Nice car," he said.

"Want to drive?"

"You mean it?" Mark gaped at him.

"Go one mile over the speed limit and I'll break both your legs," Josef said, handing him the keys.

He helped Pat into the back seat and got in beside her, letting the younger generation take the front. Pat was absurdly touched by the gesture. She knew how much it meant, to the giver and to the recipient of the favor. Men were so odd about their cars, especially cars like this one. Josef had taken her words to heart after all. He was really trying.

So was Mark; he drove as if his cargo included loose eggs and fragile old ladies. His fascination with the car kept him silent during the short drive back to the house. Josef, tense as a bowstring and trying not to show it as he watched Mark's every move, was in no mood for idle conversation either.

The weather was the sort Washingtonians brag about but seldom see: dry and clear, a perfect 74 degrees, with big white clouds moving lazily across an inverted azure bowl of sky. The plant-eating insects such as the Japanese beetles had not yet appeared, so the shining green leaves of the roses and azaleas were shapely and unmarred.

"Let's sit on the patio," Pat suggested. "It's too nice to go inside."

She had to repeat the remark before Mark heard her. He ran his hands lovingly over the steering wheel in a final caress, and tore himself away.

The redwood patio furniture needed a coat of paint, and the vinyl pads, bright yellow and orange plaid, weren't too clean, but none of them cared. Mark dragged a table close to hand and threw down a heap of notebook paper.

"I'll go first," he announced. "It won't take long; I got a big fat zip. Kathy?"

Kathy's once-fresh print dress was crumpled and dusty. Gray smudges added piquancy to an otherwise almost too perfect face.

"Well," she began, modestly fingering her notes, "I didn't find much. I only got up to 1860. The editor of the paper was a Southern sympathizer, no question about that. His editorials on John Brown and the Harpers Ferry raid were — well, the way he gloated over Brown's execution was really awful."

"That raid hit Marylanders hard," Mark said. "Remember how close it was. Harpers Ferry is right up there in the corner where Maryland and Virginia meet what is now West Virginia. It was still part of Virginia then."

"But I didn't realize how many people in Maryland really believed in slavery," Kathy said. "Do you know how many voted for Lincoln? Less than three thousand! He got fewer votes than any other candidate. Breckenridge, a Southern Democrat, got more than forty-two thousand votes."

"The western part of the state was more sympathetic to the Union than the Tidewater area, with its big plantations," Josef said. "But I don't think there is much doubt that Maryland would have seceded if she had been given free choice. The Union could not allow that. All the rail lines and roads, even the waterways connecting the capital with the North passed through the state."

"What about the Turnbulls and the Bateses?" Pat demanded. "Were there any stories about them?"

"The Turnbulls were mentioned often," Kathy answered. "They must have been social leaders, or something. They kept having parties. Peter's sixteenth birthday was a big event, it rated a whole column in the paper — dancing in the garden by moonlight, magnolias in bloom, and all that. There were about fifty guests.''

''Including the Bateses?'' Pat persisted. She was beginning to take a proprietary interest in them.

''They were what you might call conspicuous by their absence. Can you imagine not inviting close kin living right next door? The war didn't actually start till 1861, when Fort Sumter was attacked. But South Carolina seceded in December of 1860, and I guess things were pretty tense even before that. Mr. Bates —''

''If nothing else comes out of this, you'll be well grounded in one period of American history,'' Josef said, smiling at his daughter. She looked unusually pretty in spite of her dishevelment. Her blue eyes shone like the best aquamarines.

''It's more interesting when you know the people,'' Kathy said naïvely. ''Anyhow, Mr. Bates was really unpopular. There was a nasty editorial about him in 1859. It didn't mention him by name, but it hinted pretty strongly. All about abolitionists in our midst, undermining the law by stealing other peoples' property. . . . Property! They were talking about slaves — human beings. How could anybody —"

"Slavery has only been illegal in this country for a little over a century," Josef said. "We were one of the last of the so-called civilized nations to outlaw it, but it had been accepted all over the world for thousands of years."

"That's right," Mark said. "The Greeks had slaves, didn't they? And medieval serfdom was essentially the same thing; a serf could be bought and sold, like an animal."

"So maybe we are making some progress, after all," Josef said.

"Not fast enough," Mark said. But he smiled as he spoke, and for a moment Pat saw a spark of understanding pass between the two men, a look that augured well for the future.

"I'd like to read more of the newspapers." Kathy said. "It was interesting."

"Interesting, but probably a waste of time," Josef said. "You haven't told us anything we hadn't already learned or surmised, Kathy."

"How about you, Mr. Friedrichs?" Mark asked.

"Very little. I got the impression that Turnbull was living beyond his means. All those parties. . . . He sold land six times between 1850 and 1860. I don't know how much he started out with, but he couldn't have had much property left by the time he marched gallantly out to war, leaving his wife to manage as best she could while he was fighting for the Cause. He did leave her fifty slaves — one of the largest numbers recorded for the county."

"What about the Bateses?" Pat asked.

"They owned no slaves," Josef answered. "The census reports for 1860 show a household of two men, two women, and twelve household servants of the colored race — freedmen all."

The sun had sunk below the trees, and the evening breeze felt cool.

"I saw you were reading Mrs.

313

Greenhow's book, Mom," Mark said. "Truth is stranger than fiction, right?"

"Well-bred lady spies, complete with hoop skirts and smelling salts, do sound like bad fiction," Pat agreed. "But some of the so-called historical romances I've read lately have had even more unbelievable plots."

"And even more sex," Mark said, grinning. "I can't believe Mrs. Greenhow ever writhed in the arms of her lover as his hands moved softly over —"

"Did you read that trashy book?" Pat demanded in outraged tones.

"*Slave of Passion,*" Mark said. He rolled his eyes. "You shouldn't leave stuff like that lying around, my dear."

"Shame on you, Mrs. Robbins, contaminating an innocent mind like Mark's," Kathy added.

It was her first contribution to the silly little exchanges Pat shared with her son, and her tentative smile showed that she wasn't quite sure how it would be taken. Feeling that she had been given some insight into the girl's relationship with her mother, Pat exaggerated her reaction.

"Innocent, she says. You should see the books he hides under his mattress."

Kathy giggled appreciatively. Her father muttered, as if to himself, "In my day it was *Esquire*. My mother found a copy in one of my drawers, open to the centerfold. . . ."

"Well, back in those days people were uptight about sex," Mark said tolerantly, "I mean, you hadn't really advanced much since the Civil War period."

"I wouldn't say that," Josef objected. "Some of Petty's centerfolds were —"

Foreseeing another digression, Pat interrupted.

"Let's get back to Mrs. Greenhow. And no more writhings, please. I didn't finish the book, but the Turnbulls weren't mentioned in the part I read."

With his brows drawn together in the scowl that gave him such an uncanny resemblance to his father, Mark picked up a pencil and began doodling on the paper in front of him.

"It's so damned frustrating," he

315

muttered. "All this blank paper, and nothing to put on it."

"Mrs. Greenhow was only one of many," Josef said, ignoring this outburst of petulance. "There was a regular espionage network in and around Washington during the war. With the enemy just across the river, it was easy to pass on the news of troop dispositions and strategy; a man could paddle his boat across on a dark night —"

"Women did it too," Pat said, resenting the implicit chauvinism in Josef's speech. "One of Mrs. Greenhow's messengers was a girl, Betty Duvall. She drove a cart straight across Chain Bridge to Fairfax Courthouse, where the Confederates were, carrying the message in her hair. Nobody thought of challenging a simple little country girl."

"That's right," Kathy said. "I was reading a book at the library the other day, written by a woman who was ten years old at the time of the war. She lived in a town on the main road to Richmond, and she remembered a lot of

Marylanders passing through on their way south. One of them was a sweet little old lady from Baltimore — I think her name was Alexander — whose son was in prison at Fort McHenry. She went to Richmond to get him a commission in the Confederate army so he would be considered a prisoner of war instead of an enemy agent. I mean, they hanged spies."

Pat shivered. Long blue shadows lay across the table. Mark, his eyes lowered, continued to doodle. Kathy glanced at him uneasily and went on, as if hoping to rouse him from his fit of the sulks.

"She got the commission, too. She carried it back in the lining of her bonnet, can you imagine? But her son escaped. He jumped off the parapet of the fort and broke his leg, and managed to crawl to a nearby house, where the people helped him. They smuggled him to another Southern sympathizer, who passed him on, and so forth. It just shows you how many people in Maryland really believed in —"

"Mark," Pat said suddenly. Her son's

eyes were now fixed vacantly on the lilac bushes; but his hand continued to move.

"What the devil . . ." Josef began.

The chill that ran through Pat had nothing to do with the temperature of the evening air. Mark's face no longer resembled his father's. The features were Mark's, but they did not look like his; an alien, unfamiliar expression overlay them like a thin mask. And his hand continued to move.

"Mark!" Pat leaned across the table and caught that horribly moving arm.

Mark let out a yell. It was as if her touch had been a knife that slashed his arm to the bone.

"Damn it! What the hell do you think you're doing?"

His tone was offensive, and so was his dark frown; but Pat didn't mind, because both the voice and the frown were Mark's. The alien cast had left his features. He was nursing his right hand against his body, as if it pained him.

"What's wrong with your hand?" she asked.

"It hurts. You didn't have to hit me."

"I didn't. I barely touched you. What happened?"

"Nothing happened. We were talking about your lady spy, Mrs. Greenhow, and then you leaned over and —"

"You lost about ninety seconds of time," Josef said. "Let me see that paper, Mark."

"I was just doodling," Mark began. He glanced at the paper. His eyes dilated until they looked black.

Josef picked up the sheet of paper and glanced at it. Without comment, he handed it to Pat.

The top of the page was covered with Mark's scribbling. A psychiatrist would not have found it particularly interesting, for the symbols were overt expressions of Mark's feelings — question marks, spirals that went on and on without resolution. Then, abruptly, halfway down the sheet of paper, the penciled tracings became words.

"Tell her I came back. I want her to know. It was hard oh God it was hard, so hard, but I came I want her to know I came I want her I want her I . . . ."

The last word trailed off in a black scrawl, where Pat had joggled Mark's arm.

Pat dug her nails into the palms of her hands. The pain helped her control herself.

"You wouldn't do this for a joke, Mark." She made it a statement, not a question. "You wouldn't do this to me."

"Bite your tongue," Mark said. He was as white as the sheet of paper, but the insatiable curiosity he had inherited from his father was rearing its head. "Did I really write that?"

"No," Pat said. "You didn't. It's not your handwriting."

"Then who . . .?"

No one answered. They all knew the truth. They had seen the handwriting before. Spiky, bold, unmistakably distinctive. . . .The handwriting of Peter Turnbull.

# Eight

Moved by a single impulse, they fled for the house, snatching up their belongings more or less at random. The gracious blue dusk had become an enemy, inhabited by shadows.

Pat went around the kitchen switching on every light she could find. Mark, who had grabbed the ominous paper, dropped into a chair at the kitchen table and studied the writing, his chin propped on his hands.

"Amazing," he muttered. "I never knew I had the talent."

"I could kill you," said his mother in a choked voice. "How you have the nerve to joke about it . . ."

"I'm not joking. This is the most fantastic piece of luck! You know what it means."

"What it probably means," Josef said coldly, "is that your uncontrolled subconscious has expressed itself. You've had this idea in mind all along, haven't you?"

Mark looked injured.

"I didn't do it on purpose. That was automatic writing."

"One of the favorite tricks of the fake mediums," Josef said. "They claim the spirits are directing their muscles."

"Honest to God, Mr. Friedrichs —"

"Oh, I'm not accusing you of fraud. In some cases a medium honestly believes he or she has been taken over by some external force. But that force can be the subconscious, just as the spirit guides who speak through the medium can be a secondary personality."

"What are you talking about?" Pat demanded shrilly. Her nerves had been badly shaken, and she was in no mood for generalizations. "What idea?"

"I'll state it," Josef said. "Actually, Mark, I'm doing you a favor; it may sound more sensible coming from me.

"Mark believes that the poltergeist is the conscious intelligence of Peter Turnbull, and that his — er — activities are directed toward and stimulated by the girl who is the spiritual reincarnation of Susan Bates. He thinks Susan and Peter were lovers."

"I don't see that you made it sound any more sensible," Mark grumbled. "They weren't lovers. Not in the physical sense, anyhow. But . . . yes, I do think they were in love. I mean, a man doesn't come back from the grave to argue about secession."

Mark wasn't the only one who had considered the idea. Pat realized that it had been simmering in her own subconscious for some time.

"But they were first cousins," she said slowly. "Wouldn't that —"

"Prevent them from marrying? No," Mark said flatly. "Not then. And it would have been marriage that was in question, not casual fooling around; in 1860 a guy didn't dally with a young lady of good family — especially when it was his own family. But can you imagine the parents approving of such a match?"

"Star-crossed lovers?" Josef shook his head. "Mark, you stole the plot from *Romeo and Juliet*. It's highly suspect, and so is this presumed message." He picked up the paper and eyed it critically. " 'Tell her I've come back.' From the dead, one presumes. It would be difficult, I agree. 'I want her, I want her. . . .' Come, now. It was admittedly a melodramatic era, but that's a bit too much."

"I don't believe it," Kathy said. "I won't believe it. Why would he act so — so violently, if he really loved her?"

Pat started to speak, and then changed her mind. Kathy was visibly distressed; it would be cruel to frighten her further. But if Mark's theory was correct, there was an explanation for the violence of the manifestations.

Peter Turnbull, arrogant, spoiled, unaccustomed to deprivation of any kind, had been deprived of the girl he wanted, first by the intolerance of their parents and then by the final frustration. If one granted that some aspect of personality did survive death — and that was becoming harder and harder to deny — then perhaps the boy was still blindly seeking his lost love. It was not necessary to assume that young Turnbull had been malignant and vicious in life. Didn't some spiritualists claim that ghosts were by definition psychotic spirits, lingering on this plane of existence because the shock of violent, untimely death had made them unable to accept their removal from the body? If the spirit of Peter Turnbull was trapped in some such hellish impasse, their problem was insoluble. In the act of seeking Peter would destroy what he sought, and there was no way of giving him what he wanted, or convincing him that it was unattainable.

Kathy sat hunched over, her arms wrapped around her body as if she were cold, her eyes staring. Pat started up.

"It's getting late," she said, with forced cheerfulness. "I could do with a snack and a cup of hot tea. Kathy, how about giving me a hand?"

"Scotch for me," Josef said.

Mark said nothing. Like Kathy, he

stared into empty space, his lips moving as if he were praying.

## II

Canned soup and sandwiches were the best Pat could offer, but the food restored their spirits, and, as Josef said, the Scotch didn't hurt. Mark remained abstracted throughout the meal, although he managed to eat twice as much as anyone else.

When they had finished Kathy collected the dishes as if she had done that job all her life. Josef's eyes followed the slim little figure as it moved back and forth between the table and the sink. His expression was unguarded, and the baffled terror in his dark eyes made Pat ache with sympathy.

"I made reservations at the motel," he said abruptly. "For all of us."

Pat half expected that Mark would object. Instead he nodded soberly.

"I guess we'd better. At least you three —"

"You, too," Pat said firmly. "You're

not staying here alone with vases and mirrors flying around the room."

"It isn't doing that anymore," Mark said. "The last couple of times there was no poltergeist stuff. Hmmm. That's interesting."

"Why?" Pat asked.

"He's got you well trained as a straight man," Josef remarked disagreeably. "You ought to know how he thinks — if the process can be called that. He interprets everything as a sign of a guiding intelligence — an assumption which, like all his other assumptions, he has yet to prove. The idea is that this nasty apparition was awkward and maladroit at first, unaccustomed to its powers. Gradually it is focusing them, concentrating on its real aim, so that it doesn't have to waste energy in random acts of violence."

Jerry's frown altered his son's face.

"You wouldn't be able to figure that out if you hadn't reached the same conclusions," Mark said. "Why do you keep fighting it? Hell, I don't like it any better than you do! The trouble is, we're caught in a vicious circle. We don't know enough to take the steps that would enable us to learn more. We ought to be testing the thing, experimenting, finding its limitations. But we can't take the risk."

"Mark." Josef rose and began to pace back and forth, his hands in his pockets. "I've gone along with your research because the only thing we stand to lose by it is a few days of time. And because — oh, yes, I admit it — because there is a remote chance that we might be able to learn something that would enable us to deal with this — this thing. Any other method is out. It's too dangerous."

"Why do you say the chance is remote? It seems to me —"

"Because I too, in my long-distant youth, read ghost stories." Josef leaned against the counter; a faint, reminiscent smile curved his lips. "I'd climb into bed at night with a volume of Poe or Lovecraft and read till my hair stood on end and I was afraid to turn out the light. I'm tolerably familiar with the literature, including the so-called 'true' ghost stories. The White Nuns, and the ghostly carriages, the banshees and the headless horsemen. . . . I can't remember a single case in which a ghost was laid to rest by an intrepid investigator who found out what was troubling the troubled spirit. In fiction, yes. Not in fact. Now be honest. You're a screwball, but you have a good mind. Do you know of any such cases?"

The compliment was not exactly wholehearted, but Mark was rather flattered by it, although he tried to appear blasé.

"Well," he began.

"I'm not talking about the pop books written by professional ghost hunters," Josef added. "The cases they discuss are so vague, and their evidence is so illogical, that no sane person could take them seriously. I'm talking about ghosts — the kind that walk around old houses politely dematerializing when someone tries to touch them. And that, my boy, is just about all they do. Their activities are singularly aimless. Do you know of any real case like the one you have postulated — a case of a personality returning after death because of some unfinished business or frustrated ambition?''

"Well . . ."

"I don't either," Josef said.

Mark looked straight at his tormentor.

"Are you going to write this case up, Mr. Friedrichs? Or talk about it at cocktail parties?''

Josef's response was wordless. It might best be described as a growl.

At nine o'clock the others were ready to leave, but Mark had had second thoughts.

"You guys could sit in the car with the engine running, ready for a getaway," he proposed. I'll wait on the stairs, just to see what happens. If it gets sticky I can run out and —''

"And lead the thing to the motel," Josef said.

For once Pat saw her son outmaneuvered. He bit his lip and refrained from further argument.

Perhaps because he had won that round, Josef was actively cooperative

330

with Mark's next proposal — to set up a tape recorder and camera in his room. The tape recorder was simple enough; Mark's elaborate, expensive hi-fi system included recording equipment that would run for almost four hours. The camera was something else. There was no way of triggering it to go off at one A.M., although Mark proposed several unrealistic and impossible suggestions. The final result looked like a mad inventor's contraption; wires and cords ran all over the room, hooked up to the camera.

When the final cord across the doorway had been placed, Josef stood back and contemplated the maze with wry amusement.

"That might work if you were trying to catch a blind burglar," he remarked. "Although I doubt it. Pulling one of those cords will probably just jerk the camera off the tripod."

Pat glanced over her shoulder. Mark was out of earshot; he had gone down to console Jud and shut him in the kitchen.

"You helped him set it up," she said.

"I'll do anything that doesn't involve taking physical risks. Anyway, it kept him busy for an hour; God knows what he would have proposed if I hadn't gone along with this. All right, my dear, let's go."

Instead of heading for the nearest motel, Josef drove on through town and turned north.

"Where are we going?" Mark asked.

"Frederick. I figured we might as well put a little distance between us and our friend."

Having been concerned with far more vital issues, Pat had not considered the social aspects of their situation. But when the desk clerk addressed her as "Mrs. Friedrichs," a belated realization of what she was doing swept over her. As they walked down the corridor toward their rooms, Josef muttered, "You look like the picture of guilt, my dear. If we hadn't had the kids with us, the clerk would have assumed the worst."

"Why did you have to give your own name?" Pat hissed.

"Because I was using a credit card.

Relax, will you? I'm already divorced; no one is going to cite you as corespondent." He put his key in the lock and opened the door. "Here we are," he said aloud. "Cozy, isn't it?"

The room looked like all the motel rooms Pat had ever seen: shabby, characterless and bland. The color scheme was green and yellow. The pictures over the bed were prints of chrysanthemums in green vases.

Josef crossed the room to a door in the side wall and unlocked it.

"You and Kathy can share this room," he said to Pat. Then he turned to Mark. "Your room is at the other end of the wing. I couldn't get three rooms adjoining."

For a moment Mark stared blankly at the key Josef had offered him. His eyes narrowed. Then, with a slight shrug, he took the key, and his mother relaxed. After all, it was the most practical way of arranging matters; Mark and Josef had no desire to share a room. And even Mark could hardly expect the older man to take the room at the end of the hall, away from his daughter.

"You don't mind if I stick around until one o'clock, do you?" Mark asked politely.

"Not at all. Make yourself comfortable."

In addition to the double bed, the room contained the usual furniture: a desk, a chest of drawers, and a table and two chairs. Josef pulled out a chair for Pat. She shook her head.

"Thanks, but I'd better hang up my dress. I don't want to go to work all crumpled and messy."

"You aren't going to work tomorrow!" Mark exclaimed.

"Mark, I have to. I can't go on —"

"Just one more day, Mom. I told them you had flu and probably wouldn't be in till the middle of the week. Just tomorrow, and then —"

"And then — what? a miracle?"

"I've got an idea," Mark said. "If it doesn't work . . . Please, Mom?"

"Well . . . all right. But what —"

"I think I'll go look for the Coke machine," Mark said, plunging toward the door.

"Get some ice while you're at it," Josef said.

"Sure, right. Kath?"

Kathy followed him.

Pat closed her mouth on the question she had not had time to ask, and turned to see Josef taking a bottle from his overnight bag.

Why she should have chosen that particular moment to speak she did not know. In fact, the words that came out of her mouth were words she would normally not have said.

"Are you going to sit here drinking until one o'clock?"

With one angry twist of the wrist Josef opened the bottle and splashed a generous amount into his glass.

"You sound like my ex-wife," he said. "It doesn't become you, my dear."

"If that's why she left you —"

"That was one of the reasons. If it's any of your business."

Then his face twisted, as anger was replaced by horrified concern.

"My God, Pat, what are we doing?

I'm sorry. It is your business, you have every right —"

He came toward her, his arms outstretched. Pat turned away.

"No, don't. Not now, not . . . I don't know what made me say those things."

She heard his heavy breathing close behind her, but he did not touch her.

"My ex-wife was a religious fanatic," he said. "A middle-aged Jesus freak. When I married her she was devout, a little straitlaced; I found that charming, can you imagine? I thought marriage would . . . make her see things differently. But she got worse. She despised all the indulgences of the flesh, including . . . Kathy was an accident, and was resented as such. Until two years ago my daughter never wore makeup, or cut her hair, or owned a pretty dress. Marion sent her to one of those fundamentalist schools, for girls only. I should have interfered long before I did, but I thought raising a girl was a mother's job. I was a damned fool, and believe me, I paid for it. I can't say Marion drove me to drink. It's always a matter of one's own choice, isn't it? I guess I did it to get back at her. I'm still doing it."

"You don't have to tell me this," Pat whispered.

"Yes, I do. It sounds crazy, I know, but I could have admitted that she was promiscuous, or that she had fallen in love with someone else, or even that she found me boring and repulsive. What I couldn't admit was that she was dim-witted enough to leave me for an oily, unctuous evangelist. That's where she is now, in his commune in California, wandering around in a long white robe serving saintly Father Emmanuel. . . ."

"Don't." Impulsively Pat turned, and found herself in his arms. She clung to him, her hands moving over the soft tweed of his jacket, but when he bent his head she turned her face away.

"The kids will be back any second," she murmured.

"I guess Mark isn't ready for this development," Josef agreed. His hands slid slowly down her back, as if reluctant to release her. "Are you ready for it, Pat?"

"No. Not until. . . . We're in an abnormal situation, Josef. I can't trust my feelings."

"I can trust mine. I love you, Pat, I'll even put up with that outrageous son of yours if you'll have me."

"Not now," Pat said. She moved away from him and saw, from his expression, that her withdrawal had wounded him. But it was herself she didn't trust; his physical presence had aroused feelings she had not experienced for over a year, and she knew they were clouding her judgment.

"What would your husband have thought of our ghost?" Josef asked.

"Jerry?" She considered the question. "He'd have been fascinated — but skeptical. He would have been the first to slap Mark down when his theories got too farfetched."

She was interrupted by Mark banging on the door. Josef went to answer it. Something of the tension that had filled the room must have remained; Mark looked suspiciously at his mother.

"What were you talking about?"

"Your name was mentioned," Josef said. "But only in passing. Strange as it may seem to you, there are other topics worthy of discussion. In God's name what have you got there?" Mark had begun unloading various edibles onto the table.

"They are fascinated by machines," Pat explained. "Jerry always said Mark would feed a quarter into a slot if he knew it would only give him a punch in the nose."

She could see that Josef was self-conscious about her references to her husband, and that was something they would have to work out before they could come to any real understanding. Jerry would always be part of her life. She couldn't forget him and she didn't want to. In the last few days she had been able to remember him and talk about him without the gnawing ache of loss, and that was not only a miracle, it was the way things ought to be. Jerry was the last person in the world to expect her to wallow in widowhood. He would rejoice in her new happiness.

Mark arranged a row of cans and a heap of candy bars on the table and sat down with the books he had brought with him.

"I," he announced regally, "have work to do. The rest of you can amuse yourselves as you like, but please keep it down."

"Go get your mother a chair," Josef said, scowling at him.

"Please," Pat said gently.

"Oh." Mark rose and went into the next room. After an apologetic glance at Pat, Josef followed him. They returned, each carrying a chair.

And that was something else that would have to be worked out, Pat thought. Mark was a grown man. He would not lightly submit to the parental authority of a stranger. He didn't need a father, he needed a friend.

Josef was obviously struggling with the same realization, for after they had settled in their chairs he spoke to Mark in kindlier tones than he had used thus far.

"What are you looking for, Mark? Can we help?"

"Well — sure. I guess you could. I'm curious about where and when Peter Turnbull was killed. 'A cavalry skirmish, somewhere in Maryland' is pretty vague. I thought maybe one of the military-history books would have a record of the engagements White's Rangers fought in."

"If the unit was part of Lee's Army of northern Virginia, we should be able to locate it," Josef said.

"But cavalry troops didn't always stay with the main body of the army. They went off on their own, like that raid on Poolesville in 1862."

"True." Josef picked up one of the books. "We can but try. I don't understand why you think it's important, but —"

"Maybe it isn't," Mark said. "Only I got to wondering. . . . The opposing armies were so close. Right across the Potomac from each other, much of the time. Of course distances were greater then — no, damn it, I mean —"

"I know what you mean," Josef said, smiling. "It took longer in those days to cover the distance. All the same, the armies were close. This area was hit several times by Confederate troops looking for horses and supplies. Perhaps Peter was with one of those units."

"If he was," Mark said, "wouldn't he drop in on his girl friend while he was in the area?"

Josef considered the idea, scratching his chin, but Pat exclaimed impatiently, "Of course he would. Nineteen years old, swaggering in a fancy uniform —"

"They weren't so fancy," Kathy said. "Remember in *Gone With the Wind,* how they were spinning butternut cloth for uniforms, and dying captured Yankee uniforms because they couldn't get the good gray material?"

"That was after the Union blockade of the South had become effective," Pat argued. "Can you see the Turnbulls, father or son, riding off to war without the whole bit — spurs jingling, blooded horses prancing, gold epaulets and shiny swords?"

Mark snickered. "It's getting to you, isn't it? You talk about them as if you knew them personally — predicting what they would say and do."

"Get lost," Pat said.

"Okay." Mark took a book in one hand and Kathy's wrist in the other. "We're going in the next room to work. Don't worry, we'll leave the door open."

This shaft of irony was directed at Josef, who responded with a raised eyebrow, but made no verbal comment. When the two had disappeared into the adjoining room, he spoke to Pat in a low voice.

"What is he driving at?"

"I'm sure I don't know."

"Maybe I'm unfair," Josef said. "But I swear that kid would make Machiavelli look like an amateur. . . . Well, I'll see if I can find out what he wants to know; maybe then he'll condescend to explain why he wants to know it."

He applied himself to the book he had chosen. Pat tried to read too, but the low voices and occasional bursts of laughter from the next room distracted her.

Thank God, she thought, for the resilience of youth. Kathy must be a lot tougher than she looked to have survived the arid childhood Josef had described. If her mother's warped views had scarred the girl, the scars were well hidden; certainly she didn't seem to find the male sex repellent.

As time passed, it became harder for them to concentrate. Josef's eyes began to stray from his book to his wristwatch. Pat had put hers in her purse in order to resist the temptation of watching it. Mark and Kathy appeared to have forgotten the time, but when Josef said suddenly, "It's twelve fifty," Mark emerged from the next room as if he had been propelled by a spring.

"Twelve forty-five," he said. "Your watch is fast."

"Turn on the TV," Pat said.

Josef rose to do so, giving her a sour smile. She shared his feelings; trying to clock a ghost by means of anything as mundane and modern as television . . .

But the prosaic nature of the apparatus gave her an unreasonable sense of

344

security. Surely no evil spirit would invade a motel room while Perry Mason outfoxed another lawyer.

Abandoning all pretense at indifference, they sat watching Perry mouth dumb protests until Pat said suddenly, "Poor Jud. I feel guilty, leaving him."

"I wanted to bring him," Mark said. "But you —"

"He's too big," Pat said. She didn't want to explain her real objections to bringing the dog. His abject terror had increased her own. "Anyhow, he's shut in the kitchen, away from . . . I wish we could have located Albert before we left."

"Cats are reputed to be quite comfortable in the presence of evil spirits," Josef remarked.

"That's a vile canard," Pat said. "However, I think cats are more capable of avoiding unpleasant situations. Albert has not been around much the last few days. Maybe he doesn't like what has been going on."

The exchange was their last pretense at

conversation. They sat in silence for the succeeding minutes, watching the figures on the TV screen gesticulate. Perry's triumph was followed by six commercials, a late news bulletin, and the "Star-Spangled Banner," as the station signed off. Finally, when the screen had been blank for several long minutes, Josef let out a long sigh and wiped his damp forehead.

"That's that."

"Thank God," Pat said sincerely. "Let's go to bed."

"I don't suppose . . ." Mark began.

"That we want to go back to the house and see what, if anything, your apparatus has recorded? No," said Josef.

"I had a feeling you were going to say that," Mark muttered. "Good night, all."

By the time Pat had finished her ablutions Kathy was sound asleep. The girl had been stoically silent through the last vigil, but as Pat bent over her, studying her pale face, she wondered how long Kathy could stand it. Even if Josef carried out his threat of selling the house and moving away, the problem would still be unresolved in the area that counted most — in Kathy's mind. She might go on seeing apparitions even after they had ceased to pursue her; and surely her mother's hell-fire religious notions must have left unpleasant seeds of guilt and doubt in her young conscience.

Pat brushed a lock of hair away from Kathy's cheek. The girl's tight lips relaxed into a faint smile, and Pat resolved then and there that if no other solution presented itself, she would suggest to Mark that they manufacture a final, satisfying denouement, something that would settle Kathy's fears. Maybe, she thought grimly, we can burn that damned house down to the ground. Josef wouldn't wittingly cheat an insurance company, but Mark would. . . . And I'm beginning to think it might be the lesser of two evils.

Josef's room was dark and silent. He had left the door a few inches ajar. Pat got into bed, groaning as her taut muscles relaxed. The warm, sweet tide of sleep began to envelop her.

She came bolt upright, all her joints protesting, as someone knocked on the door.

"Mom? Hey, Mom, are you asleep? It's me."

She heard a muffled curse and a creak of springs from the next room. Josef hadn't been asleep either. With a curse of her own she got up and ran to the door.

"Shut up," she said through her teeth. "If you waken Kathy I'll kill you. What do you want?"

Mark, still fully dressed and wide awake, looked hurt.

"I can't find my pen. I must have left it on the table next door."

"You don't need your pen."

"I do, though, Mom. It won't take a minute. Just let me —"

He was past her before she could protest again. Kathy had not stirred. Mark tiptoed to the door between the rooms.

"I'll just slip in," he whispered. "I won't wake him up."

"I'm awake," said a grim voice from the darkness. "If I had been asleep, I'd be awake now."

"Gee, Mr. Friedrichs, I'm sorry. I just —"

"Shut up and get on with it."

"Yes, sir."

Pat heard objects rustle and rattle and jingle as Mark fumbled. There was no further comment from Josef, not even a creak of bedsprings. Mark finally reappeared.

"Thanks," he said. "I just wanted —"

"Get out of here," Pat said.

Mark gave her a wide smile full of teeth and ingratiation. Before he slipped out the door he glanced at the bed where Kathy was sleeping, and his mother's rude comment died on her lips. He cared so much it hurt her to see him.

## IV

She felt less kindly toward Mark when the incident was repeated at what seemed to her an incredibly early hour the following morning.

"Go away," she shouted — and then, remembering Kathy, she rolled over, clapping her hand to her mouth.

Kathy was sitting up in bed. With her hair tumbling over her bare shoulders and the thin fabric of her batiste nightgown showing all the fresh young curves beneath, she looked good enough to eat. Her eyes were shining as she slid out of bed and headed for the door, where Mark's insistent tapping could still be heard.

Pat fell back against the pillow, wondering whether she was tough enough to become the mother of a nubile young maiden.

"Put a robe on," she croaked.

Kathy came to a stop and turned red from the top of her nightgown to the roots of her hair. Remembering a number of things she ought to have recalled earlier, Pat added quickly, "Mark is always in a weakened state before breakfast; you don't want him to pass out in the hall, do you?"

Kathy's flush subsided. "You're funny," she said, giggling.

"That's me," Pat agreed. "Keep 'em laughing."

Mark's attack on the door increased in volume. Pat yelled, "Wait a minute."

"I'll let him in," Josef said. He stood in the doorway between the two rooms, buttoning his shirt; and as Pat rolled a weary, wary eye in his direction he grinned disarmingly. "Hi," he said.

"Uh," Pat said. Her nightgown was heavy cotton and she knew there were bags under her eyes; there always were when she had not had enough sleep. Josef glanced at his daughter.

"Get your jeans on, honey," he said casually. "The lady is correct, as always; if a passing bellboy gets a look at you, we'll have to beat him off with a club."

Kathy snatched up a handful of garments and vanished into the bathroom. Ignoring the increasing fusillade of knocks, Josef sat down on the bed. Pat was still groggy; his kiss caught her unawares, and for a few moments after that she didn't even hear the knocking.

"You look gorgeous in the morning,"

he said, his hands on her shoulders.

"You're either blind or a liar or —"

"In love," said Josef against her ear.

"Don't do that. What if one of the kids —"

"They'll have to get used to it eventually," Josef said. His warm breath moved across her cheek and mingled with hers. Pat wondered briefly how he had acquired such skills in a loveless marriage with a frigid wife. She decided she didn't care.

Finally she freed her mouth, fighting her own instincts as well as his, and pushed him away.

"How can you be so frivolous at a time like this?"

"I must have undeveloped talents for frivolity," Josef said, smiling. "I feel drunk. No, I feel better than that. Getting drunk is no fun."

"You'd better let Mark in before he kicks the door down."

"Mark." Josef's smile vanished. "That's right, I have something to say to that young man."

There was a decided swagger in his

walk as he crossed the room. Pat pushed a pillow under her back and watched him with lazy amusement. No doubt she ought to inquire why he was annoyed with Mark, but at that moment she was inclined to let them fight it out. Like Josef, she felt slightly drunk. No; it was much better than being drunk. . . .

Josef opened the door. Ruffled and red-faced, Mark stalked in, and Pat's suppressed amusement surfaced in a weird gurgle as her son's suspicious gaze moved from Josef's face to hers.

"What took you so long? What were you doing?"

"I sent Kathy in to dress before I opened the door," Josef said blandly. "Just because we are in an abnormal situation doesn't mean we can lose sight of all the proprieties." Unappeased, Mark continued to glower at him, and Josef went on, "Speaking of proprieties, I'd appreciate it if you would return my car keys. One can hardly speak of theft among friends, but it wasn't kosher, was it, to borrow the car without asking me?"

Pat sat up in bed.

"Mark! Did you really?"

"Mom, you aren't dressed," Mark said.

"Stop trying to change the subject. Did you take —"

"I just wanted to check on poor old Jud," Mark said in injured tones. "I figured you would all get mad if I suggested it, so . . ."

He handed Josef the keys. The latter inspected them.

"How are the fenders?" he inquired.

"Not a scratch," Mark replied indignantly.

"Hmmm. All right, sport. Let's get some breakfast. The ladies will join us in —"

"Fifteen minutes," Pat said.

She didn't want to lecture Mark in front of Josef. He felt enough hostility already. But she promised herself that she would have a few words to say to him when they were alone.

She knew she was hooked when she found herself hurrying to dress, in order to see Josef a little sooner. Like a high-school girl, she thought, banging her head with her brush in her haste. But it's nice. It feels good. And when she and Kathy entered the dining room, she was surprised to see that the sky outside was dark with rain. She felt like sunshine.

Josef's behavior was sophomorically infatuated. He tried to hold her hand under the table, and the way he looked at her would have been a dead giveaway if anyone had been watching.

But Mark wasn't watching. When he had finished his breakfast he sat staring vacantly at his plate. Pat offered him her toast, and he refused. Then she really got worried.

"What did you say to him?" she hissed at Josef.

He shook his head. "Not much. I'm saving it."

"He's up to something," Pat said aloud. "Mark." She nudged his elbow, which was inelegantly propped on the table. "Mark, wake up."

"Huh?" Mark started. His mother, studying him with undivided attention for the first time that morning, saw the telltale signs. "Did you get any sleep last night?" she demanded. "What were you doing?"

"Working," Mark said. "Thinking."

"That's work," Josef agreed. He exchanged glances with Pat, and some of her suspicions must have slipped into his mind. "What else did you do last night, Mark? Did you really go back to the house?"

"We better leave," Mark said hastily. "Poor old Jud must be about ready to burst. I mean —"

"So you didn't go to the house," Pat exclaimed. "Where —"

But Mark was halfway to the door, and by the time Josef had paid the check, he had vanished into his own room and closed the door.

"We may as well check out," Josef said resignedly. "When we get him home I'll string him up by his thumbs and ask him again. I don't want to make a scene here in public."

True to his promise, he said nothing during the drive. Mark was in a peculiar state, mumbling under his breath, squirming and twitching, and once, to his mother's consternation, bursting into a hoarse, sardonic laugh. Seeing Pat's alarm, Kathy patted her hand.

"It's all right, Mrs. Robbins. He's got an idea, that's all."

"If it affects him that way, he'd better give up intellectual activities," said her father, from the front seat.

"Do you know what the idea is?" Pat asked.

"Well . . ." Kathy looked as sly as it was possible for her to look. "I promised I wouldn't talk about it till he has it all worked out. If it does — we might have this whole thing settled by tonight. Wouldn't that be great?"

"Uh-huh," Pat said. She wished she shared Kathy's faith in Mark. She did not express her doubts; why should she destroy the girl's optimism prematurely?

Never before, even when it was ramshackle and abandoned, had her house looked anything but innocent to

Pat. Now, under an evil, threatening sky, it had a sinister air. The turrets and tower seemed grotesque instead of charming.

Mark led the way. He went straight to the kitchen and Pat heard Jud's yelp of pleasure mixed with reproach as Mark greeted him and let him out. Standing in the hall she sniffed, wrinkling her nose; but there was no trace of that foul aroma. That did not prove that the night had been quiet. The aura was not a physical smell, it probably worked directly on the mind of the person affected.

She lingered by the door, oddly reluctant to go farther. As she stood there, the bushes by the steps rustled. Albert's neatly marked head emerged. He eyed her dubiously for a moment and then meowed.

"I called you last night," Pat said defensively. "It's your own fault if you didn't want to come in."

Mark and Kathy went upstairs. Josef was obviously torn between curiosity and another emotion, but there was no real conflict; he turned to Pat, who was still arguing with the cat.

"Don't come in, then, if you don't want to. But you'll have to make up your mind. I won't leave the door wide open."

The cat took two tentative steps toward her, its tail at half-mast and twitching. Then it spat and bolted into the shrubbery.

"He is acting strangely," Pat said. "I wonder . . ."

Then she heard Mark call from upstairs. "Mom. Mr. Friedrichs. Can you come up here, please?"

The trail of destruction had left debris as far down as the stair landing, where shards of a broken vase glittered. A dent in the plaster showed where it had struck and shattered. The upper hall was strewn with broken glass from pictures. Every one of them had been torn from the wall. Mark's room had taken the brunt of the attack. There was hardly a breakable object left intact, including his camera; but none of the other upstairs rooms had completely escaped. It was as if some large savage animal had been let loose and had ranged up and down, searching and smashing.

# Nine

"I thought you said Peter had given up aimless poltergeist action," Josef remarked, as they stood in the doorway of Mark's room contemplating the mess.

"This was deliberate," Mark said. "It couldn't find what it was looking for, so it went storming up and down smashing things. Damn it, Mr. Friedrichs, this knocks your poltergeist theory all to hell. There wasn't a living soul in this room last night. According to the conventional theories, a poltergeist needs a human catalyst. I had the car keys, so you can't accuse Kathy of —"

He gulped, his eyes widening, as he realized the implications, but Josef shook his head, looking at Mark with grudging respect.

"You're too smart to incriminate yourself that way. If you had planned a stunt like this you'd have made damned good and sure you weren't found within a mile of those keys. Where did you go last night, Mark?"

"I'll tell you, I'll tell you," Mark said. "I'm just trying to think how to explain it."

In a stupor of distress Pat knelt down and began to pick up broken scraps. Josef took her arm and raised her to her feet.

"We'll form a cleanup team later, Pat. Come on downstairs while Mark tries to figure out how to break his latest bad news to us."

Muted howls and meows led them to the kitchen, where they found both animals waiting on the back porch. When Pat opened the door Jud bolted in, flung himself at her feet, and writhed delightedly. Albert still refused to come in, but indicated that he was faint with hunger, so Pat took a bowl of food out onto the porch.

In an effort to postpone what was

362

clearly going to be a painful revelation, Mark turned on the radio. Rock and roll blasted out.

"Turn that off," Josef shouted.

Mark lowered the volume. "Coffee, anyone?" he asked brightly.

"Talk," Josef said.

"All right, all right, I said I'd tell you, didn't I? But you have to understand the reason. I got to thinking yesterday about some of our assumptions. The discrepancies have been small, but they have been piling up, and that made me wonder if maybe we weren't on the wrong track."

The song ended as such numbers often do, trailing off in discordant howls of woe; an announcer's bright cheery voice began to report the usual international disasters: an earthquake in Iran, a revolution in South America, the failure of the latest talks between the Arabs and the Israelis.

"What do you mean, 'we'?" Josef demanded. "All the assumptions have been yours. You practically shoved them down our collective throats."

"Oh, the basic idea is right," Mark said. "I'm certain of that. What I might have been slightly mistaken about is — er — well, let me put it this way —"

"And now," said the announcer, "for local news. A shop in New Market —"

"Shut that damned thing off," Josef snarled, reaching for the knob. As he touched it, however, the content of what was being said finally penetrated. His fingers froze on the switch, defeating Mark's belated attempt to silence the voice.

". . . a number of valuable books," the announcer continued. "The proprietor, Colonel William Blake, estimates their value at approximately fifty thousand dollars. The thief gained entrance through an upper window. The police have made casts of tire tracks in the alley behind the shop, and they hope for an early arrest."

Three pairs of eyes focused on Mark.

"Don't worry," he said hastily. "They aren't yours. I wasn't dumb enough to park where I would leave tracks."

Josef rubbed his forehead.

"Where are the books?" he asked gently.

"In your trunk. I had to take a bunch of them. If I had just swiped the one, he'd have suspected you right away, since you even told him who you were and where you lived and all. Now, keep cool, Mr. Friedrichs. Don't get excited. It's bad for your health."

"In my trunk," Josef repeated. "Fifty thousand. . . . That's grand larceny, Mark. Very grand. Plus breaking and entering —"

"I wore gloves," Mark said.

Josef's face was a bright, dangerous crimson. He folded his arms on the tabletop and lowered his head onto them. His shoulders shook.

"Josef." Pat found her voice. "Mark, curse you — look what you've done." In considerable alarm she reached for Josef's wrist. Before she could locate his pulse he raised his head and she saw, incredulously, that he was gasping with laughter.

"He'll have to go away to school," he wheezed. "To Hawaii, or Tibet —

someplace where there is only one flight a month out. . . ."

Relieved and unregenerate, Mark grinned at him.

"You're a good sport," he said approvingly. "I was afraid you might be mad."

"Mad?" Josef's alarming color faded, and his mouth closed like a trap. "Mad? What would your father have done to you, Mark, if he caught you in a trick like this?"

"Uh." Mark sobered. "I hate to think," he admitted.

"Think. Because whatever it is, that's what is going to happen to you. I'll ponder the subject. Your dad sounds like a man of considerable ingenuity, but I'll try to come up with something.

"In the meantime, we must deal with the situation as it stands. Just tell me one thing. Was it worth it?"

"Yes," Mark said. He got to his feet. "You'll see. I'll show you."

He slunk out of the room. Kathy, her eyes blazing, turned on her father like a miniature Fury.

"He did it for me, Dad. How dare you yell at him!"

Her father's face softened. "All right, honey. I do understand, but —"

"He has to be punished, Kathy," Pat said. "Good intentions don't count."

"What would your husband have done?" Josef asked.

"Made him pay for the books, I suppose. But, Josef — fifty thousand —"

"That's the Colonel's estimate. We'll find out the true market value." Josef grinned. "That will be a suitable job for the young swindler: getting the prices without leaving evidence of his interest in those particular books. I'll lend him the money, and he can figure out how to reimburse the Colonel anonymously. If he gets a job right now, after school, and works straight through the summer, he'll be able to pay me back. Plus eight percent interest on the loan, of course."

The idea obviously appealed to him. He was about to develop it further when Mark returned carrying the letters of Mary Jane Turnbull. The book bristled with little slips of paper, evidence that Mark had spent the remainder of the night, after the raid on the bookstore, in perusing his prize.

"The cloth is too rough to take fingerprints," he announced cheerfully, making sure the table was clean and dry before he put the book down. "I turned the pages with my fingertips, and —"

"You are unnecessarily obsessed with fingerprints," Josef said. "There is only one chance in a million that our overworked county police would. . . . Wait a minute. Are your prints on record?"

"Certainly not," Mark said indignantly.

"It wouldn't surprise me," Josef said. "All right, Mark, what revelations have you come upon?"

"I want you to hear it straight from the horse's mouth," Mark said. "See if you get the same impression I did. I'll read it aloud."

"That will take all day," Pat objected, looking at the thick volume.

"No, it won't. I've already marked the

relevant passages." Without further ado Mark opened the book.

"Background first," he began. "These letters were written by Mary Jane to her friend, who lived in Richmond. Cordelia kept them. Ten years after the war was over she had them published, 'as a memorial to a martyr to that Holy Cause for which so many died.' " Josef started to speak; Mark raised an admonitory finger. "Wait. We'll discuss our conclusions later. I want you to hear this first.

"The ladies had been corresponding for some time before hostilities broke out. I won't waste time with the earlier letters; the first one of interest to us has the date of April twentieth, 1861.

"Surely this is the most momentous era of human history. Events follow one another so rapidly that a weak female pen can scarcely do them justice; yet, my dear Cordelia, I find relief in writing to you, since I can express my true feelings here only within these four walls. We are surrounded by enemies, the most hateful of them only a few feet from our door. The new wall keeps them from our sight, but we cannot forget their horrid presence.

"The news of Fort Sumter made us thrill with pride. The apelike monster who was inaugurated in March (would that the gallant citizens of Baltimore had succeeded in destroying him; but he stole through the city by night, like the coward he is!) then called for volunteers. On his head lies the onus of beginning the destruction! Virginia has joined the glorious roll of freedom, and to Virginia my noble father has gone, to lend his arm to the Cause.

"We are left a household of women, for my dear brother was sent away to school in Lynchburg after the incident I wrote you of. Thank God I was able to save him from its fatal consequences. His heart is too susceptible to the machinations of vile persons. It will turn now to the Cause; and if, which God forbid, he should perish, that fate would be preferable to the one his trusting heart might have been duped into seeking."

Mark stopped reading. "Nice lady, isn't she?"

"I don't know which is worse, her literary style or her vindictiveness," Pat said.

"The style is typical of the time," Mark said tolerantly. "They all wrote that way. The important thing is her reference to an incident that caused Peter to be sent away. It isn't mentioned in the earlier letters, so either some letters were lost, or Cordelia edited them for publication. But it's obvious, isn't it what the incident was?"

Josef cleared his throat. "I will admit that Mary Jane's catty remarks can be interpreted as referring to a romantic attachment on Peter's part, an attachment of which she did not approve —"

"That's putting it mildly," Mark interrupted. "She says she would rather see him dead than engaged to . . . All right, Mr. Friedrichs, I won't say it; she doesn't mention the girl's name, I admit that.

"Okay. We roll merrily on, to First Bull Run, in 1861. That was the first big battle of the war. Bull Run, or Manassas, is only about twenty miles from Washington, and a lot of the dumber congressmen and senators went out to watch the fighting. They ran like rabbits when the Union lines broke.

"In August of 1862 the same damned thing happened, at the same place. Second Bull Run. This time Lee decided to follow up the victory and invade the North. He crossed the Potomac at Leesburg, and here's Mary Jane's comment:

"Lee is in Maryland! Words, weak words — how can they express our exultation! First in the hearts of all loyal to the Cause must be the triumph of our arms, but, Cordelia, allow me to confess that my heart burns with equal fervor to behold again my honored parent and beloved brother. Yes, they were here — only briefly, for duty drove them. They succeeded in their aim of finding horses for the Confederacy. No less than fourteen mounts came from the pastures of Mr. Habitan, at Fern's Folly — a crony of those whose name I have sworn never to mention. How I laughed as Peter described, with his inimitable humor, the rage of the white-haired old man, who rained stuttering curses on those who removed his horses. War has made a man of my darling brother. Bronzed and slender, his hair bleached to whiteness, his eyes a fiery blue, he must turn many a maiden's heart. A loyal Southern maiden, one must hope. . . ."

"Dear me," Pat said. "She couldn't drop the subject, could she? I wonder if Peter tried to see Susan while he was at home."

"He'd try, if only out of spite." Josef looked disapproving. "Charming young man, wasn't he? I particularly like his inimitable humor about robbing a helpless old man.''

''He was eighteen that year,'' Mark said.

''Is that an excuse or an explanation?'' Josef inquired.

''Go on,'' Pat said quickly.

''Well, they fought after that at Harpers Ferry and at South Mountain, near Hagerstown. A lot of it was right around here, you know. Union troops, pursuing Lee, passed through Poolesville. The maneuvering of the armies ended on September seventeenth, in the bloodiest one-day battle of the war — Antietam, or Sharpsburg, as the Confederates called it. The whole countryside became a huge hospital, as far south as Frederick, with wounded soldiers in barns, private homes, and churches.''

''I remember reading that the mortality rate among the wounded was incredibly high,'' Pat said, with a shiver. ''Of course they had no idea of antisepsis then.''

''A few days after the battle, Lincoln

issued the Emancipation Proclamation,"
Mark said. "He had been waiting for a
victory, so it wouldn't look as if he did it
out of desperation. But Antietam wasn't
a victory for either side. At best it was a
bloody draw. Of course, to Mary Jane it
was a Confederate triumph.

"We ache for those sisters, wives
and mothers who have lost all, but
believe me, Cordelia, they will return,
the weary but indomitable men in
gray! And *our* men are safe. We
received a letter yesterday from Papa,
through the usual channel. Peter was
wounded slightly in the left arm, but
we are assured it was trivial. No doubt
a black silk sling adds to his romantic
looks, but I wish I could be near him
to nurse him.

"Cousin Alex was with us last week.
He is recovering from his illness and
we hope to have news of his safe
recovery soon. He was here when the
news of the infamous Proclamation
arrived, and we had a good laugh over
the irony of it; for only blacks in what

Lincoln is pleased to call "the rebellious states" will be freed on January next. There were many sulky looks when I explained this to our people. No doubt others of them will run away, but we shall do very well without them.

"One result of the Proclamation is that our neighbors have now condescended to join the fray. The old devil has taken a post with the government in Washington, and the young one has enlisted. The absence of the men will make our work easier, but I wish that one other member of that household had been removed from it."

"Guess who," Kathy said.

"Now," said Mark. "We skip almost a year. The following June, 1863, Lee again crossed the Potomac into Maryland.

"He had to win this time. The North had lost a lot of battles, but they were winning the war. The blockade, Grant pressing in the west, no help from

Europe — the South needed a big victory, deep in enemy territory. Well, they had the big one. Gettysburg.

"They fought for three days — the first, second, and third of July. For two weeks before that Lee's men were all over Maryland, burning bridges, capturing horses, generally raising Cain. On June twenty-ninth Stuart's cavalry captured some Union supply wagons in Rockville. Stuart was a dashing, brilliant commander, but that time he was in the wrong place at the wrong time. If he hadn't been fooling around in Maryland he might have arrived at Gettysburg in time. . . . It was awfully close, you know? So damned close. . . ."

"Don't digress," Josef said.

"What? Oh. Well, guess who was among the gallant horsethieves in Maryland? Right. The Turnbulls came home for a visit, and Mary Jane got off her pedestal for once.

"They have suffered so much. I have never seen Father eat with such voracity, almost forgetting his table manners. He is horribly thin. Peter says he insists on sharing everything with his men; and there has been little to share. He is too old for war. God help us, cannot we let the old men rest?

"But when I look at my brother, my spirits revive, and I know we must conquer. He too is thin, but deprivation and battle have only hardened him. He is so handsome! He wore a buttonhole of roses, the gift of some admiring girl along their route. If I could only be sure he has abandoned that other attachment! When I quizzed him about it we came close to quarreling. . . .

"They stayed only to eat, and to embrace us; Union troops are all over the area. Now they are on their way north, to carry the war into the enemy's camp.

"Mrs. Turnbull forced herself to vivacity while they were with us, but I saw that her appearance shocked my father. As soon as they left she collapsed again. I fear she is not long for this world.''

''Is that how she speaks of her stepmother, after twenty years?'' Pat demanded. ''And what's that about her illness?''

''Mary Jane mentioned it before, rather casually,'' Mark said. ''Obviously she didn't much care what happened to poor old Lavinia.'' He looked up from the book. ''And that, friends, is Mary Jane's last letter.''

''What? But that was only 1863. The war went on for two more years. Did she die, or something?''

''Something,'' Mark said. ''This is what her friend Cordelia wrote at the end of the book:

This was not my dear friend's last letter; but it was the last I could spare for the eyes of posterity. Sudden, devastating tragedy struck thereafter: an entire family wiped out, almost at a single stroke. Major Turnbull died at Gettysburg, his blood staining the bullet-riddled flag he had snatched up when the standard-bearer fell. The news of his death stopped the heart of his affectionate wife. Mary's beloved young brother was also a casualty of the great battle, though no news ever came to his grieving sister of where or how he fell. Bereaved of all she had loved, my poor friend lost her family home and lived out her days in penury and illness, in a retreat in Poolesville. I received the news of her death last year, and determined to publish these letters, as a tribute to a heroine of the Confederacy."

"She goes on and on," Mark added. "But that's about it. Well? What do you think?"

"I see one obvious discrepancy," Josef said. "The pamphlet stated that the Turnbull men were killed in a local skirmish. According to this source, it was at Gettysburg."

"Mary Jane's letter proves that they were still alive in late June of 1863," Mark said. "Of course that was before

380

Gettysburg, just before. . . . There's another discrepancy. We've been assuming the Turnbulls were with White's Raiders. Officially, the Raiders were Company B of the Twenty-fifth Virginia Battalion — and it wasn't formed till the summer of 1862. They must have been with some other unit. At least the old man was; he joined up in 1861."

"What are you driving at?" Josef demanded in exasperation.

"I told you. I want to find out where and when Peter Turnbull died. We can't do that unless we know what his unit was. Maybe it was the First Virginia Cavalry. Company K was a Maryland unit; it was formed at Leesburg, Virginia, in 1861."

Josef eyed his stepson-to-be with poorly concealed hostility.

"Mark, will you stop making mysteries about everything? Tell us what you have in mind."

"I can't! There's a piece missing, and it's the key to the whole business. You'd laugh if I told you what I'm thinking now. I was hoping you'd have the same reaction to Mary Jane's letters that I did."

"My reaction is that the book isn't worth the trouble of stealing it," Josef snapped. "You can't admit that, can you?"

"I just don't agree, that's all." Mark brooded in silence. Then he brightened. "Maybe if we had some lunch it would stimulate our thinking."

"Lunch! You had breakfast less than . . ." Josef broke off; apparently he had decided he might as well resign himself to Mark's appetite. It was, after all, one of Mark's lesser faults.

Josef rose. "I'm going in to the office for a few hours. I can't afford to lose my job. It seems clear that my expenses are going to increase drastically in the near future."

He walked out the back door, letting it slam behind him.

"What did he mean by that?" Mark asked.

Pat debated briefly with herself, and then decided this was not the time to tell

Mark about her personal plans. Anyway, she hadn't quite made up her mind what she meant to do about Josef. She could hardly marry a man who hated her son.

"I think he was talking about the possibility of selling the house," she answered, for this was certainly true, as far as it went. "He'll take a loss on it if he does."

"That's no solution," Mark muttered. "And you know it."

Before Pat could reply, the back door opened again. Josef looked even grimmer than he had when he left.

"If you think the mess upstairs is bad, come and see a real masterpiece," he said.

"Of course!" Mark jumped up. "Why didn't I think of that? Naturally it would . . ."

He dashed out the back door. Kathy followed him, and Josef met Pat halfway across the kitchen. For a few moments they stood holding one another, without speaking.

"I feel like the lover in one of those old-fashioned French farces," Josef said after a time. "Looking over my shoulder for the husband to turn up, snatching kisses in corners. . . . When are you going to tell Mark, my darling? Or shall I ask him formally for your hand?"

"He'd love that," Pat said, with a weak laugh. "Can't you see him imitating an outraged Victorian father — 'Begone, sir, never darken our door again!' No, I'll break it to him. I doubt that he will be enthusiastic."

"I'm trying," Josef said, with unaccustomed humility. "I understand how he'll feel. . . . But I can't wait too long, Pat. I feel like some idiot eighteen-year-old; I want to brag about you."

"I'll tell him," Pat promised. "But not until this is over. I can't concentrate on anything else."

"One good thing has come out of this mess, anyway," Josef said. "Damn it, Pat, I can't be too pessimistic. We'll figure it out somehow. We'll sell both the houses, move west, or south, or into New England. . . . the cursed thing must have some geographical limitations. Maybe if we leave, it will give up. After all, it was quiescent for years. You know, I can't help wondering . . . ."

Gently Pat removed herself from his embrace.

"I do know. I've wondered the same thing. Did Mark and/or Kathy unwittingly do something to stir the thing into life? Obviously Mark has information he's keeping from us. But it won't do any good to nag him about it, he's as stubborn as his father. Shall we go and view the damage?"

"It's pretty bad," Josef warned.

Pat tried not to show how shaken she was by the extent of the destruction. Kathy's room was the worst; every small breakable object in the place had been smashed. But the trail of breakage ran from room to room, and down the stairs.

Kathy and Mark were in the dining room. Mark was fingering a deep gouge in the wall. A small but heavy bronze statuette, a copy of the Michelangelo David, lay on the floor. Mark picked it up and weighed it in his hand.

"It must weigh about ten pounds," he said.

Pat leaned against the wall. "I hate to think what the kitchen must look like," she said.

"It went thataway," Mark agreed, indicating the fragments of a crystal bowl that lay in the doorway.

"Not funny," Pat snapped.

"No, I mean it. The living room is intact — didn't you notice? It came down the stairs, into the dining room, and . . . Let's see."

A short, rather dark hall connected dining room and kitchen. There were no windows, only doors leading to the basement and the back stairs, and to a series of cupboards.

Squaring his shoulders, Josef took the lead. They looked over his shoulder, with surprise and relief, into a sparkling, untouched kitchen.

At first no one could think of an appropriate comment. Mark was, of course, the first to recover himself.

"It decided nobody was home," he said. "So it went to our place. . . ."

"Theories, theories," Josef muttered.

"Well, there's plenty it could have

broken here," Mark said.

The statement could not be denied. The canisters containing sugar, coffee, flour and so on were of clear glass; the electric clock hung insecurely from a single nail; and a collection of antique plates was suspended on brackets along the walls. The cupboard doors were closed, but that, Pat imagined, would have been no problem for the poltergeist, and no doubt the shelves behind the closed doors were crowded with glassware and dishes.

"It means something," Mark muttered. "What?"

"It means I don't get to work today," Josef said. "Kathy, we've still got most of the cartons left over from the move. Let's pack the breakables that have survived, and your clothes. We'll go to a motel again tonight. Tomorrow I'll rent an apartment in the District."

"But —" Mark began. He stopped with a gulp and a start. Pat looked sharply at Kathy, who met her eyes with a candid stare. She was, as usual, standing so close to Mark that they

387

might have been Siamese twins, but if she had jabbed Mark in the ribs she had done it very neatly.

"The boxes are in the basement," Kathy said gently.

"Uh," Mark said. "Okay. I'll get them."

He went out, followed by his shadow. They returned with an armful of boxes, and Kathy said, "I'm going to pack my clothes. Mark?"

"Huh? Oh, sure. I'll help you."

As soon as Mark and Kathy had left, Josef reached for Pat's hand.

"You have to tell him now, Pat. I can't leave you in that house. If you think Mark will object to our living in sin, we can get married right away."

"I can't," Pat said agitatedly. "It's confusing. There are too many problems. All my things — and the animals —"

"The dog can go to a kennel for a few weeks, till we find another house. We'll smuggle the damned cat into the apartment, if you insist —"

"Josef, you're moving too fast. I can't decide." Then she saw his face, and remorse swept over her. "Oh, my darling, I don't mean that; I've no doubts about that. It's simply a matter of logistics. Give me a little time."

"I'm sorry," He smiled at her, and her heart thumped. "We'll work it out, Pat. Take all the time you want."

But there wasn't time; she knew that as well as he did. The alternative to the hasty decision he had urged was the unbelievable situation they had faced too long already.

For a while they worked in companionable silence, Josef handing dishes to Pat, who wrapped them in newspaper and stowed them away in the boxes. The monotonous, meticulous task ought to have been soothing; but her mind continued to flutter incoherently from one problem to the next. Close up the house . . . what would Nancy say? And the other neighbors? Rumors were sure to circulate. . . . Jud hated kennels, he grew morose and melancholy if he was away from Mark. . . . Mark. How would he take the news that she intended to marry Josef Friedrichs? The answer came only too readily. Mark wouldn't take it well. He needed time, not only to rid himself of his prejudices against Kathy's father, but to grow accustomed to the idea that his mother was a person, with needs of her own. He had to be consulted in the decision, not just notified of the grownups' wishes. He thought he could solve the case. . . . His ego would be assaulted on every possible level by what Josef had proposed.

Suddenly Pat jumped to her feet, dropping a cup. Fortunately it fell on top of a half-filled box and the newspapers kept it from breaking.

"What's the matter?" Josef looked at her with concern.

"Mark," Pat said. "He and Kathy, up there. . . . He didn't argue with us. He's helping her pack, and *he hasn't mentioned lunch.*"

Comprehension lighted Josef's eyes. As Pat pushed through the door and ran along the hall, she heard him close on her heels. He did understand Mark. Their minds worked rather similarly, allowing for the difference in age. That was probably a hopeful sign. But at that moment Pat forgot her personal concerns in a more urgent matter. What was Mark doing up there in Kathy's room? She would have laid odds that he was not helping her pack.

She pounded up the stairs, with Josef close behind. Together they made almost as much noise as Mark could have made. But the two young people did not hear them until they burst into the room. They had other schemes afoot.

They were sitting close together, at Kathy's desk. A sheet of blank paper lay on the desk top, and Mark's hand, holding a pencil, was poised above it.

Mark jumped several inches as his mother flung the door open. The pencil jabbed into the paper, tearing a hole, but Pat was infinitely relieved to see that there was no other mark on the virgin surface.

"What the hell are you doing?" she shouted.

"Nothing." Though visibly shaken, Mark tried, simultaneously, to put the pencil in his pocket and hide the paper.

"You were trying that — that automatic writing," Pat exclaimed. "How dare you! Of all the stupid, dangerous —"

"Well, we have to do something. He came through once before. I thought maybe if we gave him another chance he'd say something that —"

"You — horrible —" For once Pat was so angry that she moved faster than her son. Her hand shot out, avoiding the hand he lifted, as if in anticipation of a blow, and snatched at the paper. She had nothing particular in mind: she only wanted to claw at something, crumple it, crush it between her hands. . . . Better a blank sheet of paper than Mark's face.

Then she realized she was not the only one who was reaching for an object on the desk. A small white hand slid swiftly but surreptitiously toward something half hidden by the sheet of paper.

Pat's calloused hand slapped down hard on Kathy's fingers, and the girl let out a squeal. Pat snatched up the book Kathy had reached for.

Even in her rage and fright she knew

that the book was no ordinary object from a library or bookstore. The cover felt slick and damp under her fingers.

She stepped back and for a moment or two they were silent, staring at one another and breathing hard. Josef looked in bewilderment from his beloved, whose infuriated face was barely recognizable, to his daughter, whose big blue eyes filled with tears as she nursed her stinging fingers.

Luckily for Josef, he did the right thing. After a baffled moment he stepped to Pat, put his arm around her shaking shoulders, and included his darling daughter with Mark in an all-inclusive scowl.

"All right, you two. Speak up. Kathy, apologize to Mrs. Robbins."

Pat's saving sense of humor came to the rescue. With a laugh that was half sob, she said, "I guess I should apologize to Kathy. I didn't mean to hit you, honey; it was pure reflex. Mark can tell you I've done the same thing to him."

"She sure has," Mark said coolly. "She's a very impetuous lady. Where she loves, there does she chastise most heavily —"

"And you!" Pat turned, with pleasure, to a worthier opponent. "You and your stupid half-baked quotations! This is all your fault. Your idea. You nasty young . . . *person,* you've been holding out on us all along. What is this book? Where did you get it? It's old. It's . . ."

With a dramatic gesture, worthy of Mark at his hammiest, she opened the volume, and the words died on her lips as a sentence seemed to leap up from the page at her. She read it aloud.

"Peter told Eddie he must get the cake while cook was not looking. He didn't want to, but Peter . . ."

"It's Susan Bates's diary," Pat gasped.

Mark made a gesture of resignation and defeat.

"You've got it, lady."

## II

Mark took the little book from his mother's nerveless hand and put it gently on the desk.

"It's in bad shape," he said, reproachfully. "You shouldn't handle it so roughly."

"Where . . . what . . ." Anger and amazement robbed Pat of speech.

"So that's where you've been getting your information," Josef said. "I knew there was something. Where did you find it, Mark?"

"In the oak tree," Mark said. "You see, it was like . . ." He glanced at Kathy, whose cheeks had bloomed into a lovely pink blush, and grinned rather sheepishly. "I told you this was going to be complicated, Kath. Let me think just how to put it. . . ."

Pat collapsed onto the bed. Josef stood by her, his hand on her shoulder. Mark was too immersed in his own difficulties to see this gesture, but Kathy did; her blue eyes took on a look of guileful speculation, and she spoke without embarrassment.

"We met there, Mark and I. After you told Mark we couldn't see each other. It was only a couple of times. The tree is awfully old, there are holes in the trunk.

Mark found the book one time when he was waiting for me and I was late. It was wrapped in several layers of cloth and oiled paper."

Pat wondered, with some apprehension, how Josef would take this revelation. His heavy dark brows drew together, but when he spoke his voice was milder than she had expected.

"I'm sure you enjoyed meeting clandestinely, thwarting the heavy father. Romantic as hell, wasn't it? Well, never mind. May I see the diary, or is it reserved for those under thirty?"

"Be careful," Mark said, handing him the book. "It was well wrapped, but damp got in, all the same, and since it's been exposed to the air it has deteriorated. If you don't mind, Mr. Friedrichs, I've got a suggestion. . . ."

"Well?"

"Maybe Mom could transcribe it," Mark said. "She's pretty good on the typewriter." He grinned at his mother, the recollection of last-minute term papers hastily typed fresh in his mind. Pat did not grin back at him.

"It will take forever," she protested.

"Not so long. She didn't keep a day-by-day diary, she just wrote things down when she was in the mood, or when something important happened. And a lot of the text is illegible — rotted by damp, or too faded to read."

"But you've already read it — so I assume," Pat said. "We've got a lot of packing to do. If the poltergeist comes back tonight, it may smash the things that are left."

"Mom — trust me, will you?" Mark leaned forward. A lock of dark hair fell across his forehead, and his eyes burned with sincerity. "I'm right on the verge. I really am. Let's go over it once more. Anyhow . . ." A look of such consternation came over his face that Pat recoiled, wondering what horrific revelations were in store. "Anyhow," Mark went on, "it's way past lunchtime. No wonder my brain is so weak. You type, I'll read aloud . . . and Kathy can get lunch."

# III

Pat found it easier than she had expected to keep up with Mark's dictation. Damp had disfigured the edges of the pages, so that the only legible portions were in the middle. There were no dates; presumably they had been written on the illegible tops of the pages. Yet, scattered and broken as the fragments were, floating in time, they formed a picture in Pat's mind as her fingers reproduced the words.

Three children, growing up in the wilderness of western Maryland. . . . The girl, small and delicate and blond, dressed in the calico simplicity her father's spartan creed required: had not the Apostle Paul warned against vanity in women? Her brother, as dark as she was fair, trained to sobriety by the same rigorous faith, yet fascinated by and tempted to mischief by the imperious older cousin.

In all their schemes Peter was the ringleader and Edward was the one who got caught. It was Peter who dared

Edward to climb the tallest tree in the yard, but when the younger boy, shorter of limb and breath, was unable to get down, he was blamed, and punished. The idea of dressing up like ghosts and scaring "the darkies" was Peter's; but it was Edward who tripped over the trailing sheets in the act of escaping and was soundly thrashed by his father. Even when Peter was caught, his indulgent parents refused to punish him. "Uncle Al laughed very loud," Susan recorded, on one occasion when the three had gotten tipsy on homemade wine. Poor Edward had to eat his dinner off the mantel for several days after that scandalous affair.

Gradually, over the years, the tone of the diary changed. The early accounts of childhood mischief turned to a young girl's inarticulate record of parties and beaux. The first was Sammy Hart, who kissed Susan at a school picnic. But Sammy did not last long. "He has spots on his face," Susan recorded contemptuously. References to contemporary historical events were few and far between. Like most fifteen-year-olds, Susan was much more interested in her own emotional problems than in national disasters.

Kathy, who was already familiar with the material, made sandwiches, then took over the typewriter while Pat snatched a bite and a cup of coffee. Somehow Mark managed to read and eat simultaneously. Pat went back to the typewriter after a brief interval. She was conscious of a queer feeling of urgency, as if some sort of deadline were approaching, and as Mark read on, her fingers flicked over the keys with a speed that exceeded her best record.

"In 1859, outside events shook Susan's peaceful world.

"Father and Uncle Al quarreled again. Something about that Mr. Brown at Harpers Ferry. Usually Uncle Al laughs when they argue, but this time. . ."

"Go on," Pat said, her fingers poised.

No one answered. She looked up and saw, with a shock of inexplicable alarm, that considerable time had passed. The windows were darkening.

"The rest of that entry is gone," Mark said. "It doesn't require much imagination to finish it, though."

Pat leaned back in the chair, flexing stiff fingers. Josef bent over her.

"Take a break," he urged. "You've been working too hard."

"Want me to type for a while?" Kathy asked.

"That's okay. Let's all rest for a minute. Isn't it funny what a clear picture we're getting of these people? Mr. Turnbull sounds like an easygoing sort of man."

"I don't think Mr. Bates was so bad either," Kathy said. "He must have relaxed his Puritan ideas as he got older, because Susan talks about pretty clothes and jewelry — and he went all the way to Philadelphia to get the doll she wanted for her birthday —"

"And her mother made a complete wardrobe for it," Pat said. "A little fur muff, and bonnets, and everything."

"They sound like a nice family," Josef agreed. He added sardonically, "Too nice to be poltergeists, is that the idea?"

The others ignored this cynical question.

"The really shadowy figure is Mrs. Turnbull," Pat said thoughtfully. "Susan only mentions her once or twice."

"I guess the poor woman really was sickly," Kathy said. "I thought, when we first read the references to her being ailing, that she was a professional hypochondriac."

"Women were supposed to be fragile and fainting." Pat said. "The men loved it; it made them feel like heroes."

"Mary Jane wasn't fragile," Kathy said. "No wonder she never caught a husband — as they said in those days."

"She sounds like a tough lady," Pat agreed, smiling, as she recalled Susan's caustic comments about the big sister who spoiled so many of their games and scolded her for being unwomanly because she liked to go fishing with the boys. "But don't forget Mary Jane was already a grown woman when they were still children. She probably thought she was only doing her duty. She never did marry, did she? I wonder why."

"Maybe she was homely," Josef suggested frivolously. "Ugly women don't catch husbands, even today." He smiled at Pat.

"That shows how much you know," she said. "A well-dowered young lady could always get a husband. And I suspect the same thing is true today."

"So, maybe she didn't have a dowry," Josef said. "I suspected Turnbull's financial position was shaky."

Mark had fallen into a brown study, fingering the crumbling pages of the diary. Now he looked up at the others, scowling.

"Do you guys want to hear the rest of this, or are you enjoying your historical gossip? I mean, my God, you sound like Mom and Mrs. Groft when they get started on the neighbors."

"I guess we do at that," Pat said. "All right, Mark, I'm ready. Go ahead."

"It gets worse from now on," Mark said. "The condition of the diary, I mean. Whole pages are stuck together. The next thing I can decipher comes in the middle of a sentence. It just says,

'. . . away to school. I don't know how they found out. We were so careful. Someone must have seen us. I never saw Father so angry. Always before, when I cried, he would soften; but not this time. He found the loose board in the wall and nailed it shut. But it doesn't matter. Nothing matters now because he is gone and. . .' "

Mary's voice faded into silence as the writing faded out.

"He being Peter, I gather," Josef said. "Mark, you've known this all along. Why didn't you tell us, instead of pretending to make wild guesses?"

"I didn't know, though," Mark said. "She never mentions his name. Sure, I suspected — the way she talks about him, even when they were kids, like he was God or something. . . . But I wasn't certain till I read Mary Jane's letters. Let me go on. There isn't much more."

Unlike Mary Jane and the other literate ladies of the period, who had been conscious of history, Susan was not concerned with the great events of the succeeding years. She used her diary to express her private feelings, and as the remaining fragments showed, these were unrelievedly doleful. Reiterated expressions of sorrow and loneliness appeared on the faded paper, whose condition deteriorated rapidly as the book neared its end. Mark, who knew the material practically by heart, skipped over the fragmentary passages and focused on one that had survived.

"I must see him, though conscience says I should not. Yet how can I deny him, when he comes through such dangers, when any day may bring the news that he will never come again? If my kind parents knew . . ."

" 'Through such dangers,' " Pat repeated. "Then he must have been in the army at that time. I suppose he sent her a message somehow, when his cavalry troop was in the area on one of those raids you told us about. How foolish to take such a risk!"

"Not necessarily." Kathy's eyes were shining; and Pat thought, uncharitably, that the young of all centuries seemed to prefer romance to common sense. "He'd be safe at home — in the Turnbull house — if he could get there without being seen. I'm surprised the Federal government didn't hassle the Turnbulls."

"Why should they?" Josef said. "Two women alone, one of them an invalid? I wouldn't be surprised if Mr. Bates's influence kept them from being bothered. It sounds as if his bark was worse than his bite."

"Let's finish this," Pat said. "Go on, Mark."

"Huh?" Absorbed in some dark, deep thought of his own, Mark started. "Oh. There isn't any more, Mom. The rest of the book is illegible. Except for this."

He held up a sheet of paper. It had been folded several times. The damp that had ruined the remainder of the diary had stained the outside of the sheet, but the message, though badly faded, had survived. The handwriting, now so familiar, needed no identification. But it was not Peter Turnbull's writing that made the hairs on

Pat's neck prickle. It was the message — the same message, word for word, that she had read only a few days earlier, written to Kathy by her son. "Meet me at midnight, the same place. Love. . ." At the bottom of the sheet, in a smaller, more even hand, was the addition, "His last letter."

Pat looked up from the page and met her son's troubled eyes.

"Had you read this, before . . . ?" She couldn't finish the sentence.

"No," Mark said. "I found this book after I wrote the note to Kathy. It was the same place for them that it was for us. That's probably why Susan left her diary there, after. . . Mom. Let's try the automatic writing thing again."

"No!"

"Then," Mark said resignedly, "there's only one thing left to do. Mr. Friedrichs —"

"What?" Josef asked, visibly bracing himself.

"We'll have to tear down your basement walls."

# IV

As she descended the steep wooden stairs, Pat was again struck with a fact she kept forgetting — that the two houses had originally been identical. The upper regions were so altered by structural changes and by differences in decor that the similarities were less apparent, but here, in the utilitarian regions belowstairs, the resemblance was so striking as to be rather unnerving. The same whitewashed walls, the same low ceiling, the same depressing atmosphere. The floor of her basement was of concrete, this one was brick. Otherwise they were the same.

After his initial apoplectic objection, Josef had shrugged and agreed to let Mark go ahead. Mark was as irritating as only he could be, refusing coyly to explain what he hoped to find. One of his bright ideas had backfired. He had insisted on bringing Jud with them — with, Pat surmised, some notion of using the unfortunate animal as a sort of psychic bloodhound. Jud, not the brightest of dogs, had welcomed the excursion with gambols and waggings of tail, and the others trailed along, watching, while Mark escorted the animal through the entire house. But at the top of the basement stairs Jud had come to a sudden halt and refused to budge. When Mark took his collar and dragged him, he howled and produced a puddle — his invariable habit when deeply angry or disturbed.

"I suppose that proves something," Josef remarked with restraint, eyeing the mess on his polished floor.

"It confirms something I had suspected," Mark replied austerely. "Kath, you better take Jud home."

"Or vice versa," Pat said, as the dog retreated at full speed, towing the girl with him.

"We'll need tools," Mark said. "Something heavy, like a sledgehammer."

"All the tools I own are on the workbench," Josef said. He sat down on the bottom step, pulled Pat down beside him, and put his arm around her. Mark paid no attention. Flashlight in hand, he surveyed the walls, mumbling to himself.

". . . mirror image . . . has to be here. Or changed, for the sake of security? Psychologically. . ."

A door upstairs banged and Kathy came to the top of the stairs.

"Mark? Any luck?"

"Not yet. Come on down."

Kathy obeyed. Her father rose to let her pass. He sat down again, and the two young people retreated into a corner, where they stood whispering.

"Time," Pat said suddenly. "What time is it?"

Josef glanced at his watch. "A little after nine. Do you realize that boy hasn't asked for his dinner? He must be on to something big."

Mark walked along the far wall, giving it an occasional thump with the hammer he held. When he reached the corner he stopped, his nose inches from the neighboring wall surface, and stood still so long that his mother, whose nerves were already twitching, said sharply, "Mark, if you are going into another trance, this whole deal is off, do you hear?"

"Mom, for God's sake." Mark turned and glared at her. "You make it sound like I didn't clean up my room or something." He transferred his attention to Kathy, who stood close by him, watching him expectantly. "It's here, Kath. Down below. Must be in the floor somewhere."

He squatted, examining the bricks, and then looked accusingly at Josef. "You had this fixed. It's new mortar."

"Oh, God, give me patience," Josef said, to nobody in particular. "Forgive me, Mark. I had meant to have the bricks taken up and concrete poured, but someone convinced me that would be a sin against history. These bricks are of the Civil War period, I was told, so. . . ."

He paused, forgetting his annoyance as he realized what he had just said. "Civil War. . . . Do you suppose —"

Mark was already at the workbench, throwing hammers and screwdrivers aside, as he searched for what he

411

wanted. He returned to the corner with a chisel and mallet. Kathy moved back out of range as chips of mortar began to fly.

Josef looked at Pat. She moved a little closer to him, and his arm tightened around her shoulders.

It took Mark almost an hour to remove a section of floor two feet square. He rejected Kathy's offer of help. No one else offered. Despite the damp coolness of the cellar, perspiration was pouring down his neck by the time he finished. He then uttered a word his mother had forbidden him to use in her presence.

"Watch your mouth, bud," she said.

"Sorry, I thought I'd find. . . But it's dirt. Packed, beaten earth."

"Ha," said Josef, leaning back.

"Well, but naturally," Kathy said. Squatting on her haunches, she leaned forward to inspect the site of Mark's labors. "She'd have to put something over it, to hide it, before she had the slaves lay the bricks."

"What are you talking about?" Pat asked.

The others ignored her.

"Hey, that's right," Mark said. "Kathy. Shovel."

"In the garage," said Josef. He slid to one side so that Kathy could pass him. Again he and Pat exchanged eloquent glances.

"We've got to watch the time," she whispered.

"Almost three hours yet. Don't worry, I'll keep track."

Kathy returned with the demanded implement and handed it to Mark. He began to dig. The earth was hardpacked, but it was damp and — as it turned out — only about eight inches thick. Pat and Josef, abandoning their pretense of disinterest, watched as Mark gradually uncovered a flat wooden surface. The rusted iron ring made its function clear.

"Trapdoor," Josef muttered. "I'll be damned."

But for a moment no one moved. Mark leaned picturesquely on his shovel, mopping his damp forehead with his sleeve; and Josef, too fascinated to resist any longer, came to his assistance. He tugged at the ring, his face reddening with effort.

"Stuck," he grunted. "We need a chisel, Mark. On the workbench."

Mark pried and Josef pulled. At first it seemed that they were making no progress. The hinges gave way all at once, sending Josef sprawling. A dark, square hole gaped. From it came a breath of air as stale as death itself.

Mark turned on the flashlight. Its beam showed sagging wooden steps descending into darkness.

"Wait," Josef said, as Mark turned preparatory to descending. "Those steps don't look very solid."

Mark put his foot on the top step and pressed. The whole structure collapsed in a shower of splinters.

"Termites," Mark said. "Or damp. The floor is only about six feet down. Here, hold the flashlight."

He handed it to Josef and lowered himself, disregarding his mother's groan of protest. Josef kept the flashlight steady. It illumined Mark's sweating face as he stared up, but showed nothing else.

"I'm standing on the floor," Mark said. "Come on down,"

"At the risk of sounding like a coward, I'd like to be sure I can get up again," Josef said. "Wait till I get a stepladder."

He lowered it to Mark, who held it steady while first Pat and then Kathy went down. Pat had caught the fever. Forbidding as the dark hole appeared, she would have fought anyone who suggested she remain above. Josef was the last to descend. He brought the flashlight with him, and handed it to Mark. Not until then did Pat see the nature of the place into which they had descended.

The room had once been virtually airtight, every crack carefully sealed. It was so no longer. The insidious damp of Maryland soil had crumbled the mortar between the stones; water had seeped in and dried and seeped again, so that the lichen-stained walls bulged ominously in places. The damp had affected the objects in the room too. There was nothing left of the bed except a low, irregular platform and even less remained of what had lain upon the bed. Its shape was due more to suggestion than to actual form; but enough was there to bring a suppressed cry from Kathy.

"It's okay," Mark said — but his own voice was not quite steady. "Could be worse."

He turned the flashlight beam full on the bed.

The rotted remains of a sheet or blanket covered the shape below, but things protruded here and there: a rounded curve of skull, the end of a long bone — a femur, probably, Pat guessed.

"Human," she said softly.

"Oh, yes." Mark said, turning the light away from the pitiful remains. It illumined smaller piles of decay and stopped at one. There was little to distinguish this heap from the others — once pieces of furniture — but Mark stepped to it and fumbled in the debris for a few minutes before producing a handful of metal disks.

"Buttons," he said. "Stamped 'CSA.' He put his uniform on the chair before . . ."

"A Confederate soldier," Josef muttered. "Then this room was something like a priest's hole. The Trumbulls concealed fugitives —"

"And spies," Mark said. "You guys are really dense. Didn't you understand all those hints in Mary Jane's letters? She couldn't be explicit, not at the time she was writing, but her friend knew what she meant. This was one of the stations on the Confederate spy circuit. The location is perfect — isolated, only a few miles from the river —"

"With the Bateses right next door?"

"There was a wall," Mark said. "Remember? The houses aren't that close. On a moonless night one man, creeping through the underbrush, wouldn't be seen or heard. The very fact that it was so close to the Bateses would disarm suspicion. People would think they wouldn't dare. But it was typical of the Turnbulls — that damn-your-eyes bravado."

"This man was no spy," Josef said. "He was in uniform. A fugitive from one of the nearby battles, perhaps. Wounded, hidden by the Turnbulls. . . . Come on, Kathy, stop sniveling; it's only bones."

Kathy gulped and wiped her face with her fingers.

"She's got more sense than you have," Mark said in disgust. "You still don't get it, do you? Not just anybody's old bones. They're his."

"You don't mean —"

"Yes, I do mean. They're *his*. That's Peter Turnbull — what's left of him."

# Ten

"Prove it," Pat said. Then, as Mark took a step toward the rotted bed, she exclaimed, "No, don't . . . don't."

"I bet I could prove it," Mark said. "He was probably carrying identification. A watch, a locket with his dear old mother's hair. . . . Or, speaking of hair, maybe some of his —"

"For God's sake, Mark." Even Josef was shaken by this callous speech. "You are without a doubt the most ghoulish —"

"What's ghoulish about this?" Mark demanded, in tones of honest surprise. "This is just leftovers, like old clothes. Compared to what we've seen lately, this is clean and normal."

"You have a point," Josef admitted.

"And, since you have been right about everything else, I suppose you're right about this. Would you care to explain to us idiots why Peter Turnbull's bones are lying here, unburied and unconsecrated, in the cellar of his own home?"

"Not exactly unconsecrated," Mark said. "She covered him up. And . . . there were flowers."

From the tatters of the blanket he lifted a cobwebby coil, a fragile ghost of vegetation. It crumbled into dust as he touched it, but a hundred years ago it might have been a wreath.

"*She* covered him?" Josef repeated, sounding like the idiot he had called himself. "No, it's no use; I cannot possibly follow your . . . Mark. This is where it comes from, isn't it?"

"Yes," Mark said. "This is where, and this is why. If you'll just wait a minute —"

"Wait? Here? When that cursed thing may . . . Or does it only come at one A.M.?"

"Well, now, I wouldn't swear to that," Mark said. "We're getting awfully close.

In fact, I've got most of it figured out. That's what this is all about — figuring out what really happened. It didn't want —"

Mark's sentence ended in a choked gurgle as Josef grabbed him by the collar.

"Are you telling me, you unprintable delinquent, that you *want* the thing to come? That you deliberately, with malice aforethought, brought us down here so that it would . . . Let's get out of here."

He released his grip and turned to Pat.

"No, wait," Mark gasped. "It's all right. I can handle it. We've got to have a confrontation, right here, where it happened, that's the only way. . . . Ah. Here we go." He pointed; his voice shook with an uncomfortable blend of triumph and revulsion. " 'Look, here it comes again.' "

He stepped forward, in front of the others. Josef gathered Pat into one arm and Kathy into the other. "If we survive this," he muttered, "I'm going to kill that boy."

Pat leaned against him, incapable of

speech, as the indescribable aura invaded the room. Mark's flashlight was dimmed by the ghastly whirling light. As the light strengthened, two burning blue spots formed in its core.

Pat felt cold stone against her back. They had retreated as far as they could, and still the thing came on, moving forward with horrible, jerky movements.

Mark stood his ground. The light was strong enough to cast shadows, horribly distorted shadows, like parodies of the forms that shaped them — strong enough for Pat to see that the shadow stretching out from Mark's feet was, surely, that of a man inches shorter, broader of shoulder, with close-cropped hair instead of Mark's unruly mop.

A voice spoke, softly. It had to be Mark's, though it sounded nothing like his. Pat was unable to make out the words; but at the sound the whirling light stopped its forward progress with an uncanny, horrid suggestion of human surprise. The voice rose in volume, and changed, in tone and in rhythm.

"Don't you get it? It's all over; we

know. You can't stop the truth; you can't hurt anybody; you're dead, dead and damned. Go back to wherever you belong. In the name of the Father and the Son and the Holy Ghost, and all the saints, and. . . ."

Mark went on, mouthing an insane litany of mixed-up religious formulas, invoking every deity he could think of. Pat lost track of what he was saying; for, incredibly, the thing began to shrink and fade. For one fantastic moment — and she was never sure whether she really saw it, or whether she only imagined it — just before it went forever she saw it clear, in its true shape: the form of a woman, so emaciated as to be virtually skeletal, her straggling white hair framing a visage completely without color except for the blazing blue eyes.

Then it vanished, taking all light with it, even the feeble beam of the flashlight. A rumbling crash shook the very earth, as if the darkness had solidified and fallen upon them.

Pat would have been thrown to the ground if she had not had the support of the wall and Josef's arm. Choking, she thrust out both hands against air thick with dust.

"Stand still," Josef ordered, tightening his grasp. "Don't even speak loudly. Mark. Mark, are you there?"

At first there was no reply, only the rattle of subsiding debris, and Pat's racing heart stopped. The catastrophe — whatever its nature — had begun at the other end of the room. Mark had been closest. . . . Then her son's voice came out of the dark and she went limp with relief.

"I'm here. Part of me, anyhow. . . ."

"The flashlight?" Josef asked.

"Under a ton of dirt and stone."

"Hang on. I've got a lighter."

The flame flickered and flared. It was sufficient; there was little left for it to illumine. Half the room had vanished under a heap of earth. Mark's legs were buried up to the thigh and the face he turned toward them was streaked with blood from a dozen cuts. But his grin was broad and cheerful.

"Her last gesture," he remarked.

"Dumb stunt."

"We're buried alive," Pat said. "Not so dumb."

"Don't be dramatic, Mom," Mark said coolly. "The part that collapsed was the wall where the tunnel was. The vibration dropped the trapdoor, but it's not barred or anything. We'll be out of here in five minutes."

His estimate was fairly accurate, but it seemed much longer to Pat. They didn't even need the stepladder, which was fortunate, since it was half buried under the earth slide. This proved to be quite stable, thanks to the clayey quality of the soil; Mark was able to climb the ramplike slope to a point where he could lift the trapdoor and pull himself out. The others followed. When he had lowered the trap again it was as if he had wiped out the past half hour. Pat might have thought she had dreamed the whole incredible episode had it not been for the grubby, disheveled state of her companions and her son's scratched face. She realized that Mark's eyes were fixed on her accusingly as he mopped the cuts with a dirty sleeve, and she was about to offer first aid and maternal concern when he said,

"I'm starved. What's for dinner?"

## II

When they got back to their house, the telephone was ringing.

"Don't answer it," Mark ordered. "It's probably Mrs. Groft wanting to know what's been going on around here. She must have noticed that the wall is down."

"I guess so." Pat felt as if she had put in eight hours of hard manual labor. Even her eyelids ached. With an effort, she roused herself. "Mark, you had better shower and change clothes. Then I'll tend to those cuts."

"I can do that," Mark said. "You get something to eat."

"Mark," Josef said quietly.

"What?"

"My generation has hang-ups about hitting a man when he is off guard. Get your dukes up."

"Dukes," Mark repeated. His face went scarlet, and Pat realized that he was struggling desperately to keep from laughing. "Now, Mr. Friedrichs, you just take it easy. I don't want to hurt you. This is silly."

"Not at all. If your mother is going to render first aid, she may as well tend all your wounds."

For a variety of reasons, which she never bothered to analyze, Pat said nothing. Kathy moved forward as if to intervene, but she was too late; Josef's fist slid under Mark's raised hand and hit him hard on the chin. He fell backward into a chair, where he sprawled, his arms and legs at oblique angles.

"Do you know why I hit you?" Josef asked.

Mark's glazed eyes focused and a ghost of a twinkle appeared in their depths.

"It's a long list," he croaked, rubbing his jaw.

"No. I slugged you because you had the consummate gall to quote Shakespeare at us at a tense moment. I can't stand smart-aleck kids. Now go clean up. If you're hungry, you and Kathy can go out for pizza or egg foo gai gunk, or whatever ghastly mess you fancy.''

"Yes, sir." Mark struggled to his feet. "Right away, sir." He destroyed the effect by grinning and sketching an impudent imitation of a salute before heading toward the stairs.

"If you are going with him, you had better change,'' Josef said to his daughter.

"You're horrible," Kathy said. "I hate you!''

"Move."

He took a step toward her. Kathy scuttled after Mark.

Josef looked at Pat. Leaning against the wall, her arms folded, she regarded him unsmilingly.

"Crow," she said.

"What?"

"Flap your wings and crow. It's not going to be that easy, you know."

"My dear love, I am well aware of that. With your son, it is going to be a daily battle."

"If you can stand him, I guess I can put up with Kathy's giggling," Pat said.

Smiling, Josef reached out for her, and then contemplated his dirt-steaked sleeve in some dismay. "I'll meet you down here in ten minutes," he said. "And if we're lucky, the kids will take a long time getting the food."

## III

They had half an hour alone before Mark and Kathy returned with pizza and spaghetti and other Italian delicacies. "Enough food for an army," Josef grumbled; but Mark managed to get rid of most of it. He refused to talk while he was eating, and Josef let him enjoy this small revenge. But when Mark had shoved the last bite of garlic bread into his mouth, the older man said, "Here's your chance to shine. Or are you going to sit around smirking while we make wild guesses?"

"It was so obvious," Mark said patronizingly.

"Not to me."

"Well, look. The ghost had to be one of the Turnbulls. All the Bateses died in their beds, after lives of sickening virtue. That isn't necessarily conclusive, I admit, but the suggestion of blue eyes confirmed my suspicion that we were dealing with a Turnbull. Mr. Turnbull was fair, and so was Peter. It wasn't unreasonable to suppose that Turnbull's daughter by his first marriage had also inherited his coloring.

"Mary Jane was a ghostly figure in every sense of the word. We knew nothing about her except for the occasional references in Susan's diary. Susan thought she was an old witch — she even called her that once. Well, a lot of kids think of bossy big sisters as witches. But I got to thinking — Mary Jane did seem to hassle the kids a lot, and there she was, a spinster at almost thirty, with a younger half brother who was the answer to a maiden's prayer — handsome, domineering, sexy. . . ."

"Of all the cheap, slipshod, pseudo-Freudian nonsense," Josef exclaimed.

"Why shouldn't the ghost have been Peter, as you first believed?"

Kathy stirred. She had changed into jeans and an oversized tailored shirt. The masculine clothing only made her look more delicate. Her lowered eyes and clasped hands appeared demure, but something in her expression half prepared Pat for Mark's next statement.

"It was really Kath who figured it out," he said.

"You?" Kathy's father stared at her with unflattering surprise.

"I was the brains of the combination," Kathy said sweetly. "Mark was the muscle."

"Well, we sort of worked together," Mark said. "But Kath gave me the first . . . I mean, she had the hunch that it wasn't Peter after all. Like she said once, how could he do this if he was in love with the girl? I mean, that made sense, you know?"

"Not necessarily." Josef was still staring at his daughter. "If Peter was the domineering, arrogant young man we thought, and if he had died before he could get the girl he wanted —''

''All surmise,'' Mark interrupted. ''Peter was probably pretty cocky; who wouldn't be, in his position, with everything going for him? But we didn't find out anything about him that would support the idea that he was wicked or demented. The atmosphere the ghost produced was sick — malevolent. We got to wondering, Kathy and I, if maybe it hadn't been that way in life. Sick, hating. Peter was a soldier, he didn't have to repress anything; he could take out his anger and frustration by fighting.''

''I knew it wasn't Peter,'' Kathy said dreamily.

''Sheer irrational romanticism,'' her father grumbled.

''Maybe,'' Mark said. ''Maybe the idea came from . . . somewhere else. Anyhow, once we had decided Peter wasn't the ghost, we had to find another candidate. Mary Jane was a distinct possibility. That's why I was so mad when you didn't buy her letters.'' He gave Josef a sidelong glance and added, ''The book filled in the missing pieces in Susan's story, and gave us the final clue. Only I was too dumb to see it at first."

"The clue was the fact that Mary Jane was a Confederate spy," Kathy explained. "Remember the reference to Cousin Alex? That was Colonel Alexander. I told you about him — the man who escaped from Fort McHenry and broke his leg when he jumped from the parapet. The book said he was passed on from one Confederate sympathizer to another. One of them was Mary Jane. She had to be careful when she referred to him, in case her letters to Cordelia were intercepted."

"And how do you suppose she got those letters to Richmond?" Mark asked. "Enemy territory, in wartime?"

Josef gave Pat a hunted glance. He was being beaten back on all fronts, but he fought every step of the way.

"Okay, I'll buy the spy part. But how you got from that to Mary Jane's illicit passion for her brother —"

"The letters reeked with it, Dad," Kathy said, in a fair imitation of Mark's most superior tone. "And, like Mark said —"

"As Mark said," her beleaguered father interrupted.

"As Mark said, she was always spying on the kids and tattling to their parents. She was the one who caught Susan and Peter — you got that, didn't you?"

"Well, I —"

"Susan said in her diary that someone must have seen them together," Kathy persisted. "And Mary Jane bragged about being the one who saved Peter from the fatal consequences of —"

"All right, all right." Josef put his head in his hands. "I'm dizzy trying to follow your logic. Let's see. Given the fact that Mary Jane was a spy, you leaped to the conclusion that there was a secret room in the house."

"That was really dumb," Mark said. "I should have thought of that much earlier. The houses were twins, weren't they? There was a tunnel in the Bates house —"

"But I assumed that was constructed by Mr. Bates, years after the house was built," Pat exclaimed. "It wouldn't follow that there was a matching tunnel —"

"Not necessarily, no," Kathy said. "But I was reading a book about old houses, and secret rooms and passages weren't uncommon in architecture of that period. It was all part of the fake Gothic stuff. There was a place called Pratt's Castle, near Richmond, built in about 1850, that had a secret spiral staircase and a hidden room where guns and ammunition were stored during the Civil War. And Mary Jane would have to have someplace to hide fugitives, especially with the Bateses so close. Mark is right, we should have figured it out sooner."

This time Josef made no objections. The certainty in Kathy's voice overruled simple logic. Pat knew that he had been convinced, not by the girl's reasoning so much as by his own irrational sense that this theory somehow fit — not the facts of the case, but its atmosphere.

"I'll buy it," Pat said. "But, Mark, how did you know he — his body was still there? You did know, didn't you? You couldn't have identified those poor anonymous bones unless you expected to find them.''

''Come to think of it,'' Josef said, recovering. ''They still haven't been officially identified. Have you any solid evidence on that, Mark?''

''It's rather complicted,'' Mark said patronizingly.

''Translation: he hasn't got any evidence,'' Josef said, in an audible aside.

''I'll try to simplify it,'' Mark went on, without appearing to hear the comment. ''The fact that Peter Turnbull's body was never found has bugged me all along. Then there was the discrepancy in the stories of how the Turnbulls were killed. One said it was at Gettysburg, the other that it happened during a minor skirmish. So I — I mean, Kathy — got the idea that maybe there was some truth in both stories, but they got garbled, as history often does. We know the Turnbulls were alive in late June of 1863, just before Gettysburg.

"Not all the men who died in the war died in the famous battles. The cavalry especially was running around the countryside all the time. So we thought, suppose Peter was killed in a skirmish after the battle, during the retreat? We looked up Company K, the unit we thought the Turnbulls might have joined. And . . ." Mark reached for one of the books that always surrounded him, and opened it. "The unit fought at Gettysburg, all right. It also skirmished heavily at Williamsport while covering Lee's retreat. This is Manakee's *Maryland in the Civil War*. He says: 'For more than a week after Gettysburg, Maryland roads were alive with soldiers, all the way from Washington County to Baltimore and Washington. Constantly ranging between the two armies were cavalry units of both sides. Often they clashed in small, briefly fought engagements.'" Mark looked up from the book. "By July seventh, the Confederate army had reached the area near Hagerstown, but they couldn't cross the river because Union cavalry had destroyed their pontoon bridge, and the river was swollen by heavy rains.

"Now that campaign was Lee's last invasion of the North. If Peter was killed 'somewhere in Maryland,' it had to be during that period, since we know he was alive in June of 1863. If you consider the retreat part of the Gettysburg campaign, well, you could say he was killed 'at Gettysburg.' "

Mark paused. He looked meaningfully at his mother and then directed his gaze toward the kitchen. She remained oblivious, and with a pained sigh Mark went on.

"This part is — well, I admit it's somewhat hypothetical. But, I mean, like, you have to have a theory so you can search for evidence that will prove or disprove it, right?"

Josef looked as if he were about to expostulate at this peculiar description of the scientific method, but Mark swept on.

"The trooper who told about Peter being shot didn't actually see him fall. Suppose — just suppose — that he wasn't killed. Suppose he was only wounded."

"But he did disappear," Josef argued. "He'd have reported to his unit, or been identified as a prisoner of war, if he had survived."

"Well, we know what happened to him, don't we? I mean, Mr. Friedrichs, all this is Monday-morning quarterback stuff. I'm just trying to explain how I — we — figured it out in advance.

"I kept thinking about the fact that all this happened in Maryland. Not so far away from here, really. And I thought, suppose it was me. I'd try to make it home if I was hurt." He looked at his mother; and although she knew quite well that Mark was deliberately working on her emotions, her eyes grew moist. "I mean," Mark went on pensively, "care of the wounded in those days was grim, even in regular hospitals, and the Confederates were on the run. They piled wounded men into springless wagons and bumped them along those muddy roads. . . . Maybe, even, Peter was cut off from his men and couldn't get back. So — he started home. He knew about the tunnel, and the secret room, and Mary Jane's work with the spy ring. He'd figure he could get back to his unit via that route, after he had recovered. Can you picture that journey? It must have been terrible for an injured man. But he made it — into the arms of his loving sister . . . who killed him."

"Wait a minute," said Josef, after he had recovered his breath. "This isn't history, this is straight out of Sophocles or Euripides. How do you know the poor kid didn't simply die of his wounds?"

"He did," Mark said. "I never claimed she actually murdered him. She let him die, when she could have saved him — or at least made a good try at saving him. Oh, for God's sake, it's so obvious! If she didn't have something to hide, why did she brick up the hidden room, with his body still in it? They didn't hang enemy corpses over the city gates, the way they did in the Middle Ages. Peter would have been buried properly, in the family graveyard with his father, and with the conventional religious rites. That sort of thing meant a lot to people back then. It would have meant a lot to Mary Jane. She could have raised a big corny gravestone over him, with some sloppy epitaph on it. Yet she left him on the bed where he died like a — a dead animal. She shoveled the dirt over the trapdoor — it had to be her, there was nobody else to do it — and ordered the slaves to lay the brick floor. Why? Why would anybody do a thing like that, much less Peter's adoring big sister?''

Mark paused, as if waiting for an answer. Neither of the adults had anything to offer, and Kathy, smiling smugly, remained silent.

"All right, let's get back to the ghost," Mark said. "If Hiram's story can be believed, Mary Jane had appeared before, but it took Kathy to rouse her to furious activity. Kathy still can't see any resemblance between her and Susan Bates — although it was strong enough to strike Jay. Remember when he said she reminded him of somebody? But Kath has to admit that the circumstantial resemblances are considerable. She's the same age, the same coloring, and she — er —"

"Was emotionally involved with the boy next door," said Kathy calmly. "What Mark means is that the emotional atmosphere was similar to what had gone on over a century eariler in these two houses. I don't mean you, Mrs. Robbins, you've got good sense. But Dad acted like a nineteenth-century heavy father, and Mark — well —"

"How about you?" Stung, Mark forgot his manners and his tact. "It wasn't me that broke down in tears when he said we couldn't go out."

Kathy blushed. "That is irrelevant. The point is that our behavior stirred up the old hate. That, and the fact that Mark found the diary. But that — oh, well, Mark, we might as well tell them. We don't think that was an accident."

"Peter?" Pat asked.

Mark nodded. "On several occasions we were conscious of another presence, one that was trying to help us. It was relatively feeble and ineffectual much of the time, but it laid a couple of clues on us that we were too stupid to interpret."

"You were," Kathy said. "I knew it all the time."

"Oh, well, she kept insisting Peter wouldn't hurt the girl he was in love with," Mark said. He added disgustedly, "I told her that wasn't evidence."

"People who live in glass houses," Josef remarked, "should not criticize other people's logic. So you — Kathy — decided that the constructive force was Peter?"

"Obviously," Kathy said. "Last night, when Mary Jane was rampaging through our house, he led her off. The trail ended in the hall — at the basement door. He was trying to tell us to look in the basement."

"But the real giveaway was the message I got with the automatic writing," Mark said, seeing that this last statement failed to carry conviction. "We completely misinterpreted it. It wasn't a threat. It was a quotation — from Peter's dying words. He had fought his way back to her, through incredible pain and suffering. When he was dying and delirious, he called for her. He wanted her to know he had tried to come back to her. And that is why his sister let him die, instead of trying to get help for him.

"Help was available. It was only eighty feet away. After reading Susan's diary, you know her parents weren't cruel, vindictive people; can you imagine them refusing their nephew the medical attention that might have saved his life? Peter was in uniform, he wasn't a spy; the worst that could have happened was that he'd have been interned as a prisoner of war. But with Mr. Bates being a big wheel in the government, he could have gotten the best possible medical care.

"When Mary Jane realized that her brother was dying in that damp little room, all she had to do was walk across the yard and knock on the Bateses' door. She didn't. We know she didn't, because he's still there."

"Maybe he was on the verge of death when he got there," Pat said. "Maybe she didn't have time —"

"She had time to help him undress and put him to bed," Mark said inexorably. "He had time to babble and plead to see his sweetheart. Even if Mary Jane couldn't have gotten help in time to save his life, she could have heeded his dying wish and brought Susan to hold his hand and say good-bye. The vindictiveness, the awful jealousy, that kept her inactive then drove her insane after Peter died. She couldn't even share him after he was dead. That place in Poolesville that Cordelia mentioned — there was an insane asylum there, one of the first in the state. Read Cordelia's epilogue again, with that in mind. Cordelia wouldn't mention the word, nice people didn't go crazy, they suffered from melancholia or went into a decline. Mary Jane was crazy. She died insane. It's no wonder her spirit couldn't rest. It was caught, like a fly in a spiderweb, in a single moment of time — the hour of Peter's death. Alive or dead, she hated Susan Bates and blamed the girl for her own crime, the way guilty people do. She got her revenge on

Susan, all right. The girl must have died a thousand times during those years, not knowing what had happened to her lover, hoping against hope he'd come back. . . . When she finally gave up hope, she married that creep Morton. She didn't live long, luckily for her."

"I hope it's true," Josef said, after a period of appalled silence; Mark's passionate description had affected them all. "I'd hate to think you could invent a story as gruesome as that."

"I didn't invent it," Mark insisted. "We can probably prove the bones were Peter's, if you want to dig them up again. Personally I'd fill in the hole and plant a cross or something on the top and leave well enough alone. He wouldn't care. He wasn't bothering anybody. Mary Jane was the ghost, and she's gone. I took care of *her.*"

They let this egotistical statement pass, for varied reasons; Kathy because she didn't want to jar Mark's male ego any further, Pat because she was reluctant to state what she really believed: that Peter Turnbull had finally found strength enough to deal with the threat to his sweetheart.

Pat never knew why she chose that moment to speak. Now that the emergency was over — and her own instincts, even more than Mark's assurances, told her that it was — there was no need for hasty decisions. She had meant to prepare Mark for the step she planned to take in slow, subtle stages, giving him time to appreciate Josef's good qualities — and getting him enrolled in a college some distance from home. Instead she blurted it out, interrupting Mark in the midst of his self-glorification.

"I'm going to marry Mr. Friedrichs, Mark."

Silence descended like a pall. Pat twisted her hands together. Her palms were damp. Mark's face had gone completely blank.

"Well, that's a relief," he said at last. "I mean, not that I think marriage is necessarily the best relationship, but for your generation . . ." He smiled in a kindly fashion at his speechless mother.

"It will be nice," he conceded, "for you to have somebody around next year, when I'm away at Princeton."

Josef reached for Pat's hand.

"Do me a favor, darling"

"What?" Pat managed to get this word out.

"Don't ask him how he knew."

The publishers hope that this Large Print Book has brought you pleasurable reading. Each title is designed to make the text as easy to see as possible. G. K. Hall Large Print Books are available from your library and your local bookstore. Or you can receive information on upcoming and current Large Print Books by mail and order directly from the publisher. Just send your name and address to:

G. K. Hall & Co.
70 Lincoln Street
Boston, Mass. 02111